MW01688711

The Underground Chameleon

An Android Against Authoritarianism

Lynn Tharp Hesse

This publication is fiction set in a hopeful dystopian future. Any name associated with a real person is purely unintentional.

© 2024 Lynn Hesse and Lynn Tharp Hesse
All rights reserved. LynnHesse.com

This publication may not be reproduced, stored in a retrieval system, or transmitted in whole or in part, in any form or by any means, electronic, mechanical, photocopying, recording, or otherwise, without the prior written permission of Lynn Hesse or the Publisher. Short quotations may be used by newspapers, magazines, and other publications, and online blogs as part of reviews, articles, or reports, but must attribute author and book title. **AI NOTICE:** Author AND Publisher reserves the rights, and Distribution and Retail Platforms have no rights to, reproduce and/or otherwise use the Work in any manner for purposes of training artificial intelligence technologies to generate text, including without limitation, technologies that are capable of generating works in the same style or genre as the Work, unless Distribution and Retail Platforms obtains Publisher's and/or Author's specific and express permission to do so. Nor does Distribution and Retail Platforms have the right to sublicense others to reproduce and/or otherwise use the Work in any manner for purposes of training artificial intelligence technologies to generate text without Publisher's and/or Author's specific and express permission. For permissions, write:
lynnhesse85@gmail.com
Subject Line: Undercover Chameleon

Cover design and interior layout: Angela K. Durden
iStock licensed cover background graphic: 1486587303.jpg
iStock graphic creator: onurdongel
Editor: Susan Pierson, finelineproofs.com

ISBN: 9798990587007

THE UNDERGROUND CHAMELEON

9 798990 587007

SUSPICIOUS UNDERCURRENTS PUBLISHING

To
Milton Dale Tharp, my dad,
and his inspiring
bedtime stories including
The Belch Fire Eight.

Prologue

By day, I am a crime and mystery writer and Teddy Strange, my grandson, is a college student and private investigator in what's left of the good old U.S. of A. Of course, nobody but me and Teddy's creator, my deceased husband Jack, knows or knew my grandson is artificial intelligence working for the Underground. The Underground is composed of people leaning right and left who believe the Bill of Rights should be reinstated. We must be cautious.

Teddy is drinking a cup of coffee inside Black Jack's, our favorite coffee shop in North East Atlanta. It's a bit too trendy for us since the neighborhood has gentrified, but we have our reasons for sticking around. My husband used to own it. My grandson fakes a satisfied smile as he drains the cup, then types a message on his phone. He is probably texting on that gosh awful CatchYas. He likes the smell of coffee. Although he tells me he only kind of tastes it, drinking the dark brew makes him "fit in" and helps to acquaint him with human addictive behaviors.

I stretch my aching back and scan the room. Everyone but a gray-haired man in the corner typing away on his laptop is younger than me. I need a yoga workout and a massage. My latest deadline for Women Against Violence Magazine has chained me to the computer for three solid days and left my short story writing in need of attention.

Because Teddy doesn't need to rest or sleep, I envy him. I'm oldish, over 65 years of age and tend to run out of steam around the eight-hour mark and may or may not get a second wind. For some of my lanky cohort's late-night P.I. adventures, I'm tucked safely in my bed.

Usually around breakfast time the following morning with those sun-streaked curls framing his high cheekbones, his skin the color of the African desert, he traipses in. I listen. His storytelling skills are excellent, and he doesn't object if I write it down verbatim or embellish the details in my novels. He understands we need money to support our modest lifestyle, but he is programmed, as most AIs are, to value human life and the survival of the planet beyond all else. He reminds me of my Jack in so many ways.

01

"What are you researching?" I asked and leaned in toward Teddy. The coffee shop was humming with low-grade conversations.

"Nothing in particular. Scanned all the latest on the dark web about a new conservative cell group called Reboot. Hothead rednecks mostly, but I want to watch them for any signs of cyber sabotage with the presidential election coming up."

Our last president had been assassinated by a democratic senator after a rigged election. With the country in turmoil and conservativism at a new high, the vice president, now our Commander-In-Chief, had spearheaded the Congressional movement to amend the constitution and extend the presidential term from four to six years, rescinding the twenty-second amendment. Because the rules for eligibility to vote or even casting one's ballot were meant to be confusing, essentially, the president could stay in office for a lifetime—a dictatorship.

"Any P.I. work?" I asked.

"A Trans woman approached me to spy on her lover. I'm considering it, but I got the impression she was plotting something for a third party."

"Because?"

Teddy uncrossed his legs. "Her numbers were off, too normal, like she was talking about going shopping when she was talking about Ger-Ger—her pet name for Gerald—and the other woman."

"I see. You think she is a plant by the government." I patted his hand. The physical connection was for me, not him. Although programmed to respond appropriately, Teddy doesn't understand the human need for touch.

His eyes went back to his cell. "It's my duty to report Trans activity, but we both know what the state will do."

"Send her to prison or, worse, put her in a facility for the insane. Besides, how would you know for sure about their sexuality? You're just human."

He grinned, keeping his attention on his cell.

I stared out the window at the bleak rain. "Back to a potential job. You do what you think is best, but don't be too picky. The first of the month is approaching."

Christy, a young woman in jeans and a holey T-shirt, approached with a coffeepot in hand, and Teddy put on his best version of a nineteen-year-old awkward face. In actuality, he's about two years old because Jack finished making my grandson the year he died. My practical husband knew he was dying, and I'd need a companion.

"Hi, Mrs. D.S.," Christy said. I've asked Christy to call me Dorothy or Ms. Saunders, but she prefers to call me Ms. D.S. in tribute to the famous mystery author Dorothy L. Sayers.

"Would you like some more coffee, Teddy?" A dark strand of hair flopped into Christy's eyes, and she brushed it away, exposing a blush.

He nodded. So handsome. Like Christy, if I didn't know better, I'd think he was your everyday attractive young man.

"I would like a warm up too," I said, trying to keep amusement out of my voice. "How is your mother, Christy?"

"Good. She went to her first art class yesterday. Her back is better. Teddy handled that foreman guy like a pro. I mean, he is a pro, but whatever."

Teddy had worked an employee compensation case for Christy's mom and made sure she got her benefits by hacking into the boss's computer. Kiddie porn sites dominated this guy's screen history. The charge, if the Feds anonymously found out about the sites, was twenty-five to life, another one of the changes since President Gainey took office. I halfway approved of this law because I worked for many years in Child Protective Services and saw firsthand the children emotionally damaged by pedophiles.

Teddy glanced down at his cell.

"I'm sure Teddy was glad he could help," I said.

My grandson focused on Christy. "Of course, 'To the future in justice.'" He swept his hand up as if opening a superhero cape, making Christy laugh. My grandson had misquoted our Underground motto, "May the future hold justice for all." Dangerous. He enjoyed testing others' reactions. Sometimes, he acted all too human.

*****

Standing at the stove, I heard Teddy slam the front door shut in the living room, an annoying human habit Jack had programmed into Teddy as a "little surprise" for me. "I'm in here. Breakfast is ready," I said.

Teddy lumbered into the kitchen and draped his jacket over the back of a dinette chair. The morning light streamed through the bay window and reflected off his glasses. "Hi, Grams." He closed his eyes and sniffed for my benefit. "You're cooking bacon, my favorite smell." Then he walked over to the stove and gave me a world-class hug. He was programmed to give me at least three hugs a day. Somehow, Jack knew I'd need hugs after my grief subsided.

I handed my grandson a cup of black coffee, raised up on my tippy toes, and gave him a peck on the cheek. "Sit down and tell me about your night."

Teddy pulled a padded bar stool underneath him and traced the swirls in the black marble island top.

I returned to draining the bacon. I knew he was reorganizing his data to make it easier for me to understand. "What case are you working on?"

"I met with a strange woman at a local bar last night. A clairvoyant, if she is to be believed. She wants me to spend tomorrow night at her Victorian home in Oakhurst to find out who is taking objects in the night. She claims her dead twin sister's prized possessions have disappeared, one by one, during the past month. No break-ins. Local police dismissed her as delusional."

"What objects?"

"Trinkets and toys from childhood, an empty pink tin—a gift from a lost love—and the list goes on."

"How old is your client?"

"I calculated thirty-seven years of age. Neither sister married. Independently wealthy. They lived together in the family home after their parents died in a plane crash over the Swiss Alps. It happened on the girls' eighteenth birthday."

"Was there conflict between the sisters and the parents?"

"Reading Elsbeth's skin temperature, blood pressure, and capillary flow…" He looked at me and realized he was slipping into robo-speak. "She acted distraught about the plane crash, but her internal body readings conveyed she wasn't unhappy her parents were dead."

Unless Teddy's operations were on the fritz, he had monitored her perfectly. "Hmm, when did the sister pass?" I finished scrambling some eggs and divided them onto two plates.

Teddy hesitated. "January seventh will mark the one-year anniversary of her sister's death."

"How did she die?"

"Car accident, but no autopsy. She veered off the road and hit a pole."

"Of course."

"Meaning?" Teddy carried the plates to the dinette table where I'd already set the table with cutlery, maroon cloth napkins, and a Christmas cactus with pink blooms.

"Meaning I don't believe in clairvoyants, and I'd check out that Swiss Alps story. I bet they killed their parents," I said. "The dead sister felt guilty, committed suicide. Your potential client feels nada remorse. But she does believe in the spirit world. So—"

"Please, Grams, you're jumping to a conclusion. Again." He rolled Jack's old desk chair out and sat down at the round table.

"We'll see. I bet they couldn't get their hands on the family money until daddy and mommy left this earthly plane." I sat down facing the window seat. A brown finch pecked at the birdfeeder outside the bay window, and the buds on an azalea bush promised white blossoms in our spring-like December weather. "Now, dig in. I have a full day of writing and cleaning before the writing group comes over at six this evening."

"Do you want help to prepare?"

I placed my napkin in my lap. "If you'll clean the bathrooms. I'll get the rest of the house."

He nodded and nibbled on a piece of bacon.

"The plastic gloves are under the sink." I looked over my shoulder toward the kitchen. "I wouldn't mind if you made my famous blueberry scones for the meeting."

"It's your recipe, but my measurements are more precise."

I grabbed Teddy's hand. "You're the best grandson." I stopped myself from adding, I love you.

02

Liz and Ed knocked on the door fifteen minutes before the writers' meeting scheduled time. As prearranged, they came early, in case we needed to pass information between us from the Underground. Today they helped put out refreshments, and we chatted about the latest shooting in Kirkwood. "It was domestic related," Liz said. "Nothing political or military. I checked the couple for ties to subversive organizations. Their backgrounds reek of the corporate god, SUBLIGHT. No children. No foreign connections other than a timeshare condo in Italy. The Grangers didn't vote in the last election, IEDOs.

Insulated Educated Dropouts were not a new phenomenon, but now it had its own acronym coined by a well-known national commentator. Liz was the best at tracking online. If she cleared the Grangers, they were clean.

"Have you bought a new couch?" Ed asked. He rubbed the shabby slipcover made of inexpensive cotton. "I love the understated browns and golds. It's so you." Ed, a local artist, was known for using bold colors on his canvases.

I snarled. "I like comfortable and subdued with the world in constant turmoil. I quake if my home isn't up to your standards."

Somebody knocked.

"Make yourself useful and answer the door." I pointed. "I haven't finished making the coffee."

Ed backed toward the entrance. "If you would let me get my hands on…"

I entered the kitchen area out of direct ear shot and rolled my eyes for Teddy's benefit.

He held a tray with a coffee urn and scones, intent on delivering them into the living room.

"Hold up," I said. "Ed is at it again with another interior decorating critique. I need a minute."

He set the tray down on the kitchen island. "The nosy old goat." He touched my shoulder.

I laughed because the phrase sounded like something Jack would've said. Tears welled in my eyes. "I do miss your grandfather."

"He was a charming genius like me."

I grabbed a tissue and blew my nose. "As much as I respect Liz and Ed, he gets on my last nerve. Okay, I'm ready to have a nice evening and forget everything else."

"You go, Grams. Are you reading pages from the sequel manuscript tonight?" Teddy asked.

I pulled up my drooping slacks and rolled over the waistband. "No, I have a surprise tonight. I finished the rough draft of the novel set in Arkansas' Boston Mountains in the 1800s. My heroine escapes the clutches of a serial killer and steals a horse for her getaway. Tomorrow, will you be a beta reader for me and double-check the historical references?"

Teddy handed me a dessert plate. "Gladly. Have one of my gram's prize-winning scones."

I took a bite. As the scone melted in my mouth, I thanked my lucky stars for the good in my life.

*****

My best friend, Barbara Lowery, stepped out of the downstairs bathroom, tucking in her blouse around her slim waist.

"Oh, there you are," I said. "I thought you'd left without saying goodbye."

"You know I'd never leave without giving you a hug and stealing a scone or two to take home for breakfast. Or did Helen eat the last nectar of the Gods? She is gone?" Barb looked around, swinging an imaginary gun from right to left and back again.

I laughed. "Teddy stored your scones in a reusable square." The square was a piece of cloth sealed with an antibacterial agent during manufacturing.

"He's an angel."

We walked together toward the kitchen, and I touched Barb's shoulder. "During the discussion about your manuscript, you seemed a bit miffed at Helen's comments."

"You could tell, huh? She messes with my chi. I wonder why she didn't pick up on it and stop droning on about the comma splice and split infinitive. I noted it the first time she mentioned the errors."

"In her way, she was being helpful." I passed the kitchen island and opened the dishwasher. Barb came around to the counter and handed me the dirty mugs from the sink as I filled the dishwasher in my slapdash way. Teddy had a precise way of loading the dishwasher, using every inch of space, but I could never get the hang of it.

"Right. She can store it where the sun doesn't shine."

"She writes crime, not literary fiction. Maybe she can't think of anything useful to add to the discussion." I nudged Barb's elbow.

"I admit Helen isn't my favorite person. Too perky." Barbara lifted her breasts for effect.

"I can't wait to read what happens next in your story. I'm rooting for your midwife to seek revenge. Poison would be a nice touch."

"I'll let you know when I know."

She patted the storage square lying on the kitchen island. "Are these my yummies?"

"Yes."

"Such a nice young man. You're so lucky Jack found Teddy through social media when he did. I know your grandson is a comfort."

I kept my eyes on the dishes. "Yes, he is. Jack had good timing."

"Imagine never knowing your daughter had a child until years after her death."

Emily had died in a climbing accident in her early thirties. I regretted our last phone conversation. It had ended on a sour note. She had wanted money again. Jack and I had said no.

I straightened up and forced a smile. My dear husband had died a few months after he finished creating Teddy. I hated deceiving my friend, but Jack made me swear not to tell anybody about Teddy being AI. Besides, Barbara was a devout Catholic and totally against the personal use, let alone the creation of AIs. We never discussed politics or our differing views on women's rights either. We were an unlikely pair to bond, but we had.

We finished stacking the dishes and Barb gave me a hug. "Now, where's my sweater?"

"Over there, in the living room."

"Oh yes, next to my purse." She moved with ease across the floor.

I caught myself envying her grace. As a former dancer and long-time yoga enthusiast, she stood with poise and seemed to glide in and out of rooms without effort.

"I took it off during the riveting discussion about split infinitives." She put on her orange sweater, fluffed her short gray hair, licked her fingers, and ran them over her thick dark eyebrows, knocking her glasses askew. "Will I do, Miss Dorothy?"

I laughed. "Always, my dear."

With her tote draped over one shoulder she said, "Let's meet for drinks next week." She blew me a kiss and shut the front door behind her.

03

It amazed me to watch my grandson, the P.I., work. First, he set up the cameras in the Folk Victorian's nooks and crannies while I kept Elsbeth busy. She appeared as normal as the librarian who lived next door to me, but then what did I know about clairvoyants?

"Was anything taken last night belonging to your deceased sister?" I asked. "I'm sorry. What was her name?" I sat on a maroon velvet couch with an embossed floral design. The lit fireplace and the dim light from two stain-glass lamps gave the room an amber glow.

"Daphne is my twin and no, nothing else of hers seems to be missing," Elsbeth said. She placed her cup of tea on the antique side table.

Her pale, slender fingers rubbed the base of her thirty-something throat between her open collar. "We're still connected, although her body perished. I feel her presence stronger than ever since the anniversary of her death, January 7th."

"Of course." I took a sip of excellent Earl Grey tea. Despite myself, I looked around the room for signs of the supernatural. Atop the mantel, a clock struck midnight. The first chime made me shiver. "How did she pass?" Asking questions against what I already knew tested the client's honesty.

"There was an accident and the car burst into flames.

"I'm so sorry."

She nodded.

"I understand she sends you messages. Has she indicated where the missing items might be? Or who took them?"

"It's the same male figure in a dark cloak every night. I have seen him leaving by the French doors in the parlor on the other side of the vestibule."

Elsbeth had evaded the issue about whether she had communicated with Daphne. Some clairvoyant.

Lanky Teddy loomed behind Elsbeth. His serious artificial-intelligence demeanor was in contrast to his patchy peach-fuzz chin. "Please show me where you saw the intruder," he said.

As we walked to the parlor, I noticed a blue crystal vase on the entryway table and a painting by Gauguin above it, probably originals, but even copies of the artwork were worth more than Daphne's missing books, toys, and the sentimental powder tin. Teddy had reported Elsbeth had grimaced when she had mentioned Daphne's lover on their initial client interview. He recorded any human telltale signs of stress, a useful tool in the private investigation business.

Teddy scanned the room, made a sketch, and walked the perimeter of the parlor. He knocked on the wood paneling between the built-in bookshelves on either side of the fireplace. "Ah, we'll use this room as our base of operations."

He retrieved our bags from the foyer and unfolded the craft table inside the doorway. Within five minutes he was pressing keys faster than I could think.

Elsbeth watched me walk to the French doors. Two sets of luminous cat eyes stared through the glass panes at us. "Let me guess. The cats are named Daphne and Elsbeth."

The calico cats took off, streaking across the backyard. They set off the motion-activated floodlight that lit a garden path leading to a utility shed.

"No, CeCe and Dede." Elsbeth locked the French doors and shut the blinds. "It's foggy outside and damp inside. I'll go get you a blanket."

I dropped my bags on the floor. "No need, dearie. These old bones come prepared." I lifted my stadium blanket and sleeping bag from my rolling suitcase. "You go on to bed. We'll keep watch over you and the house tonight."

Her wide Bolero pants swept the floor as she seemed to float toward me. "Don't be alarmed if you hear a dog barking. Daphne's dog died within days after her death and his spirit roams the house."

I nodded, trying to hide my disbelief.

Teddy stood up and guided our client between the table and the wires strung across a Persian rug to an electrical outlet.

"Are you sure you'll have enough lamps in here to work?" Elsbeth stopped and wrapped her arms around herself, embracing the blackbird print on her shirt.

"Ma'am, we'll be fine," Teddy said. "Grams and I should have good news by tomorrow morning. Now, you must sleep and let us do our jobs."

The foyer light bounced off Elsbeth's straight black hair and porcelain skin as she turned and left without another word.

"Don't you think it's strange the intruder didn't bother taking at least Daphne's cat?"

"Maybe," Teddy said.

"What now?"

"We wait."

"Won't the thief see us?"

He handed me a note. "I doubt it," he said, walking back to his seat. "Back to my research for political contributors who gave over two hundred dollars." He tapped the keyboard.

The note read, "The Swiss Alps story is hinky. Elsbeth wrote a paper, 'Control the Narrative Through News Manipulation' in her freshman year in college. Be on alert."

"Nevermind explaining anything," I said, tucking the note in my pocket. I took out a flashlight-taser combo and a Jacqueline Winspear mystery reader from my tote. I kept reading the first line over again. "Is that federal campaign law still in effect from 2025?"

Teddy scowled. "Yes. Will you please let me finish uploading this photo to EyeSpyU.com?

Arrogant rascal. As Jack's widow, I swear before his death, my husband assembled Teddy in our basement as much to exasperate me as to be my companion. My artificial-intelligence grandson acted so much like Jack, it made me want to hug Teddy's neck, then strangle him in the next moment.

A quarter past three in the morning, Teddy stood up. "Daphne's alive. Found her on two websites, plus her own." He showed me the computer screen.

"She runs an herbal shop in Seattle. Why the deceit or retrieve her own things from the house while her sister sleeps? I don't get it. Is she afraid of Elsbeth?"

Teddy cocked his head.

"You think Elsbeth killed them. Can you prove it?" I asked.

"Not beyond a reasonable doubt, but Daphne could enlighten us." I followed Teddy's gaze to the curtains.

An athletic duplicate of Elsbeth with frizzy red hair stepped out from behind the curtain, wearing a black cloak over black jeans and a turtleneck sweater. "Did you hear me in the crawl space connected to the secret panel? It's been a while. It was just right for a ten-year-old."

"Something like that," Teddy said.

"Tell us what happened." I stepped closer to Daphne.

She shot me a warning glance, gauged the distance between us, and paced. "Yes, well, I kept up with the repairs in the house. Last year, I was working in the basement on a water leak when a knuckle bone popped through a cement crack. I found Mom and Dad buried in the basement underneath the concrete floor. No mistaking their engraved anniversary watches. I panicked and left."

Teddy stepped closer. "When I explored the house and set up the cameras, I saw the telltale signs where you had dug and the shoddy repair work."

"Why fake your death or take items from the house? Why not go to the authorities?" I asked.

"They would've thought I helped her. Besides, what prevented her from killing me too? I was getting the hell out of here when I swerved to miss another transport and hit a stupid billboard pole. The eyesores. I crawled out, and my vehicle burst into flames. I had picked up a hitchhiker at a recharge station. She didn't..." Daphne brushed her jawline with the back of her hand.

"Make it," I said. "Go on."

"I wandered around aimlessly for a while, but I came back. I despise Elsbeth. I wanted to drive her mad, maybe force her to confess. Mother and Father loved me best, and she took them from me. You two should go." She clutched her coat near her waistband.

As she moved past me, I saw the glint from a hatchet hidden inside her cloak.

"She will pay," Daphne said.

I tasered her thigh. She dropped to the floor in spasms.

Teddy keyed 911 in his cell. "Really, Grams. I had everything under control."

04

Before the police arrived, I reminded Teddy to switch on his system blocker and to omit details from the incident only an AI would know.

"Yes, Grams, as soon as I store the original data, scramble the video, and take down the cameras." He hurried out of the living room, leaving me with Daphne. I understood he meant to protect everyone in the house, including us, from the State Censor Review Board. Its affiliate members scoured videos for subversive ideas or disloyal citizens and potential threats to the government.

Teddy's advanced covering and personality chip designed by my ingenious husband prevented humans from detecting my grandson's origin, but the newest model of AI was equipped with a sophisticated scanner that was rumored to detect unregistered, pirated non-humans within seconds. The police departments used some AIs in the field, usually hand-me-down models from the military, but most worked inside the lab for the Crime Scene Discovery Unit.

Teddy had an Underground sympathizer inside the unit, a Georgianna or Georgie Cooper. If she showed up, I would breathe a little easier. My cell beeped. A text alert warned me I was past my mandated med time.

I reached into my tote, took out the newest government-issued "Wellness Helps All" reader, then touched my temple. The reader, about the size of a cell phone, monitored my blood sugar and pressure, heart rhythm, and vitamin levels as it checked my body for bacterial and viral infections. The coronavirus worldwide deathly pandemic in the 2020s shut down the world's economy for far too long, and caused the United Nations in collaboration with The World Health Organization to mandate global daily screening for adults over sixty-five and children under eighteen, the hardest hit demographic and the largest group of carriers, respectively. Thus, one of the reasons Jack made Teddy nineteen.

"I need to find a sanitizer. Quick. You'll have to come with—" A knock on the door made me jump. I motioned for Daphne to stay put and flashed my taser in her direction. My bluff worked. She flinched.

The young woman didn't know I only had a hand taser without projectile electrodes as I moved further and further away from her.

Georgie Cooper opened the door as I crossed the parlor threshold. I stood facing her, allowing the tension to drain from my body. I must've looked pale.

"Dorothy, are you alright?"

"Yes. Are you alone?"

"Yeah, but not for much longer." Georgie glanced over her shoulder.

"I'm so glad to see you," I said. "We have a situation."

After a brief summary of events, I excused myself and left Georgie alone with Daphne, who sat in the parlor with a defeated expression on her face. I went into the bathroom to wash my hands. The reader screen blinked the critical five-minute limit advisory and a blue-pack image popped on the screen.

A hologram healthcare case manager, HHCM, appeared and repeated three times "Sanitize and Be Well, Dorothy" and then instructed me to wash my hands or hold up an uncontaminated hand for review. "You have ignored our three previous reminders. Your med waver expires in three minutes. Notification to the state is eminent," the machine repeated.

I did as I was instructed. 'Big Brother' was watching. I put the monitor upside down in one of the slits built into the home sterilizer box required by law in every home. The appliance operated like a back-in-the-day toaster. I pushed the lever down and washed my hands. The monitor popped up in the sterilizer, and I dislodged it. A thin waiver rolled out in a blue cellophane-like covering and hung in mid-air.

It reminded me of the old receipt printing process at gas pumps before paper receipts and petroleum-powered cars were banned. It required a yank to release the filled prescription. I spread my free hand toward the screen, then used the same hand to dislodge my daily dosage. The waiver and its covering melted in my mouth, leaving a hint of lemon on my tongue. The hologram said, "Excellent. Have a safe social-distancing day." The hologram disappeared.

I took a few more minutes for personal hygiene. It had been a long night, and it was only four a.m. Outside the bathroom, I heard voices and doors opening and closing. I assumed the police had arrived.

When I returned to the parlor, Teddy, Georgie, and a uniform officer stood next to a seated detective as he questioned Daphne. I didn't spy any robotic AI officers on the scene.

I studied how my grandson and Georgie, as she prefers to be called, were standing side by side talking about the case, their heads tilted toward one another. She touched Teddy's arm, glanced over her shoulder at me, and smiled.

They walked toward me, and we convened in the foyer.

Teddy slid his phone into a pants pocket and faced me. "I'm going with Georgie to the basement to document the scene downstairs. Would you stay up here with the detective? He will have questions for you." I noticed Georgie's eyes lit up as Teddy talked. I liked and respected Georgie, but I estimated she was in her late twenties. At least ten years older than Teddy appeared. She was beautiful, a new-age petite Liz Taylor with violet eyes and olive skin in a compact, shapely body. I recognized age wasn't as important now in relationships with age-redefining drugs, but then Teddy was an AI. It was too confusing for this old widow.

I nodded. "Of course, who is with Elsbeth?" I looked at the staircase. "Surely she heard the commotion and came downstairs."

"She seemed to know what was occurring without leaving her bedroom," Georgie said. "I slipped upstairs after the detectives arrived. Elsbeth had written out a confession about killing her parents in long-hand using an unsanctioned paper journal." She lifted an evidence bag containing the rare item.

"That won't help her during sentencing," I said.

"Nope. Just the paper carries a minimum sentence of five years in confinement. They've been banned since I was a kid. Imagine an elegant woman like that killing her parents when she was a teenager. Anyway, a female detective has Miss Elsbeth Winchester detained inside an unmarked police car. Interviewing her." Georgie pointed toward the frosted etched-glass design in the front door as if we could see the roadway.

I nodded toward the detective watching me from the parlor, reset my heavy tote on my shoulder, and excused myself while Teddy and Georgie headed in the direction of the basement. The detective finished with Daphne and gave her his matrix digital business card or MBC.

"As I said, I'm Detective W. E. Barden. Stay here in the district for a while until I can wrap up the case. I may have more questions."

Daphne wiped her eyes and straightened her shoulders. She caught my gaze. "The detective has promised to bring my sister to justice. It won't bring my parents back, but thank you for stopping me from making a big mistake."

"You're welcome."

"I'll go make some coffee while the two of you talk." Daphne left the room, leaving behind air full of grief and regrets.

"Nice enough young woman," the detective said. He was stocky with auburn, unruly hair, as if hundreds of short cowlicks were stuck together. His large, callused hands holding his laptop would've looked more natural lathing a piece of wood. The detective invited me to sit down.

"You won't be charging her with anything?" I asked.

"Why bother? The D.A. won't be interested in an almost attempted domestic murder foiled by a senior sleuth and her P.I. grandson. However, I'll look into the death of the unfortunate woman who died in the car fire, a hitchhiker, if Daphne is to be believed. Should I find any foul play, she may be charged yet." He kept his countenance serious, but his eyes danced with mischief. "Unless you want to prosecute because you were in fear for your life and that's why you zapped her with your taser? By the way, do you have a permit?"

"I observed a small ax on her person. She indicated her sister would pay for their parents' murders, so I tased her. Would you like to see the permit?" I reached for my tote on the floor.

"That's not necessary. I ran your name through the system already. Just messing with you." He grinned.

"I see." I didn't find Detective Barden's humor off-putting. Instead, I sized him up as a sharp-witted man. Playing his game, I pursed my lips at him for effect, hoping I looked like a disapproving schoolmarm.

"Now your grandson's history is a mystery. His parents must've lived off the grid in a W-5 Zone. No cyber trail to speak of. That's odd."

In general, the party line was the W-5 Zones were small, forested areas dotting America to maintain the quality of the air. In actuality, only squatters, criminals, and the homeless hid out in these areas, and the air quality remained poor. I cupped my hands in my lap. "We never found a birth certificate for Teddy. It must've been a home birth. We found a 2036 state-required immunization record for my grandson, so he must've been born in 2030. His mother was killed in a climbing accident out west near Yosemite National Park and we—sorry—my husband is now deceased, and I didn't know where she was for many years. Of course, we were notified by the authorities when Emily died. There was an I.D. in her backpack. We'd declined chip insertion for our daughter."

"When were you aware your daughter had passed?"

"October 2036." I would never forget that date.

"Sorry for your losses," he said with tenderness in his voice.

"I take it day by day. It's been almost two years since my Jack transitioned. Teddy keeps me busy, and I write fiction—mainly novels."

The detective tapped on his laptop. "The father? Was he in the picture?"

"No. Emily never revealed his name."

"You didn't know Teddy existed for approximately fifteen years?"

I realized Teddy would need to tweak his face soon to appear in his early twenties.

"Approximately. As you pointed out, Emily lived off the grid. We didn't know about our grandson until he turned up on our doorstep. Well, my husband saw an old photo on social media of his mother taken by a friend and tracked him down. Long story."

"A boy's real-life adventure story of survival for ten to eleven years alone in the W-5 Zone."

"Not alone," I said, collecting my thoughts, preparing to tell him the standard lie about a veteran from Civil War II fostering Teddy.

"The details about the foster parent can wait for another time. Please give me your account of what happened here." He held up a finger and turned the camera on the laptop toward me. "I must advise you that you are being videotaped as a witness. This recorded evidence will be on file with the State Central Office for seven times seven years and can be used in this case and any other case where the facts intersect or otherwise are deemed necessary to prosecute a person suspected of committing a crime, including yourself. Are you clear on what I just told you?"

"Yes." Teddy and I joined the Underground to fight against this type of intrusion by the state. The

Bill of Rights no longer existed in our constitution, but I remembered when "inalienable rights" in theory, at least, couldn't be taken away by the government without a warrant, and you had the right to remain silent and to have a lawyer present during questioning.

I gave a concise statement mentioning the licensed cameras but leaving out whatever I thought might alert the detective to Teddy's real identity, and then I swore to the validity of my statement and steadied myself for questioning about the scrambled video.

Instead, Detective Barden gave me his MBC card. "That will be all for today, Ms. Dorothy L. Sayers, I mean Saunders." He flashed his dimples. "You can expect a call from me later."

I hadn't mentioned I wrote mysteries. His reference to the twentieth century distinguished crime and mystery writer surprised me. I noted Barden was a thorough man who came across as non-threatening on purpose, plus he seemed knowledgeable about my genre. I wondered if he played chess.

05

Teddy and I sat at the dinette table where I could look out at the squirrels and birds playing around a sweetgum tree. Half of the bird species were extinct from the gray sooty air, but a clever college student and entrepreneur had saved a lucky few with an immune supplement added to bird seed bought over the counter by citizens like me. Perhaps they would adapt and survive. While we ate what my people called goulash, a combination of macaroni, onions, green peppers and, in this case, ground turkey in a tomato paste sauce, I rambled on. "I will be happy when spring comes." I buttered yet another piece of bread.

Teddy nodded.

"I do love yeasty bread, as my expanding waistline proves. I'm ready for the azaleas and irises to bloom. Do you remember the glorious pink blooms on the azalea bush last spring? Barbara does give the best presents. When did she give that prayer plant to me?"

Teddy blinked at the plant on a shelf, but I knew he was checking his archived data. It was seven years ago, the day after your birthday. You said, 'Well, damn, my best friend forgot my sixtieth birthday.' She gave you a belated birthday card that you put away in your cedar chest. It read—"

Darn Jack and his photographic memory. "Thank you, Teddy. That's more than enough information. My aches and pains remind me every day I'm getting older." Barbara's card had contained a not-so-humorous comparison to human organs wearing out after sixty and robotic systems breaking down after twenty-five years. Both prospects gave me anxiety.

He gave me his best pouty look and took a huge bite of the spicy macaroni dish.

"Oh, stop it. Tell me about your new case."

"A woman approached me at Jack's and interrupted my ritual of sipping my mocha latte—one of my best performances yet. She was five feet six inches, light brown hair, late twenties, with a tiny moon-shaped scar on her chin. She wore twenty-two-carat gold hoop earrings with a charm bracelet that she'd had since her high school days. A cheer charm gave that away. Pricey name-brand sports attire. Rather thin—twenty percent body fat."

I held up my hand. "Please, who and what did she want your help with?" I sprinkled more salt on my goulash.

Teddy shot me a look of disapproval. "Julie Farnsworth. Her brother is missing. He went on a vacation to Hawaii a month ago and never returned."

I covered my mouth full of salad with my napkin. "I'd like to get lost in Hawaii. Tell me we need to fly there to find him."

Teddy raised his eyebrow.

I swallowed and dropped my napkin in my lap. Never enough money was a constant in our lives. "Don't worry. I'm joking. Kind of. Tell me more about this brother. His name?"

"Jonathon Farnsworth is a successful businessman — pharmaceuticals — married with two children. He left for a conference without his family two weeks ago."

"Does the wife fear he took another woman with him to Hawaii?"

"Probably, but the sister told me her brother had been despondent lately, something about company politics and pressure to merge with another mega corporation."

"I take it he wasn't in favor of the merger?"

"Correct."

"What's your first step?"

"I have an appointment to meet with the wife, Mrs. Chantel Farnsworth, at eight-thirty this evening in Newnan. She wants to put her children to bed before I interview her. Traffic should die down by the time I need to head south."

"Excellent. Would you mind if I tagged along?"

'"You're fine company, Dorothy' as Grandpa Jack would say." Teddy grinned, but his hand holding a fork froze in mid-air. "I will, will, make sure you're returned safe and sound to your residence as programmed—" He jerked his head back and forth. "—as grandpa wished." He darted his eyes from me to objects in the room. "A reboot is required."

The stutters, a result of a malfunction in the warning system, had happened only once while Jack was alive. It couldn't happen again and certainly not in public. "Maybe you should upload your annual program update and age your frame and outer appearance before your next birthday celebration in April."

He didn't respond. Jack's workroom, now Teddy's, was in the basement where my AI grandson preferred to refresh his systems.

"Go on then. I'll see you in fifteen." I brought his hand down. "Dear Teddy, we must stick together and make sure we each don't break down and fall to pieces."

*****

The ride to Newnan on I-85 South was uneventful as we discussed his pending upgrades. We agreed spring break was a perfect time. He could be out-of-service for the upload up to twenty-four hours, but I would tell everyone he was on a trip to Florida. I was so relieved I let Teddy navigate my restored 2030 electric Renault but that made me nervous again. The Global Positioning Coordination System, replacing the old GPS and collision avoidance system, was new on the market, and I didn't trust it. Teddy laughed at me when I reminded him that GPCS isn't one hundred percent correct or perfect in anticipating a collision. "I know I'm being silly to visualize dying in a crash while the powder-blue metal of my car folds in and crushes me, but having my hands on the wheel comforts me. I can avoid the other convenient transports or CTs traveling in the same direction. I feel in control."

"Right," Teddy said.

"Please be careful, grandson. Some deranged people don't register their plans with the Ministers of Transportation. 'Why travel in a curved line when you can cut straight across,' as the saying goes."

"Yes, Grams. I'm aware."

Many numbskulls refused to obey the guidelines for driving between major cities or hubs, skimming no more than six feet above the deteriorating interstates. The understaffed air marshals have their hands full with smugglers using camouflaged traveling contraptions and signal scramblers; mere traffic violators aren't a priority. "Although the drones have caught some non-compliant citizens on camera and tickets are sent out, as I can attest. I'll never live down my speeding ticket last year."

Teddy glanced at me. "Is your blood sugar low?"

"Stop monitoring me. I'm not a lab rat."

He kept studying me.

"I took my meds, but I'll eat a snack." I took out a pack of nuts from my purse, poured the contents into a palm, and stuffed them in my mouth. "Drive on," I said in between chewing.

The rest of the trip, we exchanged little conversation.

Mrs. Chantel Farnsworth lived in a modern glass and steel house with sharp angles and panels that could go down and provide bullet-proof, if not bomb-proof protection. I found it interesting a pharmaceutical rep and his wife needed in-home, governmental-grade security. "Perhaps Jonathon isn't what he appeared to be in my initial search of the web," Teddy said.

"The security system is unexpected."

We parked and walked toward the house. I took in the immaculate surroundings, white stones and boulders and an occasional cactus replaced a lawn. The drawbridge entrance, disguised as a walkway, crossed a thirty-five-foot-wide mote. I tilted over the railing and saw humongous fish circling in the water."

"Careful, those are piranhas," Teddy said.

I'd heard about breeding the aquarium species for outdoor conditions, but I'd never seen any before today. "These people take security seriously."

Teddy knocked on the door. "I'll screen the house for a vault or panic—"

The door opened. Chantel didn't look like a mother who had worked hard at the office all day, ran errands on her way home, cooked supper, and put children to bed, or a wife worried about her missing husband. We introduced ourselves as she posed in the doorway in a salmon-colored silk gown and robe, holding a martini. She studied us and lingered on Teddy. "Well, look what Jules has hired to find Jonathon." She smiled and then, as if she remembered her manners, "Please come inside."

The inside of the house exuded a sterile extravagance. The marble floors shined in the atrium with a domed skylight. We followed Chantel down two steps into a living room with columns. A black shag area rug half the size of my house was lying underneath two white leather couches. They formed a forty-degree angle with a pair of plush mustard-color chairs with a bold poppy print—no doubt Ed would approve. The mistress of the house tucked herself in the corner of a couch and crossed her legs. She waited a bit, then motioned for us to sit. "Now, how may I help you?"

Teddy looked down at his electronic notepad and pretended to scan his notes. "Has your husband contacted you since he left for Hawaii?"

"Not since he landed. Not unusual. We aren't the type of couple who need to check in with each other multiple times a day. In fact, our paths might not cross for days at a time because I work at a lab most evenings. He works long days." She shrugged.

"Excuse me," I said. "What do you do at the lab?"

"I'm a scientist at E.I. Vance. Today is my off day. We employ a live-in nanny for the children to answer your next question."

"How old are your children?" I asked. Teddy always forgot these lead-in questions not directly related to the case.

"They are five and seven, a boy and a girl."

"What nice ages."

Teddy cleared his throat as if mucus ran down his non-existent sinus passages. "Had your husband indicated he was troubled about anything or anybody before he left on his business trip?"

"Nada. My husband's happy countenance is a constant." She leaned forward. "Rather annoying if you aren't a flaming optimist."

Because we didn't react, Chantel plopped back into the couch cushions. "We rarely speak about his office interactions. I'm not allowed to talk about my research."

"You develop new drugs? Test them?" I asked.

"Yes, among other things I can't talk about."

Teddy studied her. "Ms. Farnsworth, Jonathon's sister, told me the merger under consideration worried your husband. Why?"

"I don't have any idea. I don't meddle in the financial or political dealings within the corporate structure. As I said, I'm a scientist. Running my lab, the house, and raising my children are my priorities." She yawned.

A wife who has a missing husband and doesn't mention him as one of her priorities. Interesting. Teddy gave me a knowing glance.

"Are you sure Jonathon didn't do anything out of the ordinary before he left?" Teddy said.

"No, wait. He did leave a notarized updated copy of his will on his desk. It's our custom to review our wills every other year with our solicitor, but he mentioned taking his name off the deed and leaving the Farnsworth family home to Jules. I didn't object. I wouldn't live in that eighteenth-century monstrosity if you paid me, and it's worth little in today's market."

"The next question is rather delicate." I paused to sense her anticipation of the next question. Her face remained neutral. "Was your husband having an affair?"

Her eyes widened for a fraction of a second. "I wouldn't think so. As I said, he's a happy man with a family he adores and a job he likes. He considers himself a success. He has his crew of golfing buddies, and we do set aside time to be alone together."

"Weren't you concerned when Jonathon didn't answer any of your texts or phone calls and missed his flight home?" I held her gaze.

"Yes, of course. What are you implying?" She pushed her hands down on the couch cushion as if bracing herself. "I'm not good at expressing my emotions, but Jules told me she would handle it. After forty-eight hours of turmoil, the police took a report, acted like it was my fault, and assumed he was a runaway spouse. Never happen, not his style."

"I checked with Jonathon's supervisor, and Jules checked the airlines to see if he had booked another flight. Nothing. He did check out of his hotel on the day he was supposed to return."

"Do you know what time he checked out of his hotel?" Teddy asked.

"No. Why?" Chantel scooted to the edge of the couch.

"To chart a timeline. I can find out."

Chantel closed her eyes for a beat. "Please. I am tired. My day started at five o'clock this morning."

I stood up. "One more question. Would you give us the name of Jonathon's best friend and his golfing buddies?"

"I'll text you the list. Harry Dewall is his closest friend." She walked over to a chrome desk or armoire. It was hard to tell with the generic style. She took a digital imprint card from a drawer and handed it to Teddy and directed her next comment to him. "Here is Harry's contact card with the club's logo. He is the director of our club where Jonathon golfs. I'm sure you'll find him there."

Chantel escorted us to the vestibule without another word. The door closed behind us. I grinned. "There was a vault room, right?"

"Yes, and it's a large area containing supplies, what you would expect to survive for two weeks during a disaster, but the painting collection was a surprise."

"I'd say that's not all Mrs. Farnsworth is hiding."

06

Teddy backed the Renault into the garage and hit the release button on the seatbelt.

"Wait a moment," I said. "I think we're being watched."

He turned toward me, laughed like I had said something funny. "I'll scan the area by connecting to the surveillance system."

"I could be wrong. Just a feeling."

"You're spot on. Detective Barden is parked in the shadows in the parking lot near the retaining wall."

I opened the passenger door. "I wondered when he would show up. Let's go. Act as if we haven't discovered him."

Inside, we scrambled around, checking our security measures. The screen shields went up anytime we left the house, so they were in place in the basement. Teddy's AI scrambler didn't seem necessary. Besides, the detective might stay longer than fifteen minutes. We were in the middle of going over what we should say, and then the detective knocked at the door.

I opened the door and Barden flashed his badge. "Remember me from the Elsbeth and Daphne Winchester case?"

"Of course. Please come inside, detective." I stepped back, opening the door wider.

"I have a few follow-up questions before I close out the case file."

"How may we assist you?" I asked. "Please sit down." My mind was racing back to the case where I tasered Daphne to prevent her from killing her sister with a hatchet.

"I decided not to charge Daphne for plotting to kill her sister, but Elsbeth will be tried and punished for her parents' murders, as the state requires." Many prisoners were put in suspended animation or in colloquial terms, "freeze-dried and put in a drawer" for serious crimes. When and if they were reconstituted, they were never quite the same mentally or physically. I hated to think about dramatic Elsbeth hooked up to the machines.

"What about the burnt hitchhiker killed in the car crash?" Teddy asked.

"The state has categorized her as a runaway, a Jane Doe. No suggestion of foul play. I had to push for the results. Otherwise, our medical examiner, the governor's son-in-law, can be a tad lazy and the bodies stack up at the morgue." He shrugged.

"Has the M.E. checked the dental records of the victim?" Teddy leaned forward.

"No, not yet. As I said, the current M.E. isn't known for his industriousness. The test won't be run unless Missing Persons Division links the case to a felony. About the scrambled video..." The detective suppressed a smile and looked at both of us like an amused parent. "I know Teddy had time, means, and opportunity to mess with the video before I got to the premises. What I'm curious about is why?"

"I assure you it was an error on my part." Teddy combed his hair back with his fingers. "I got flustered when Grams scuffled with Daphne and—"

"Teddy is protective of me. My bones break like eggshells." My bone density was like a thirty-year-old, but I was banking on the detective not bothering to check my medical files. The application forms for the release of medical records were endless.

"How long have you known Georgie Cooper?"

I glanced at Teddy, a rookie mistake betraying my nervous reaction.

"Our P.I. work intersects sometimes with criminal behavior that requires evidence collection," Teddy said. "We met about a year ago."

I stood up. "Would you like a cup of coffee?"

"No, thank you. I'll be brief." Barden motioned toward Teddy. "Because you seemed fond of Georgie, I wanted to give you a heads up. Her name popped up on a recent Federal watchlist for suspected Underground activities. Anybody who has been in contact with her will be thoroughly assessed. I know you passed your annual personal and home inspection a few months ago, but be prepared for more inconveniences. Can't be too vigilant."

I sat back down. "We don't have anything to hide."

Barden flashed his dimples. "Maybe, but we're all more than meets the eye." His gaze lingered on Teddy. "I'll be in touch." He put his hands in his trench coat, drew out a burner phone for each of us. "Or in an emergency you can call me directly."

*****

The next morning at Jonathon's golf club, Teddy and I waited in the gift shop as a clerk went to fetch Harry DeWall. It seemed unusual for the employee to leave the floor when he could've called or texted his employer, but we didn't have an appointment. Teddy had insisted on making an early, unannounced visit to the club before his social justice final exam, his short-film presentation at the college this afternoon. Everything was virtual these days, except for some finals for first and second-year students. They met with a counselor or a state inquisitor slash advisor afterward. Most students loathed the exercise, but Teddy loved it. I mean, if AIs can be thrilled, he was. "Rather like playing a game of chess," Teddy had explained.

Harry showed up smiling and extended a huge hand toward Teddy, who stared, then shook the man's hand. The custom went out of style with the 2020 COVID-19 virus except with jocks in some sports communities. Harry's thick, middle-aged neck and large biceps offset a slight paunch visible through his cherry-color golf shirt. Some men preferred short sleeves year-round, a habit I never understood.

"Harry DeWall here, the director of this beautiful golf club and spa. Be happy to take you on a tour of our facilities. Always glad for people to drop by." He focused his attention on me.

"Thank you, no," I said. After brief introductions, I stressed the urgency of our visit. "We're here about Jonathon Farnsworth. We're P.I.s investigating his disappearance.

May we go to your office or a quiet place to talk?"

His happy-go-lucky countenance clouded, and he glanced over his shoulder at the clerk. "I don't want to be disturbed for a while."

The skinny clerk nodded.

"Please, follow me." Harry took us down a hallway, past a bathroom and a tiny room with an open door. Its walls were painted sky blue, complimenting an extra-long massage table. Maybe Harry had his own private massage room. His head skimmed close to the eight-foot ceiling, and he was bowlegged and slightly pigeon-toed. His walk reminded me of a duck's waddle. At the end of the hall was his office. Besides a cluttered desk, trophies lined the shelves around the room, and photos of tournament winners covered the walls. A couple of file cabinets filled the rest of the sparsely furnished space.

The cabinets with combination locks struck me as odd. They were "old school," an expression from my mother. Companies were required to go paperless unless grandfathered in, a lengthy process, but also, locks meant sensitive material or something to hide. Why would a golf club need locked cabinets? This place was the second location in less than twenty-four hours where I'd seen security that didn't match the risk assessment.

Harry waved at two chairs in front of his desk, inviting us to sit as he plopped down behind his desk. "How can I help you?"

Teddy said, "We understand you knew Jonathon quite well. When was the last time you spoke to him?"

"It's been almost three weeks. He was supposed to show for nine holes, but he didn't. Not even a text. Finally, he called before he left for Hawaii and apologized. We usually golf the second and fourth Wednesday afternoons of each month."

"I see. Is it unlike Jonathon to miss a round and not call you?" I asked.

"Harry's face worked hard at hiding his feelings. "It's not like he broke any friendship rules, but I always reserve a spot on the schedule for us. The Jonathon I know is steady as you go."

I readjusted my posture. "So, it was Jonathon's habit to call you if he couldn't make your regular game?"

"Right, as I said." His eyes darted toward the cabinets. When he focused back on us, he asked if we wanted a cup of coffee or water.

We declined.

Teddy took out his phone and hit record. "I hope you don't mind, but the details are important. When was the last time you spoke to Jonathon?"

"It must've been the Monday or Tuesday before he left. Monday, I think. I work on Sundays, and I typically take Mondays off. Didn't call me at home much. I'm a bachelor and Jonathon hated to interrupt me while I was entertaining." From Harry's reddening face, I assumed he now remembered I was in the room. "He usually called me at the office unless we were planning a fishing trip or something special."

"Do you fish at a stocked lake?" I asked. The fish in the lakes and ocean weren't contaminated by the government's low standards, but because of the pollution, the independent health organizations advised against it.

"Yes, Heritage Lake mainly."

"Anyway, I was eating my usual breakfast of three eggs and half a pound of bacon at home when the phone rang. He razzes me about not watching my weight." He patted his stomach, then his face clouded over again. "I hope he's all right."

"Had he shared with you any problems he was having at work or at home?" Teddy brought us back on topic. His AI programming didn't understand the illogical human rambling-talk technique of allowing the subject to get comfortable with the interviewer before asking pertinent questions.

"We never talked about his work. He played golf to get away from all that."

"How about his family, his wife?" I asked.

Teddy twisted toward me with bulging eyes, his signal to let him handle it.

"He loves his two little ones, a boy and a girl. His wife is too uptight for my taste. I see her around the club working out and having lunch with her snooty friends, but Jonathon usually doesn't complain about her."

"What do you mean?" Teddy asked.

"The last time we played golf, he told me Chantel wanted another child, pressuring him, but he thought they should wait another year until the market settled down."

"Did he say they were in debt?" Teddy leaned forward, no doubt checking Harry's physical responses to see if he would lie.

"Not exactly. Her family has old money. They'll never go under, but Jonathon likes to be his own man. He keeps most of his financial dealings to himself."

I couldn't help interrupting. "Away from his wife?" I asked as my tote slipped off my lap to the floor with a thud. I felt like a klutz, plus my expensive surveillance camera was inside my bag. I bent over, retrieving my purse.

"I hope so. She's a piece of work." He turned toward Teddy. "Look. He wasn't messing around. I would know. He's the kind of guy you can count on."

He glanced at his overhead monitor as an announcement of a club luncheon flashed on the screen. "I'm sorry. I need to check on the kitchen staff before my next appointment, a tour of the club at noon."

As we stood, Harry said, "Anything else, be glad to help. Update me when you can. Jonathon and I go way back from high school days. I'd hate to think…" He brushed a hand over his mouth.

"No problem," Teddy said. "Miss Dorothy or I will call you."

As the three of us stood up, Teddy flexed a palm in Harry's direction to prevent an offer of a handshake. I exchanged matrix business cards with Harry and then Teddy and I left.

Walking back to the parking area, I said, "When did I become Miss Dorothy?"

"Sorry. Referring to you as Grams makes us both sound like amateurs."

I checked my emotions. "I think Ms. Saunders will do in these situations, but not at home."

He nodded.

"What do you prefer? How should I address you during business hours?"

Ted or Teddy is fine. If I were to change my last name, I'd use Stringer.

"Stringer, not your mother's alias?"

"No. I prefer Stringer to Strange. Jack's stories about his father running a paper route as a boy are some of my favorites."

Surprising myself, I agreed to the change. Teddy's reasoning, or what I'd call sentimentality, got to me. Life is full of surprises. In a matter of seconds, our relationship was on a new footing.

At the Renault, Teddy paused before advising the car doors to unlock and open. "Mr. DeWall knew more than he admitted. He lied about not knowing what was bothering Jonathon before his disappearance."

"Yes, I thought so. One thing is clear, he doesn't like Chantel Farnsworth one iota."

On the ride back to the house, I stewed over what had occurred with Detective Barden the previous evening.

Teddy gave me a sideways glance. "What do you make of Detective Barden? What's he up to?"

"He could be setting us up or not. Warning us about Georgie was interesting."

"You think he's Underground?"

"Maybe. If he is, he's deep cover. I'll get Liz and Ed working on the connection."

Silence filled the car as my mind swirled around possible scenarios. The landscape flashed by. I found the bedraggled road signs and grass growing in the cracks on the interstate disturbing. "The other option is he's a spy for the state or a double agent. It's too early to tell. Let's review the facts of the Farnsworth's case so I'll stop thinking about the enigmatic detective."

"Good idea."

My grandson had stored the results from the interactions we encountered and could play it back with visuals when we returned to the privacy of our home, but I wanted answers. Now.

"Damn it. I forgot to tell Liz and Ed to find out why Jonathon needed major-league security before his disappearance."

"You are assuming it's Jonathon, not Chantel who needs the security," Teddy said.

"You're right. Chantel's the scientist. Why didn't we ask more pointed questions about her work at E.I. Vance?"

"She wouldn't have answered them. Remember, she made it clear she couldn't talk about it. Dictate the Vmail to me you want sent to Liz and Ed and I'll encrypt it. Do you want the hologram option?"

"Not necessary this time. Here goes: Need info ASAP concerning scientist Chantel Farnsworth and her pharmaceutical rep husband, Jonathon. Both work for E.I. Vance

Pharmaceuticals. Their house has governmental-grade security. Why? Our case: the disappearance of Jonathon Farnsworth while on a business trip to Hawaii." I studied Teddy, admiring his ability to drive and compose a Vmail without effort. "Oh, and please add the info about the possible merger and the couple's DOBs and their address for Liz. She hates it when I leave out the initial details. That should do it for now." My stomach growled. "I'm a bit peckish. I need to eat."

"I could order a delivery of crab Rangoon and fried rice from Thai City. They can leave it on our porch."

"Perfect."

He ordered by asking our onboard computer to call Thai City as we pulled into a roadside recharging station pad in the middle of an abandoned rest area. I didn't find these sites as disheartening as the abandoned gas stations located in the strip malls and discount shopping malls left to decay along the interstates. I placed my hand around the handle of my taser being vigilant for robbers as Teddy backed the rear portion of the Renault into position and hit the exchange button. The recharging module lowered, locked, and left the front seat section of the Renault uncovered and exposed for forty-five seconds. We couldn't move forward and escape if drive-by thieves hacked our computerized door code and forced their way into our vehicle.

I noticed a boxy silver Galaxy Plutonium about the size of a Hummer of yesteryear with dark-tinted windows circle in the parking lot and hover. Thank goodness, the recharging engagement signal on the steering panel turned from red to green.

Teddy ordered the Renault to start up, move forward, and maintain the maximum safe speed.

I glanced back. The Plutonium took our spot at the recharging module. I exhaled with a sigh.

"Smooth sailing now, Grams." Teddy checked the rearview and side mirrors, confirming we weren't being followed. "Why don't you rest while I reorganize the data for a thorough review after dinner. I'll direct us home. The sonar is on, and I'll set my scanner to alert me if a vehicle comes from any direction within six miles of us."

"Make that ten miles, and we got a deal."

"Okay, but the—"

"Operation manual says to travel five to six miles apart to avoid collisions, but that's assuming transports aren't traveling beyond warp speeds."

Teddy smiled at me as if I were his child. "Yes, Grams. We have a deal."

I don't remember opening the air pillow tucked inside the panel between the front and back windows, but I woke up with my head on it, refreshed, as Teddy parked the Renault in the garage.

The Tai food was on the porch and smelled heavenly, and I rummaged through the bag and pulled out the sauce packets. "Only two packets of soy and one for the crab appetizer. I get dibs on the sweet and sour sauce."

Teddy pursed his lips. "Then I get an extra piece of crab Rangoon."

"You drive a hard bargain. I trained you well."

Inside the house we divvied up the food onto sunflower stoneware plates at the counter. The emptied takeout Citsalp containers would disintegrate as soon as one of us dipped them in antibacterial soapy water. My grandmother, a staunch recycling advocate, would be proud if she was still walking around on the planet.

Swallowing his food, Teddy touched an ear lobe. "Liz and Ed are calling back. You want to talk to them?"

"Sure. Please put them on the house speakers."

"Liz and Ed here," Liz said, the usual spokesperson for the duo.

"What did you find out about Chantel and Jonathon Farnsworth?" I asked.

"I was about to give up when Ed remembered a way, a back door, based on a computer program he developed while he was in college. It worked. You're right, Chantel has some major cyber security. She was a big cheese in genetic engineering before going with E.I. Vance. She is the director of the lab, making the new anti-aging and reversal drugs. The proposed merger would put genetic cancer tracers in her lap and give her the power to test and eventually redesign genetic codes in fetuses."

Ed joined in the conversation. "Jonathon comes from a Catholic background and probably objects on moral principles, but the merger is with Xetrov, an extra-terrestrial company, complicating matters further."

I dipped a corner of a rangoon-stuffed triangle in the scarlet spicy sauce. "An ET company merger would lead to the availability of valuable resources for the earth, but the deal has major ethical drawbacks for the right-to-lifers, not to mention the anti-ET coalition backlash."

"Everyday man loses again for the one percent to win," Liz said.

"Yes, but—"

"Exactly," Ed said. "My Liz is a wiz." Ed's manners—in fact, his whole personality—irritated me, but he was a genius in some areas. He had solved an art heist case for us last year because of his unique skill set.

"Yes, Ed. Can you check over some paintings Teddy scanned in the Farnsworth home vault and get back to me about their worth and authenticity? I realize your appraisal will be limited by the quality of the scan."

"No problem. Can't wait."

"I am downloading the scan now," Teddy said. "Stand by."

"What about Detective Barden?" I asked.

Somebody sighed on the other end of the line.

"I have another impatient caller waiting," Liz said. "Nothing unusual on Barden. Yet. I'll Vmail you the list of pertinent details on the Farnsworths. It will be encrypted using our R-code from six months ago. Be well." She disconnected the call.

I understood "impatient caller" meant from the Underground. The six-months reference was a misdirect—a red herring—for any audio hackers. Our encryption keys were color-coded. R, or red code, was used as a red flag when Liz and Ed thought the chances were high the government was listening to our conversation. This case was becoming a complicated maze, and we weren't close to finding Jonathon.

07

The next morning, after an invigorating yoga session in the living room, I immersed myself in writing a suspenseful scene about the art heist of an Edward Hopper painting from the Thyssen-Bornemisza Museum in Madrid, Spain—loosely based on one of our past cases. In the background noise, I heard Teddy in the kitchen, opening and closing cabinet doors.

He brought me a fresh cup of coffee and patted me on the head. "I'm leaving to go to the university library. I'll catch the Blue-Sky Transit. The research librarian insisted I see the materials on Jonathon with my own eyes. Did you ever read that email about Barden and Farnsworth from Liz?"

"Not yet. Have a good time," I said, continuing to type. The dinette table wobbled a bit as I hit the laptop keys. My con-artist protagonist's bent sense of right and wrong fascinated me. Two hours later my rear end was numb, and I realized it was raining. I stretched and walked to the bay window to watch the drizzle. A wooden birdhouse on a wrought iron pole swung in the wind.

It was after two o'clock in the afternoon. I wondered how long Teddy would be, but decided not to text him. Although I had read the confusing email from Liz about Jonathon and Detective Barden several times, I wasn't ready to discuss it. Something was off. It gnawed at me but it wouldn't surface.

I felt the familiar foggy brain and nausea symptoms when my blood sugar drops. I needed protein. I managed to fry an egg and slap it on a piece of bread. I sat on a stool with my elbows propped on the center island counter while chewing and holding my head up with one hand. I hoped I'd recover before

Teddy returned, but he came through the kitchen entryway and slammed the door. Rain dripped from his curls.

I straightened up with effort.

He watched me for a second, then opened the refrigerator, retrieved a container of orange juice, and poured me a glass. "Really, Grams, you need to take better care of yourself." He grabbed a tea towel draped over the oven door handle to dry off.

I drank the juice and, delaying the inevitable reprimand, I stacked the glass and the silverware on my plate as if I was designing a sculpture and smiled. "Let me take my meds before the state health hologram chastises me." I headed for the bathroom under the stairs.

"Wait. One of my jobs is to take care of you." He folded his arms, still dripping wet, mimicking one of Jack's gestures when he was upset with me.

I ducked into the bathroom.

I returned five minutes later to find him in the same stance.

"Sorry," I said. "I got carried away with my writing. Was in the zone. I do feel better. Now, go change clothes and tell me what you found out about Jonathon." I handed him a towel I'd brought back with me from the bathroom.

He undressed to his underwear, toweled off, and threw his pants and shirt in a corner. Modesty wasn't Jack's strong suit or stressed in Teddy's code.

I diverted my eyes and handed him another dish towel from a drawer underneath the center island.

My oblivious grandson rubbed his hair vigorously. "The librarian wasn't there. Never came to work, so they said." He tossed the towel on the back of a dinette chair.

"Did you call him or her on their cell?"

"I tried. The personal phone number I found online for her was a bad number." Teddy frowned, a gesture of stress or concern that Jack had programmed into Teddy, making him appear human.

"That doesn't sound good. Now, we might have a missing librarian. This case gets curiouser and curiouser," I said. "Go put some clothes on, and then I'll tell you about Liz's email."

*****

When Teddy returned from his bedroom, he wore sweats and tennis shoes. He combed his hair back with his fingers and took the cup of coffee I offered him. He didn't need to warm up. His body temperature stayed the same no matter what, but I liked to pamper him.

I remained quiet.

"Why are you procrastinating about sharing the contents of Liz's email?" Teddy asked.

"I wanted time to sort it. When my gut tells me one thing and my head another, I have learned to stop and make sense of it before I move on."

"Your intuition kicked in." There wasn't a hint of sarcasm in his tone. Jack's scornful tone toward my hunches was absent.

"Yes, it's a human trait, although your grandfather would dismiss my remark because he didn't believe in a soul."

"The immortal soul, a spiritual or immaterial part of a human being or animal." He inclined his head. "By definition, I don't have one."

"No, but by definition, you can't choose evil. However—"

"Evil, vile, destructive behavior—"

"Thank you, Teddy. Believe me, life, as well as this P.I. business, has defined evil for me. I fear your librarian is dead. Liz suspects Jonathon is or was an undercover agent from the Underground, but her security clearance isn't high enough to confirm."

"Logic demands, if dead, my inquiries led to the librarian's demise." He held my gaze.

"I'm afraid so. The aftermath of free will, or in your case, a program with a learning curve, causes good and evil. Some would say gray issues of consequence, but that's a discussion for another day. What exactly did you ask the librarian to obtain?"

"I wanted to scan Jonathon's birth records and marriage certificate etc., because, as you say, something was off about the online records."

"Too clean?"

"On first inquiry. Jonathon is listed as a ward of the state. However, the librarian may have found information about a birth mother living in Hawaii within Jonathon's will—filed days before he left."

"So, Chantel misled us about the will. Hawaii, here we come."

"She left out info, yes, but Jonathon did leave the family home to his sister."

"And we can't afford a family trip to Florida, let alone Hawaii. But I can dream."

"Changing the subject, now. What about the vault full of art at Jonathon's house and Detective Barden?"

"Nothing. The art looks to be legit, bought at auctions—my guess it's Chantel's hobby—and Liz found absolutely zero red flags on the detective. No complaints, no reprimands in his personnel jacket. He was a bit of a rebel in his academy class but tested out number one in academics and tactical pursuits."

"Your assessment?"

"I can't figure him out, and until I do, I'm treating him as an agent sent by the state."

08

The next morning, over our first cup of coffee, we flipped a quarter from Jack's coin collection for the leftover crab Rangoon. "Heads, I won," I said. The breakfast of scrambled eggs and warmed-up leftover crab Rangoon hit the spot. "Don't pout, Teddy. There will be other tosses." If I hadn't done the honors, I might have thought Teddy allowed me to take the last triangular pouch of yummy.

"I don't pout. Besides, I need to empty my food disposal depository." He excused himself and went to the bathroom. Upon his return, Teddy nibbled on half of a bacon sandwich and then wrapped up the remainder. He placed it inside a three-sectioned tray on the storage belt unit. It would be sorted into a packaged meal using other leftovers compatible with Teddy's or my dietary habits. I loved the way it sealed, labeled, and dated the contents.

He looked so serious. "Statistically speaking, the odds were and are against you."

I wiped the tabletop and handed Teddy the dishcloth to clean the counters. "I don't gamble anymore. This doesn't count."

Teddy turned to the sink, but I knew what he was doing. He was considering what, if anything, to say next and dipping each takeout container, one by one, in the sink and watching the warm soapy water dissolve them.

I sat down at the table and opened my laptop. I felt lucky. Risking a lecture by Teddy, I surfed the net for a bargain flight. "You could practically JetRocket to the moon for what it costs for an economy flight to Hawaii."

"Because federal regulations forced the airlines to install costly plastic cubicles, and then the activists insisted on sanitized air being piped into each passenger's enclosed space, the ticket prices have skyrocketed. No pun intended." Grinning, Teddy joined me at the table.

"One could argue the protestors lost more than they gained. Still, we humble and poor deserve to breathe air without life-threatening viruses infecting us just as much as the first-class passengers."

"Agreed, but I think the previous standards with shields instead of cubicles and filtered air inside the cabin were adequate."

"Perhaps. Granted, it was convenient for the head of the lobbying group who supported the protestors to bring a win to the table on the same day she announced her candidacy for governor."

"Getting back to the matter at hand, without gold Gainies handy, we could BlinkoTime with Jonathon's mother. I have the number," he said.

"I hate it when you're right." It was true we didn't have half of a Gainey—worth about five hundred dollars in old currency—between us.

"When you didn't share Liz's info, I did a quick interface with your computer system."

"And... I hate it when you break our privacy rule."

"I dislike it when you withhold intel and disregard our agreement about spending limits."

I glared at him, but he looked away.

"Anyway, while I was in there, I updated your security system," Teddy said. "It needed it."

A knock at the front door made us scurry. I dropped my laptop into a safe hidden in the floor, and Teddy grabbed his AI buffer from the freezer and eased it into his abdomen port, projecting human organs throughout the inside of his mainframe. The outsourced device drained power: he could only sustain it for fifteen minutes.

The floor covering slid back into place, hiding the safe. The pounding shook the front door. Teddy and I held each other's gazes. Whatever was out there wasn't human, or our security cameras would have alerted us before the first knock.

*****

Patriot Act 2044 required all homes to be inspected randomly, once a year by military police, but this was our second visit in less than six months. I hoped this visit wasn't because of our association with Georgie or our recent case. Teddy hit a special button on the stove he had installed. It connected to the basement panels, making them unfold and slide into place, hiding his AI maintenance shop.

I opened the door to find a bomb-detector robotic arm stretched out, ready to knock again. The arm was attached to a round machine about the size of my twenty-year-old vacuum cleaner. An officer stepped forward and read the part of the Patriot Act, reminding citizens to comply. "Do you understand what I have read to you? Will you cooperate?"

"Yes." Mentioning our inspection from last August would be futile.

"How many occupants are currently inside?"

"Two," I said.

"Names and ages?"

"Dorothy Saunders, sixty-six, and Teddy Strange, almost twenty. We are the only residents."

"Citizen Strange is nineteen years old," the robot announced.

"Yes. Please step aside."

A military police officer dressed in combat gear took a stiff-legged step closer. He reminded me of a commercial television character made out of tires I'd seen as a child. My grandmother's favorite pastime was watching true-crime stories on the tube before independent and corporate channels were replaced with state-run announcements. "The inspection won't take long. You may follow and record, but please do not interfere."

The officer meant or else we would be arrested. He motioned for the robot to step inside and scan the house, including the basement through the floor. Jack and Teddy's secret panels, made from a unique combination of materials, created a shield that diffused light and, for all practical purposes, erased the maintenance shop behind them. The shield held. The AI signaled the human officer that all was well by flashing a greenish-blue light.

I made myself take a breath. "My grandson is on his way out to study with a friend. Is that okay?"

Again, the robot emitted a green-blue glow. Teddy had passed the human-figure test, but in a matter of minutes, his power source would be running out.

"First, let me see his identification papers," the officer said.

"Teddy produced his driver's license encoded with a background check and a student ID."

"Please place your index finger on the screen." The officer held up a minicomputer the size of a man's wallet. I noticed the index finger on the officer's left hand was missing.

Teddy complied. Jack had made sure Teddy's fingerprints were unique.

The officer's computer beeped. "You may leave."

As protocol mandated, Teddy would drive to Liz and Ed's house less than a mile away for an emergency power boost. I sat down at the desk table I never used for writing and took out a tablet containing trite manuscripts from my college days. "May I write? I am a fiction writer."

"Of course. 'We disrupt only for your safety and others.'" He quoted one of the many slogans from the Good-Citizen campaign.

I turned on the video camera, hit record, and wrote a bunch of happy nonsense about a summer vacation Jack and I had taken at the only remaining national park, Yellowstone, renamed Gainey's Gift. The president had left the area pristine and chose not to extract the mineral resources because the First Lady had spent many summers of her childhood there. I tried to concentrate on writing, but I flinched as the officer opened drawers and went through my things. He found a campaign button for the minority party candidate from the last so-called democratic election in the back of the kitchen junk drawer. He tossed the button into the robot's trash bin. "You won't be needing this anymore." The officer turned his upper torso as if his spine rotated from screws in his neck and lumbar spine.

I cleared my throat but held my tongue.

"Reminder: you must log all of your business calls."

"Yes, I am aware."

The officer stared.

I added, "Thank you." Teddy and I logged the calls that were innocuous and used a GoSure filter system for the rest. The officer continued his search.

Thirty grueling minutes later, the officer asked me to sign an acknowledgment of service and gave me a copy. I couldn't wait to close the door behind him and the robot. I remembered when private property was synonymous with personal privacy.

*****

I picked up Teddy, and we decided to swing by Black Jack's for a cup of java before we called Annette Collins on the West Coast, four hours behind us. Apparently, Jonathon's mother kept her family name and never married. With the trying morning behind us, we indulged in a cheese and fruit platter and divine croissants with a jam compote on the side.

The high-tech BlinkoTime Cafés weren't on every corner. We hopped on the train and headed for the newest section of the Fourth Ward. The homes had tripled in price in the last five years during its second gentrification wave within twenty years. Young families moved in and paid inflated mortgages or bought turn-of-the-century fixer-uppers. A few yards still had trees. "I remembered when Atlanta was known for its plethora of trees."

"I bet it was beautiful when you were a kid." Teddy glanced up from his phone. The landscape blurred by as the train picked up speed between stations.

"It was, and the shade helped beat the heat." Atlanta didn't have four seasons anymore. We had a rainy, cool season in January and February, and then it turned warm and got hotter each passing week. By mid-August, the temperature jumped into the low hundreds to the mid-teens, killing the flowers and grass. The homeless fled to the cool tunnels built when the infrastructure failed about ten years ago. They outsmarted us all.

The first café was a block from the BeltLine, a walkway with on-site art installations looping the city. The newest BeltLline installments were electronic billboards with advertisements. I quit going there years ago after the city council allowed hoverboards and flying bicyclists.

Teddy held the door open for me at Mirrors Delight. The red and gold state colors motif turned me off. A huge mirror against the back wall bounced our reflections back at us. The place was set up like a rat maze. The sides of the maze looked as if it would reach my shins on my 5'4" body. I wasn't known for my long legs. The individual mirrors were in cubby holes against the side walls. The short clerk behind the podium counter with gates on either side sized up Teddy. "You'll need an extra-tall mirror or adjust by standing back. Be an extra twenty surpas, plus, if you're calling outside of the continent—"

"We're calling Hawaii, ten to fifteen minutes," I said.

"Okay. The descendants of Queen Lili'uokalani of Maui are running a special this week because of the Hula Dance Fest." The clerk looked up from his computer.

Teddy stepped around me and leaned his upper body over the desk. "No. A regular mirror will do. Calling Honolulu. Anytime today."

"Chill, doo." He handed Teddy two clip-on microphones and conjoining carotid phone hookups. "Just forty regular surpas."

"Make that thirty." Teddy pointed to the chart listing prices above the clerk's head."

"Right. My mistake."

"Your governmental surveillance rating?" Teddy asked.

The clerk put his elbows on the counter. "Officially, they spot-check about fifty percent of the conversations, but I'd say it's more like sixty."

We approached the maze in a single file. Teddy turned around. "The clerk's a jerk, but he was telling the truth about government surveillance."

"Got it. I'll use security protocol." We had developed a strategy of interviewing that gained the maximum intel while it minimized the risk of attracting the National Security Service's attention."

Teddy handed me a keyword list on his phone.

I scanned it. I'd memorized most of the red-flagged words, but there were a few new ones.

"I updated the list yesterday. Don't use the highlighted ones."

I stumbled over a sharp curve in the maze, and Teddy caught my shoulders and righted me.

The blood rushed to my face. I hated needing help like a doddering old fool.

He assessed the surroundings. "Let's take the second-mirror slot. That mirror is tall enough for me to see."

After several seconds, Annette appeared in the mirror wearing a spaghetti-strap dress with an exotic-bird pattern and no makeup. We introduced ourselves as P.I.s.

Annette's hologram's reaction was concise. "I won't speak to anyone from a private detective agency."

"Please don't hang up. Jonathon Farnsworth is missing, and he was last seen in Honolulu," I said.

"What did you say?" Annette's voice sounded shaky. Her skin was flawless, no lines or bags around those baby blues. Expensive work.

"We have reason to believe he's in trouble. Weren't you acquainted with Jonathon's late father from your college days at Harvard?" Jonathon would've been born during Annette's senior year at college and placed in an orphanage.

She stared at me. Catatonic.

"Have you heard from Jonathon?" I asked.

"Never heard of him. Please don't call here again." She shut down the connection.

Undercover Chameleon

09

The next day, Georgie met us at The Bird for a late lunch. The new owner was an Underground sympathizer, a fourth-generation hippie or Four-H, so he swept his place for incoming surveillance continually. He believed in a free press and displayed framed covers of The Speckled Bird with political satire cartoon drawings from the 1970s. Most of the younger patrons shook their heads at his funky ideas, but they savored his rebellious art.

The state's restructured CIA had distance surveillance equipment available to pick up conversations from anywhere within a two-block radius, but it was expensive to run. We hoped if there had been a "good citizen" complaint report lodged against the establishment, it hadn't reached too far up the city's official chain. We needed to talk to Georgie without using word protocols.

Somebody with influence liked the place, but powerful people lost favor. We feared The Bird would be open one day and vacant the next, like other businesses that the government shut down without warning. Sometimes, the proprietors disappeared.

"Why so urgent? What's this about?" Georgie sat down in a patio chair.

"Wait a sec." I scooted around in a chair, trying to get comfortable. Finally, I took out a small pillow from my tote. Let people stare. "I hate these wrought-iron chairs with a passion."

Teddy looked off into the distance.

"We had a visit from Detective Barden," I said. "Somehow he knows you're on the government's watchlist, so we are too."

"Sorry about that. They've suspected me for about a year, but they haven't enough intel to bring me in."

"They don't need a reason," Teddy said.

The all-smiles waitress appeared and we ordered. The waitress left.

"Usually, you'd be right, but my uncle is second in command in the CIA. He thinks I'm an angel and most of the time, I am. My life consists of my forensic work, research, and swimming. I rarely date, and I am discrete in my personal life."

Teddy looked down. If I didn't know it was impossible, I'd believe my AI grandson blushed.

"What security precautions are you taking?" I asked.

"I install a new firewall every thirty days and sweep for hackers with a new software called NotToday. My flat's security is the best around, but we all know the CIA can breach any commercial system." Georgie raised an eyebrow. "I don't conduct sensitive inquiries on my cell phone or business computer."

"Then you're using burner phones and repurposed home laptop temps," Teddy said.

Georgie cocked her head. She knew he was aware that low-cost temps or home laptops with a shelf life of nine months were hard to hack because they were developed for educational purposes during the COVID-19 pandemic for low-income children. NATO dictated the devices be free of spyware.

"Yes," Georgie said.

"Don't you just love it when a social problem can be solved through global cooperation," I said.

"Yes, or go through Liz and Ed. Recently, they hooked me up with a dealer." She meant a black-market computer dealer."

Her frankness in a restaurant made me nervous. I looked around. "I see. Teddy introduced you to them?"

"I hope that was all right."

I wrestled with my ire. Teddy had broken our rule to discuss with each other the possibility of allowing a new person into the inner circle of our section of the Underground network. It was unlikely Georgie was a spy, and I trusted Liz to run a thorough background check on her or any other perspective new member of the team, but I was furious.

The happy waitress brought us our drinks, BLTs, and slaw.

"I haven't any objection, but there's a procedure—a few steps—Teddy chose to skip. I'm afraid you'll be monitored by us as well as the CIA for a while."

Georgie nodded. "As I would expect." She picked the tomatoes off her sandwich.

Teddy avoided looking my way and took a huge bite of his sandwich.

"Georgie, what's your opinion of Detective Barden?" I asked.

"Seems like a stand-up guy for a state officer. Doesn't take himself too seriously. But I wouldn't suspect him of being a sympathizer or, for Gainey's sake, a double agent." She placed some slaw on her sandwich and munched.

The phrase "for heaven's sake" had become a politically incorrect phrase to use in conversations after the Christian right threw away their 2038 election by backing a moderate candidate during the runoff. It made me flinch every time I heard the president's name being glorified. I stewed over the fact Teddy had said little during our luncheon and let my two younger companions eat for a bit.

I put my sandwich down. "Why would the detective take a chance and alert us about your name being on the list?" I asked.

"I have no idea. Maybe he worked with Dad before he quit the force and started his law practice. I'll check." Georgie gulped down the last of her coffee and left half her food. "Sorry, I gotta go back to work. I'll text you."

"Were you advised on the communication protocols?" I asked, realizing I sounded snarky.

She flashed me a put-on smile and slid her chair under the table. "Yes, I'm familiar. Later, Theodore."

She walked away with a bounce in her step, hair bobbing to and fro across her neck. Teddy watched her leave, too, but I suspected for different reasons. For the first time, Georgie's confidence and her girl-next-door manner seemed a perfect cover for a spy.

We sat in silence and finished our meal.

*****

Against my will, I was chauffeuring Teddy to the university library in the sweatpants and

T-shirt that I'd worn to bed. I patted Teddy's knee, making him look at me. "I'm sorry," I yawned, "for being snippy with you. I'm not at my best early in the day. I prefer outings or appointments in the afternoons."

He tapped on his phone screen. "Yes, Grams. Sorry, I needed to meet with my project partner. This was the only time he could do it."

The express train was out of order. It wasn't Teddy's fault. His research paper about the flashpoints for protest and cultural change was due in less than twenty-four hours. He would pull another all-nighter, his customary way of completing major assignments. Unfortunately, he'd messed up my morning rituals of rising slowly and stretching for ten minutes before coffee and toast. "We need to meet up later and discuss the Farnsworth case," I said. "It seems our leads have dried up."

I pulled over inside the drop off lane and pushed the auto-open button for Teddy's door.

He slung his satchel over his shoulder and stepped out. "Okay, if the train is still out-of-order, I'll catch a ride home with Dell, my project partner. See you for supper."

I plastered a smile on my face. "Have a super day, dear."

Traffic was a nightmare. I couldn't go around, under, or over the other cars. Waiting through multiple light changes at a major intersection, I turned on the radio. A tiny hologram popped up on the dash-panel screen and reported the daily headlines. Another driver honked for me to drive forward. Photos flashed on the screen. I lost the name of the first man arrested, but the second smuggler of stolen goods was Raphael Denton, one of our Underground operatives. It couldn't be a coincidence if Georgie had met Raphael or Raph for her recent black-market purchase.

At home, I threw my purse on the divan and headed straight for the refrigerator, pulled out a meatloaf leftover dinner—now my brunch—and a bottle of red wine. It had to be five o'clock somewhere. A hefty glass of wine plus an empty plate made the day look brighter. I called Liz using a secure line.

"Is that you, Dorothy? You sound tipsy." Liz sounded amused.

"Yes, I've had a glass of wine with my brunch. To my dismay, Teddy got me up at the crack of dawn, and I drove him to the university. Of course, I got caught in rush hour traffic on the way back. But what I called—"

Liz coughed and kept coughing. "Could we talk later? Something has come up, an emergency of sorts."

We were being recorded on her end. The phrase "an emergency of sorts" was our code for "shut up or heads up," so I played along. "Is Ed okay?"

"Yes. I mean, it's not deadly serious. A wasp stung him in the garden. Gotta go. I'll call as soon as I can."

Liz was in the middle of cleaning up whatever mess was created by the operatives' arrest. I wondered how I could help and sent an encrypted email to Liz and then Ed. I didn't receive a response email for thirty-five torturous minutes: "They've arrested Alfie and Raph. They're in detention at Claymore. Trying to get more info. Possible Alfie attempted TOL." Liz signed it Prissy, my nickname for her.

If Alfie attempted to take his own life, TOL, he must have feared the worst. The new Mindsweeper drug was more effective than sodium amytal or pentothal, but the side effects, if used more than a couple of hours, produced a burning-alive sensation. The detainee died in agony.

I sent a text to Teddy. I need you to come home, sort of an emergency.

He wrote back. K. Express train up and running. Be home in twenty.

I made a cup of strong coffee and paced until Teddy walked in. He hugged me straightaway. "I saw the dark web chatter about Raph and Alfie being in Claymore. Have you contacted Liz?"

"Yes, I'm still waiting for a complete response about Alfie's possible TOL in an encrypted email. Everything points to a leak and Georgie."

Teddy's face remained expressionless.

"Logically, we should wait for Liz's update, but human life is at stake," I said. "What is the risk assessment if we call Detective Barden's private number?"

"About fifty-fifty."

"We could meet him in a public park in a blind spot, and you could monitor his vitals— see whether he's lying."

"What does your intuition tell you about the guy?" He held my shoulders and saw I was determined. "Let's do it," he said.

*****

The wind had picked up and cut through my short cotton jacket. "I told the detective to meet us at one in the afternoon on the far side of Peacock Park near the viaduct. Will that block any audio surveillance?"

"It should help, but I'll scramble anything I detect. We weren't tailed," Teddy said.

"If it wasn't a life-or-death situation, I might've enjoyed the brisk stroll over here." I pointed at Detective Barden under the bridge. "For goodness' sake, he's smoking a pipe. I haven't seen one of those in years."

The detective took a compact-sized tin out of his coat pocket and tapped the pipe's bowl on the edge, emptying the tobacco. He watched us approach, unflustered, although we had seen him engaged in an illegal activity. He smelled like dried fruit and autumn leaves. With dimples complimenting his square jaw, he tipped his head toward me. "Now we both have compromising information on each other."

"Yes, I suppose we have." He wasn't going to let us forget he let the video-tampering incident slide on the Winchester twins' case last month.

Barden was enjoying the irony and was content to wait as Teddy scanned the parking lot.

"It's clear, Grams, go ahead," Teddy said.

"What can I do for you?" Barden asked.

"Georgie may've passed sensitive information to the authorities that resulted in the arrest of Raphael Denton and Alfie Combs."

"The two Underground operatives, yes. They're being detained at Claymore's Homeland Security Compound for questioning or torture. Whatever the state deems appropriate."

His sarcastic tone surprised me. "Did Georgie have anything to do with it?" I asked.

"I can't be certain one way or the other. My best guess is no. Too obvious. Georgie is a shrewd woman. She reminds me of a master chess player I once had the pleasure of playing. He let me think I was holding my own, but he controlled the long game. He surrounded and checkmated my king without me tracking."

"How do you know so much about Georgie?" Teddy asked. I could've sworn a nervous tick flickered over his AI face.

"I was her father's friend and partner when we worked vice years ago. Just young bucks. Georgie was small—four or five years old."

"You keep an eye on her. Why?" Teddy asked.

"I owe her father and her mother. Nothing you need to know other than they came through for me at a low point in my life."

"Why use the past tense in reference to your friendship?" I asked.

"He and I disagreed about a criminal case involving a serial rapist. Jerry, by then a new up-and-coming lawyer in hot Atlanta, got the scumbag off on a technicality. I voiced my dissatisfaction on the courthouse steps, punches were thrown, and as a result, I toted some suspension days. I got over it. He didn't."

"Teddy, the time?" I asked.

"We've been talking three minutes."

I turned to the detective. "I want to keep this short."

"I agree. Less chance of a random surveillance scanner picking up our conversation." Barden opened his coat and revealed a mini blocker. "This should help, but let's keep it under five minutes to be on the safe side."

I nodded. "Are you able to get a message to Alfie or Raph?"

"I'll do you one better. Some human rights advocates caught the sympathy of a territory governor's wife. If all goes to plan, your friends should be on their way to the county hospital in about two hours. Look for a Claymore van. This is the route." He unrolled a fist. There was an old-fashioned hand-drawn map on a slip of paper. Forbidden paper.

I gasped.

He started to hand it to Teddy, pursed his lips, and then gave it to me. "Memorize, don't scan it. There shouldn't be a paper or cyber trail. Burn it." Releasing carbon emissions or the act of burning materials was prohibited. He gave me a couple of long matches from the box.

"How do we know we can trust you?" I asked.

"You don't, but I suspect Teddy has been reading my vitals. What options do you have?" He set his tweed cap closer to his ears and left, heading toward downtown Atlanta.

"He knows about you," I said.

"Or guessed. The detective isn't lying, but he probably omitted some details," Teddy said. He turned around and stood between me and the nearest entrance. "Hurry up."

The wind blew the map in my hands back and forth, making it hard to read. It showed Constitution Road to Bouldercrest Road to I-285 South to Riverdale Road. I reviewed it again, and then I lit a match against the viaduct wall and burnt the paper, stamping the ashes out with the heel of my boot.

"We better go." He made a whirling motion with a finger, our sign for a nearby flying drone. I stuffed the extra match in my jacket pocket and took Teddy's arm.

*****

The next two hours were all-hands-on-deck. We met in person at Liz and Ed's house. They had called in the five-person rescue team. Within twenty minutes, Ed's chic living room was transformed into an incident room with a wall full of data tacked up using pieces of electrical tape. The squad stood by in their tactical gear. Our crews used non-lethal tranquilizer guns, but the guards wouldn't.

Teddy set to work creating a smoke-bomb screen for the operation.

I briefed the squad commander about the route of the van, and she took it from there. Because the need-to-know protocol kicked in the moment Alfie and Raph were arrested, I walked home alone, leaving the car for Teddy in case the impromptu command post got raided. He stayed behind to help handle any technical glitches and to destroy evidence if necessary.

I arrived home exhausted, closed my front door, and I burst into tears. Teddy had kissed me goodbye with his usual casual manner, though his calculations for a successful mission were low. I trusted our network to do their best to save our guys, but the dangers were real. I could do nothing but wait.

*****

At six in the evening, Teddy came bounding in through the kitchen entrance. It was disconcerting; he never looked worn out. He led me down to the basement and put up the shields. "We did it. Raph and Alfie are in one of our safe houses in South Georgia."

"How are they? Did anybody get hurt?"

"The team is fine. The operatives, too soon to tell. Raph was beaten, but he'll mend. He's being debriefed. Alfie was experiencing a high level of pain and placed in an induced coma to allow the antidote to work."

"So we don't know if Alfie or Raph exposed us?"

"No, but there were only two guards on the van transport and—"

"And there should've been state officers if they thought our guys were of value and still withholding any intel."

"Maybe. It did seem too easy. We'll keep them under close surveillance using a new protocol so they won't be familiar."

"Did your smoke bomb work?" I moved toward the stairs leading up to the main floor.

"Really, you must trust me. All of Grandpa's designs are uploaded in my programs." He looked incredulous and followed me into the kitchen.

"The execution by the team was sloppy but adequate for the extraction." Teddy sat down at the island.

"Do you want something to eat?" I felt such relief he was home. I couldn't help myself. I turned and hugged Teddy's neck. "I'm so glad you're safe." He allowed me to brush a stray curl off his temple.

"Thank you, Grams. I'm at your service day or night." He grinned, replicating Jack's smile.

I swear my AI loves me.

10

I was revising a short story about a bigamist found murdered in Dunwoody. How could I still find mistakes in the dialogue after it sat for twenty-four hours plus five or six read-throughs? Frustrating. Teddy came into the kitchen and fixed himself a PB&J sandwich. Last night I couldn't keep my eyes open. Fatigue had set in after supper, and I had left the dishes for Teddy to clean up and went to bed.

"May I have one of those sandwiches? I need to stop this treading-water exercise in futility called my writing."

"Besides, you still want to talk about the Farnsworth case."

"Yes, how did you know?"

Teddy munched on his sandwich while he slid a ridiculous sideways grin from one corner of his mouth to the other.

"Oh, stop it. Suggestions on how to proceed?"

"I did find out something interesting. Harry DeWall booked a ticket for Hawaii on tonight's redeye flight out of Hartsfield."

"That is curious. I think you should—"

"Already asked Dell Matthews for a favor. He has appropriated his dad's company jet to fly me to Hawaii. Tonight. He won't be able to stick around. I figure I can take the jet train back if necessary." The jet train was an inexpensive means of travel comparable in comfort to the second-class train seats during the wild west era. This modern version skimmed over the land and water masses, but the drivers were known for using the autopilot and sleeping. All things considered, it was a bumpy ride. The train hit and smashed small objects or debris blown onto the so-called safe route, but the worst were the unfortunate small animals crossing in front of the train and not picked up by its low-grade radar. The demise of a fun-loving porpoise jumping in the Pacific last Christmas hurt my heart. I read later the company fired the driver because their precious train was damaged and gave hush money to the right environmental commissioner.

Teddy handed me a sandwich.

I took a bite. "Wow, this cherry jam is excellent. May I join—"

"There's room in the jet for you, but it's more expensive for two in the hotels and restaurants. I'll be traveling light." He meant I couldn't take my bed pillows, transcutaneous electrical nerve stimulation unit, and thirty other things an oldster needs to be comfortable.

I closed my computer and held my head up high. "Right, I'd cuss out loud but that's beneath me. By the way, Julie's second payment transferred into our bank. We can afford for you to report in by hologram once a day." I expected resistance.

He set his jaw, but he held out a hand. The out-of-style custom bothered his logical programming as unhealthy. He was offering me a concession. "A deal?"

"Deal." We shook hands.

*****

My best friend called at five forty-five in the evening. I know because she called as I waved goodbye to Teddy from the doorway. My grandson and Dell, two young men—technically an AI and the other human—drove away in a sleek black limo. If Dell's rich father could afford a plane, I guess a limo was nothing special.

"Your timing is intuitive, Barb. I want to cry and pout because Teddy left to investigate in Hawaii without me. Am I a spoiled child?"

"Never. Just at odds with your human limitations—probably physical needs and funds, I suspect. We all go through this dear, but really, you have an exceptional, vibrant life."

"For a woman over sixty-five."

"For anybody. What do you say I bring a bottle of wine over to your house, and we watch old movies and eat pizza?"

"Best deal I've had all day."

*****

The following evening after supper, I dropped exactly one plate in the dishwasher rack before Aaron Copeland's lively strings from "The Revivalist Flock" portion of Appalachian Spring alerted me my cell was ringing in the downstairs bathroom. I had never gotten used to keeping it in my hands or close by. "How do young people get anything done?" I said punching the green icon.

Teddy laughed. "You left your cell in the bathroom again. Didn't you?"

"Dang state med check. Why aren't you using the hologram?"

"Maybe next time. I'm meeting somebody soon, so I only have a minute."

"Go on. Are you staying in a decent hotel?" Teddy hated checking in with me, but I needed to hear his voice and know he was okay. Plus, I was curious about the progress of the case.

"I'm in an air B&B. Quite comfortable."

"Does it meet your required needs?" Teddy knew I was asking about recharge unit capabilities. He needed a quiet ten every forty-eight hours to keep going. Unless it was an emergency, he wouldn't use the on-site recharge station, but otherwise he would find a discreet off-site location listed on the dark web and use untraceable never-ever coins for payment.

"Yes. I have nothing to report other than I've located his hotel, and I have him under surveillance." Teddy was letting me know he'd bugged Harry's room.

"Good."

"There's a convenient coffee shop across the street from his hotel. I'm sitting there now. I'll call you tomorrow with more news."

I pictured him sitting outside the shop wearing his favorite running shorts and his baseball cap. Women adored his muscular legs, and he used his boyish charm to extract information from them. Teddy found waitresses a fountain of information and ended up befriending most of them. My contribution—I had taught him to tip well, but like Christie at Black Jack's, Teddy usually helped them as much as they helped him.

"You better," I said to dead air.

*****

Liz knocked on my door at nine the next morning and interrupted my writing. Odd. "Where's Ed?" I asked. She'd never just showed up at my abode, and I couldn't imagine her ever going anywhere without Ed. I peered outside, expecting the irritating man to appear.

"Shut the door. I left him at home. He's fine. I needed a break and a drink."

"Okay." I tried to wipe the surprise from my face. "There's half a bottle of white on the counter near the bread and toaster drawers."

Liz walked toward the wine. "Plus, we should talk. Have you swept the house today?" She meant had I swept for bugs and signs of incoming surveillance.

"Yes, automatic timer, every hour."

"Do you have anything stronger? Whiskey? I could use some in my coffee."

I joined her in the kitchen and found Jack's bottle of Kentucky whiskey in the back of the cupboard. I doctored a cup of coffee and handed it to her.

She gulped it down as I watched.

"What's wrong?" I asked.

"Alfie and Raph were found dead this morning in the safe house. It was staged to look like they killed each other."

I grabbed for the counter. "I don't understand. How? Why make it look like—"

The security detail, two of our best guys, were shot execution-style and dumped in the woods. Miles away from the safe house."

"That doesn't make sense."

"I can't answer your questions, but I feel responsible. I missed something, Dorothy, and four good men are dead." She laid her head on my shoulder and burst into tears. Efficient, matter-of-fact Liz fell apart in my arms.

11

Our Underground contacts within the main branch hadn't reached out, and Liz and I decided convening a gathering at her house was too dangerous. We waited. The half-empty whiskey bottle sat on the table between us. In the meantime, Liz searched the dark web for any signs of a private contractor being engaged for a hit in our territory, and I distracted myself by writing a rough draft of yet another short story.

The due date was looming for a detective story set along Florida's shrinking coastline. If I won the contest—a big if, considering I hadn't sold anything in months—it wouldn't pay a utility bill, but it would boost my morale.

The soft evening light filtered through the bay window and for a moment, I sat watching one scrawny bird peck at the feeder. Climate change was in overdrive. The bird population had dwindled since the NASA 39A launch to Mars three years ago. I had no idea why my brain paired the spacecraft launch with the bird's survival probability outside my window.

My laptop stared back at me. I typed for over an hour—in the zone. A tragic tale took shape. The main character's story emerged loosely based on an elderly man I knew from the community pool whose entrepreneurial schemes lost him his wife of thirty-five years.

In my head, the imaginary character's gravelly voice reminded me of Detective Barden's. The character's need for attention, bragging manner, and disregard for others' wishes made me think of Richard, my college flame. "I think I'll name my new protagonist William Richard Helms." I had forgotten Liz, not Teddy, was in the room with me.

"What?" Liz's brows met in a scowl. She continued to type at a fast pace, boggling my mind.

"Would you like something to eat? Fried egg sandwich?"

Liz stood up, took hold of the edge of the table, and flattened her back. With her body in an L-shape, she squatted. "No, thank you. I need to get home. I'm sure Ed has cooked supper."

"Did you find anything?"

"I have a thread I'll follow up on tonight. At home, I have some scrambling equipment Ed coded that I trust more than your system. No offense about Jack's design."

"None taken." My cell buzzed, and Teddy's hologram flashed near the kitchen counter.

Liz gathered her things. "Hi, Teddy. I'll let your grandmother fill you in about what's happening here."

"Tell me what? Why didn't you text me?" Teddy's image faded in and out, but the audio was loud and clear.

Liz smiled and passed by me, shaking the quarter-full whiskey bottle in the air.

I nodded.

Sympathy crossed Liz's face. She tucked Jack's bottle with the last of his beloved whiskey under her arm and shut the front door.

I stood up and faced Teddy's image. "Awful what's on the news. How long do you have?"

*****

I brought Teddy up to speed, being careful to use security-word protocols. I rambled on, sprinkling my conversation with the local media propaganda quotes, and my grandson nodded without displaying any human reaction. "Did you receive any of this news in Hawaii? I asked.

"Not a word."

Because the national news had been censored, I wondered why the local news hadn't. "Liz thinks the so-called suicide pact of the two men was a travesty."

"Human energy wasted on emotions when rational thinking is the best tool."

"I must say it's not like you to judge human frailties, but our Jack did—"

"Red is apparently Henry DeWall's favorite color." By using red in the sentence, Teddy was warning me the hologram transmitter wasn't as secure as usual. I needed to stick to the protocol."

"How do you know?"

"The maître d' remarked that DeWall wears a red-collared shirt with a club logo on it everywhere he goes… even in the pool."

"Let's hope it isn't the same shirt every day. Do you think when he changes the color of his shirt it will be a signal for Jonathon to surface safely?"

"Yes."

"How much did that info cost you?"

"I tipped him well, like you taught me. He'll be a good source while I'm here investigating."

"I'm calculating that DeWall's room needs a random security check by staff. He's the kind of guy who would leave his computer in a drawer."

"You're the P.I. Any other links to our missing person?"

"Maybe. Gotta go. Be careful. I love you, Grams, and I'll call you tomorrow." His hologram disappeared.

I knew he added, "I love you" to sound normal, but it warmed my heart anyway.

*****

My morning ritual of toast and coffee sat cold on the kitchen counter. I tried to write for over an hour, gave up, and turned on the news. Neither Alfie nor Raph's family considered a funeral. As the custom dictated, they cremated their dead, but a combined memorial service in the spring for the men was planned at Callaway Gardens.

I hadn't realized the men were lovers. According to Liz, they had kept their relationship a secret from everyone except a few close friends because the state registered gays and isolated them by ordering they live in segregated ghettos. Their wills requested the service to celebrate their lives together, and Alfie's addendum left detailed instructions about the music. Coltrane.

I sat down on my beige couch and parted the curtains. My hands were shaking. Why did humanity continue to muck up the world? The January day was sixty-five degrees, sunny with cumulus clouds in a blue sky and a cool breeze. Idyllic. Two young men in their prime were dead, murdered, and would never see another gorgeous day. My neighbor and his dog walked by on the sidewalk. The dog—secured on a state-color red leash—barked at me while the middle-aged man looked straight ahead.

Maybe the people who went to Mars didn't miss Earth. I felt old. A nagging thought crossed my mind that I needed to update my will. After my death, I wondered if Teddy would continue on without me or power off. We had never discussed it. I couldn't think of a thing to do to help the Underground right now. The downstairs bathroom door creaked open. Teddy kept putting off replacing the misaligned door catch. Instead of shutting the door, I darted into the bathroom and grabbed the toilet brush and the bleach cleanser. I scrubbed, scrubbed, and scrubbed. The acrid smell hit my sinuses, making my eyes water as I emptied my mind of nothing but making the porcelain sparkle.

*****

By midday, I had run backgrounds on half of Jonathon's boring friends, and I was wiping down the baseboards in the guest bedroom upstairs. My cell—still plugged into the charger on my bedside table—rang. I ran to the phone, a bit disappointed it was Barbara, not Teddy.

"You sound glum and out of breath," Barbara said. "What's wrong?"

"Cleaning the house. Teddy is in Hawaii. Remember?"

"So sleuthing alone isn't as much fun?" Humor not pity filled her voice.

"I'm tracking some leads but—"

"Listen, most cases you solve the problem or puzzle before Teddy. And you have loyal friends and family." Barbara had been a widow for ten years, and her daughter and son rarely called her. She filled her days with writing and exercise classes.

"You're right. Please save me from myself before I wash the blinds and windows."

"Wait a minute, unless you want to come over to my house and clean. Just kidding. How about I buy you a margarita and some shrimp tacos at Nathan's—Oak Grove Shopping Center? Afterward, we could browse the electronic book and podcast archives at Tales and Things. That should cheer you up. Meet me in an hour."

"Make that an hour and a half. I need a shower. Maybe I'll even change into something besides sweats."

"Oh good, and try a little lip gloss. Coral is your best color."

I huffed. Barbara never stepped outside her condo without makeup, not even to feed her feral cat. Bless her heart.

"I love you scrubbed and au naturel, but it wouldn't hurt." On that critical note, Barbara ended our conversation.

12

From a corner booth, Teddy watched Harry chat up the barmaid. Her breasts heaped above a red bra that peeked out of her black spaghetti-strapped T-shirt. Tattoos covered her arms like sleeves displaying mini-Japanese opera characters. Teddy noticed the middle-aged woman kept cleaning the bar but glanced up at the aging-jock as he reached for the bowl of bar nuts close to her chest. She didn't move away.

However, Teddy observed her flinch and her breathing and pulse rate increase. Harry was a big guy, and the bar was almost deserted on a slow Thursday night.

The waitress excused herself and walked over to Teddy. "You want anything else?" She looked at Teddy's glass with melted ice cubes. "On the house." She nodded toward Harry. "That guy in the striped shirt has been here all night drinking and keeps asking me questions about my personal life. Might be waiting on someone, but he's creeping me out."

Teddy put down his cell and let her read his second-hand Notre Dame University T-shirt and see the Cosplay game he was playing online. He replaced his living-in-a-separate-reality nerdy expression to compassion. "Sure. I can stick around. I'll take another Jack on the rocks."

"Thanks. My boss should show up any minute."

*****

The Aloha Bar was closing up, and Harry paid his tab to the bar owner, a nice-enough burly Hawaiian dressed in whites like a martial arts instructor minus the black belt. Harry crossed the room, headed for the door, and glanced at Teddy seated in the corner booth in the shadows wearing a ballcap. There wasn't any change in Harry's pupil dilation. He didn't recognize Teddy. As Grams told him right after he was initiated as an AI, "In some ways you're superior to humans. We have limited eyesight and our true vision is regulated by intelligence and intuition or the lack thereof." Teddy set an internal reminder to call Grams tomorrow at ten a.m. EST—after her breakfast and meds.

He left enough to cover two drinks—a tip the barkeep would remember—and his matrix business card on the table and then followed Harry out the door. The street appeared deserted except for Harry, but Teddy could assimilate the sounds of some people laughing on a hotel patio. Somebody picked at a guitar. The breeze swept Teddy's man-made hair off his face. He associated a programmed memory from Jack's childhood of a pleasant afternoon at a beach in St. Augustine, Florida. Jack was seven or eight years old, collecting shells. The tide was coming in and the waves tickled his feet. The bathing suits were retro. His parents were packing up and calling for him to dry off.

"Hey buddy, do you have a spare surpas?" A homeless guy grabbed at Teddy's T-shirt. Teddy stepped back and using his one-hundred-and-eighty-degree vision, he saw Harry cross the street.

Something was off about the homeless guy. He looked dirty, but a faint smell of expensive cologne was seeping through the reeking getup of mismatched clothes and oily long hair. An undercover cop? Teddy stored the facial-recognition data, turned away from the scraggly guy, and tailed Harry.

*****

I poured myself a cup of coffee and heard the hologram's tinkling notification sound behind me. "Damnit," I said and whirled around.

"How many cups today?" Teddy asked.

"I refuse to answer. You look as if you're in the room, a triple-A image. Wish I could hug you."

"Yes, Grams, I know you do. Are you taking your meds? Eating? Doing your yoga?"

I messed up in the aftermath of Jack's death and forgot to take my meds. The state worker had evaluated me and reminded me about what happened to elderly offenders who couldn't keep their med schedules. I plastered indignance on my face.

"I never skip a meal and with the government tracking my med intake, what other choice do I have? They would put me in a state-run home. I'd rather walk into traffic or jump off a bridge. And yoga, not today, too early."

"Jumping off a bridge is unadvisable, because you would cease to exist, but walking into traffic with transports, traveling above your head wouldn't hurt you."

"It's a phrase of exaggeration and stop using that 2020 speech pattern."

"Storing data." Teddy blinked.

Sometimes he faked an AI program several steps below his superior rating to annoy or entertain me. I wasn't sure why Jack programmed him that way.

"Stop kidding around," I said. "I've traced nothing of interest about Jonathon's upwardly mobile friends, except one guy has two families living in separate cities. The allure of a bigamist personality eludes me. What have you found out about the case?"

"Not much. I thought I tracked down Jonathon's paternal family on another island. It didn't pan out, but Harry changed his shirt to a striped number, and I tailed him to a bar. Still no sign of Jonathon."

"Nothing else?"

"I left Harry at a massage parlor with my mite drone to watch him. Sex is a messy business. Makes me glad, well, you know. Anyway, I went through his hotel room. He had locked his computer in the safe. I cracked the password in thirty seconds. It was golf. He's a genius."

"And?"

"I documented his emails and chats and traced the IP addresses on incoming. Nothing suspicious so far, however—"

"You want to spend another day."

"Yes. It might be nothing, but I want to find a homeless man who bumped into me outside the bar. I almost lost sight of Harry."

"What piqued your interest?"

"His smell."

"Why?"

"Expensive cologne underneath the grime de stinko."

I laughed. "Teddy, you slay me, and before you start, it's another expression."

"Yes, Grams. Have a day to remember. Love you."

*****

Sitting in the coffee shop across the street from Harry's hotel, Teddy accessed the city's security cams on the street where the Aloha Bar was and searched the footage for the homeless guy.

Last night, he had stumbled into the area within minutes of Harry's arrival at the bar.

Teddy widened the search a bit and backed up the footage a few more minutes. The homeless guy had gotten out of a van parked two streets over, checked his wire, and changed his upright stance to a slump.

Now, the only problem was to find out if the guy was working for the state or Feds.

Teddy stopped on a frame and scanned in on the license plate. He hacked into the state's mainframe. The Department of Transportation registration info on the van associated with the homeless guy was redacted beyond recognition, a sure sign it belonged to the Feds or Central Intelligence.

13

I suspected I heard Teddy come in the kitchen door in the middle of the night. I slipped on a faded pair of Jack's plaid PJ bottoms underneath my oversized T-shirt, and to be on the safe side, I grabbed my taser and crept downstairs. The door to the basement was ajar, and I called out Teddy's name.

"I'm here, Grams. Need a recharge."

I tossed the taser on the counter. "A heads up would've been nice. Would you like some coffee? I'd love a chat."

"Sure. Give me fifteen."

I puttered around the kitchen, preparing toast and bacon.

He poked his head around the door. "That smell." He sat down at the kitchen island and reached for a piece of bacon and nibbled.

"Strong coffee. Just the way I like it," I said standing across from him. I devoured my sandwich with a smidge of mayonnaise. Delicious.

He waited for me to finish. "You're cheating again. I detect processed cheddar cheese and the saturated fat of—"

"Please, don't ruin the moment." I pushed my empty plate aside. Teddy insisted I be on a healthy diet regime. I wasn't.

"Fine. I ran a home and perimeter security check while downstairs. We can speak freely."

"Tell me about the train ride home. Any fatalities or dangerous encounters en route? What did you find out about the homeless guy?"

"The train ride was bumpy but otherwise uneventful. No mishaps." He gave me a look of disdain.

"Don't judge me. Boredom sets in and the mind searches for distractions."

"Moving on. I scanned the street cams. Based on license plates of the van, the homeless guy is a Fed or CIA."

"How do you break into a system without being detected?"

Teddy pulled his mouth to the side. "The state might detect a breach, but grandpa taught me his brilliant anti-tracking techniques. Plus, I've improved them. Redacted registration. Central Intelligence has blocked my hacking efforts so far, but I'll work on it."

"Either way, they're watching Jonathon as a potential Underground threat, or our missing person is actually a part of an Intelligence investigative team checking into E.I. Vance Pharmaceuticals."

"There are other options. Feds could be on an unrelated op. Harry could be the operative."

I rolled my eyes.

"Or Jonathon could've gone rogue," Teddy said, "but the two alternatives you mentioned are the most likely."

"Thank you. Does any of this relate to Alfie and Raph's assassinations?" The three days since their deaths felt elongated and full of foggy-brain turmoil.

"Probabilities are low, but I'll encrypt a message to Liz and Ed for follow-up."

"Good. Now, you go do your thing and I'll write. You've inspired the beginnings of a short story about a master-of-disguise operative posing as a homeless person. I need two to four thousand words by the next critique meeting."

"When is it?"

"You know very well it's the fourth Thursday of each month."

"Yes, in two days. You give new meaning to the word procrastination."

"I worry when you're gone, and then the loss of poor Alfie and Raph… I wish I'd known them better."

"I wonder why two closeted gay men didn't reach out to you to go shopping."

I sat up straighter. "Oh, hush. Okay, fashion isn't my thing, but I didn't pout much while you were in Hawaii without me. Barbara and I visited—"

"And drank wine."

"Yes. She makes me laugh."

"As long as you don't slip up and talk about the Underground while intoxicated."

"Honestly, I would never, under any circumstances."

He patted my hand. "I only meant your meds and the wine aren't a good combination. I would hate it if the Underground needed to eliminate a breach in security."

I couldn't tell if Teddy was pulling my leg. "Meaning me or Barb or both of us would have an accident?"

Teddy raised his eyebrows, making two foreboding arches on his forehead. "Pro-Gainey Barbara."

The doorbell rang and adrenaline flooded my body. "You can't be serious. Barbara is harmless."

The doorbell rang again.

"For the love of… That's her now."

*****

"You must tell me about Hawaii," Barbara said to Teddy. "I bet you met an island girl and had the time of your life. You bad boy." Barbara looked radiant. Gossip fed her soul.

The fact that she wore a pink cashmere sweater, pearls, and metal-gray slacks while I still had on Jack's PJ bottoms and a raggedy T-shirt didn't faze her.

"I was there on a case. But I did meet an interesting waitress."

"Do tell." She sat down, placed her elbows on the table, and laced her fingers, placing her chin in her hands–drama queen. I held my breath, wondering if Teddy was sexually active and what exactly that meant in AI terms.

Teddy let Barbara savor the moment. "Alas, she was too old for me."

"You tease."

"Why don't you leave my grandson alone and tell me why you showed up at my door so bright and early."

"I come bearing my latest manuscript for your critique and an invitation to the fashion event of the season, The Southern Benefit Gala."

"Oh no, I'm not going. I hate those things." I handed her a cup of coffee.

"It's either you or ask Herman Gentry, the poor deaf man, to escort me." She turned toward Teddy. "See why I must live vicariously through you?"

"Don't act pitiful. Your downstairs admirer has treated you like a princess for years," I said.

"He did buy me a diamond tennis bracelet for Christmas." She dangled her wrist in front of us. The bracelet caught the light streaming from the alcove window.

"Sparkly," I said. "Where is the microchip?"

She dug in her purse and pulled out an eyeglass case for contacts. The chip was in the case, a sliver of round gold.

I took out tweezers and lifted the microchip into a computer receiving device about the size of my thumbnail.

"If you would let the state put a chip in your arm, I wouldn't have to go through this," Barbara said.

"Not unless they force me."

"In a couple of years, I won't be able to order these outdated things. They track everything and everywhere you go anyway."

I must've looked dumbfounded.

Red crept up Barbara's cheeks. "I mean…" She shuffled the contents of her bag and closed it. "Cameras and mics are everywhere. I think my church's confessional booths are state-wired since the last threat on Father Dugan's life by that fanatical abortion group."

"That's an unsettling thought. You're messing with my chi, yoga gal," I said.

Barbara reached over toward a built-in bench by the window covered with potted plants. "I noticed your philodendron leaves are brown. Consistent watering would help. Should I bring over some plant fertilizer?" With benevolent haughtiness, she had executed a perfect deflection. I played along.

"No. I still have plenty of fertilizer from the last time you so kindly saved my plants."

Barbara scanned her pink-polished nails. "I'm going to stay and make suggestions until you agree to go to the gala."

"You're evil."

"I'll take that as a yes."

*****

Finally, Barbara left, and Teddy cleaned up the kitchen while I excused myself and went upstairs to change into a clean pair of sweatpants. At the bottom of the staircase, I pulled a shirt over my head. "I really don't know why I bother. Who decides on what's daywear versus sleepwear?"

Teddy was staring at me with my writing computer open beside him on the desk.

I stopped talking. He motioned for me to remain silent and played Michael Jackson's song "Beat it" through the house speakers. "Wanna dance?" he asked over the music.

He lowered his voice and walked me to the kitchen counter. "I've swept this area for devices. This microchip Barbara gave you contained advanced spyware, a trojan. If you had plugged it into the computer, they would have had access to every device we own."

I grabbed the edge of the island counter and sat down on a stool. "Who is they?"

"I'm not sure right now, but tell me you haven't broken security protocols with Barbara or how you accessed her other manuscripts."

I sat up straighter. "No. I have not, but I did fall asleep during the wine and movie night."

"For how long?"

"I don't know. She covered me with an afghan, and I woke up the next day on the couch."

"She could've dosed the wine and let them in to snoop or plant UF bugs or whatever." Only the government's elite squad of spooks used the outlandish expensive Undefeatable Flat bugs.

"It's possible but I can't believe—"

"That Barbara would be a good citizen and collect evidence on Underground rebels?"

"Okay, you're right. What now?"

"I've already alerted Liz and Ed. They're on the way over here with a security team to sweep the entire condo."

*****

The five-member security team dressed in pest-control overalls entered the house.

A thirty-something redhead with short, cropped hair took charge. I recognized her from the Underground briefings. She put her equipment case down on the floor. "If you have any allergies, you might want to leave for a couple of hours. The stuff we use to get rid of bugs is pretty strong." She retrieved a small whiteboard from her case and wrote: LEAVE ALL YOUR DEVICES ON THE TABLE.

We complied.

"I hope you don't mind. We, Edgar and I, brought along some trainees. They're young and eager to implement the newest techniques in pest control."

"Yes, that's fine," I said. "We'll be at Black Jack's Coffee Shop. Just give us a call when you're done."

Teddy stood up. "Your personal body cams will be running?"

"Required protocol. It protects the homeowner and our reputation. If you would sign my laptop agreement before you leave, giving us permission. I'll send you a copy and receipt of the work order when we're done." The woman pointed toward the door.

We said our goodbyes and took our cue to depart the premises.

At Jack's, we ordered coffee at the counter and instead of sitting at our usual table in the middle of the room, we chose a table in a rear corner. "It's silly, I know, but I feel better with a clear view of the entrance and the register," I said.

"'Paranoia is just a heightened sense of awareness,' John Lennon," Teddy said.

"A Beatles band member doesn't make for a legitimate philosopher, but I'll take it." I patted Teddy's forearm. His stored historical data about me had motivated him, not human sympathy, to say something to reassure me. Still, I felt better and would rather be with Teddy if the worst happened and we were arrested. My dear AI grandson would destroy himself if taken into custody. However, I wasn't sure I'd have the guts to commit suicide if it came down to it.

We spent the next two hours playing chess. Teddy scanned the room and moved his chess pieces on the board effortlessly. He was always several moves ahead of me. Sometimes, if I played an erratic game, I won, but not this one. I got up to go to the public restroom, and the manager stopped me in the middle of the shop. He spoke in a low tone, "You have a phone call on my business cell. What's up?"

"I'd rather not explain right now. Are you good with that?"

The emaciated, long-haired dude, maybe sixty, studied my stressed-out countenance. "Sure, whatever you need, Miss D. I love a woman of mystery." His face lit up and his wrinkles disappeared like he'd discovered a hidden Christmas present.

"I appreciate it. Can we go?" If he was flirting, I wasn't in the mood.

"Sure." He motioned for me to follow him to the back. I double-timed it to keep up with his long stride. He took me into a walk-in freezer slash personal com center and pointed to a state-of-the-art signal scrambling device.

Now, I was surprised. I took the phone he proffered.

"This room is soundproof but nowhere is state proof. Push the red button on the keypad near the door when you're ready to leave. You have two minutes," he said as he closed the door.

14

Inside Liz and Ed's bomb shelter, fourteen Underground members settled in folding chairs around two craft tables butted together to form a conference table. The chairs scraping against the tile floor made me wince. I placed my tote pillow on the cold metal seat.

Liz summarized the speculations that one or both, Georgie and Barbara, were state spies. "On one hand, I vetted Georgie," Liz said, "and Teddy knows her to be a truthful person based on his body scans. However, the timing of Alfie and Raphael's assassinations is within days of giving

Georgie a black-market contact, and I don't believe in coincidences. Now Barbara, a conservative Gainey supporter, either knew she was passing on a compromised microchip to track Dorothy and Teddy's communication devices or she didn't.

"How could she not know?" A young member asked.

"Barbara's of the older generation. Some of them don't update their security systems except during their annual state inspections. Too trusting. It's possible a state operative switched out her microchip during an inspection, after a purchase if she stopped somewhere, like a coffee shop, en route home, or she bought a trojan-infected chip over the counter. As we know, "good citizens" employed through sympathetic companies are asked to randomly sell products over the counter with spyware incorporated and packaged by the state."

Teddy scooted his chair out and gave himself some leg room. "I propose we enter and gather intel in their homes to see what evidence exists to eliminate suspicion or prove these women are spies." Breaching the sanctity of one's home went against a human right we all held dear. The table fell silent.

"I second the motion, but with limitations," Liz said.

"Such as?" I asked. The taste of bile flooded the back of my tongue, and I squirmed in my uncomfortable chair. I felt like a traitor to my beliefs for entertaining the possibility of carrying out the motion under any circumstances and torn by my loyalty to my best friend, Barbara.

We use our AIs to enter upon invitation and scan for hidden compartments and copy laptops etcetera," Liz said.

"In other words, we don't sanction rifling through their underwear drawers, but anything else is up for inspection. Plus, we humans don't put ourselves in harm's way."

Teddy made the human sound of clearing his throat. "We are here to serve. Besides, it's logical, the least invasive, and the fastest, safest way to gather intel." I knew he was right but still.

"Let's remember we owe it to Alfie and Raph to find their killers," Liz said. "We should vote."

Ed knocked three times on the table with his knuckles. He was in his element as the parliamentarian, all military justice, his artistic side not anywhere in sight. I found him obnoxious in either mode. "All in favor, raise your hand." Thirteen members lifted their hands. I alone didn't. Now, I felt like a coward. "The motion carries. Meeting is adjourned. Teddy and Helen, please stay for a briefing."

I went home, but I wasn't happy about it. Not for the first time, the Underground's sanctioned actions blurred the lines of integrity and violated principles set forth in our mission statement: to uphold our American Constitution, the original version, and promote the reincorporation of The Bill of Rights as foundational. Technically, I could absolve myself because I didn't vote for it, but I should've offered an alternative plan. No, I was culpable and if anything happened to Teddy, I'd never forgive myself.

*****

Teddy glanced at Helen as she slid into the seat left vacant by Gram at the council table.

She tapped on the craft table with the huge First Nation eagle ring, the one she wore on the middle finger of her left hand. "Barbara is in my critique group," Helen said, "and we butt heads a lot. She thinks everyone has the same opportunities as she does inside her privileged bubble, but I could ask her advice about Delta's upcoming wedding table settings, buy a bottle of expensive wine—dangle a carrot—and gain an audience with the queen of drivel." Helen was a neighbor's AI, a grandfathered-in model, but they presented themselves to the world as an adopted auntie and niece relationship.

"I see your sarcasm program is working," Teddy said. However, your suggestion is sound. I'll call Georgie and accept the invitation to a housewarming or renovated-flat party. The E-vite has been pending thirty-two hours. Because of the Underground operations concerning the assassinations, the timing wasn't optimal but now—"

"I hear she flirts with you." Ed pushed his chair back. "Perhaps a sexual advance will be necessary."

"I can't help Georgie with her biological need to reproduce."

"No, but maybe she wants a boy toy." Ed flipped a hand in the air and posed.

"That's exploitive," the young woman said with a thunderbolt shaved into her side part.

Helen put on her shawl. "Just act like you're interested. Kiss her. You can remain a celibate AI if you want. Women like to be held and kissed."

"I don't need your input to complete my mission."

"What I meant to express is that you're a rendition of an attractive young man, and she has a normal human sexual drive. It's an option."

Teddy placed his Citsalp coffee cup in the water bin. "We'll see, as Grams says."

Ed walked them to the door. "The security protocols are to be followed to the letter. You put yourselves and the Underground at risk if you're compromised."

They raised a hand and spread their fingers toward each other, giving the Underground solidarity sign.

*****

Teddy surveyed Georgie's flat. It was stunning from a minimalist point of view. The concrete and steel exterior theme was incorporated in wide open areas with compact earth-tone couches and chairs lining gray marble walkways surrounded by thick dark glass partitions. They separated a small Japanese garden with an adjoining exercise patio and lap pool area from the rest of the flat. The panels had remained black until the housekeeping computer lit them as the guests approached. The automated kitchen used voice activation and a bot chef, complete with an apron, appeared. The classic round service model skimmed from the center island to the stove and inserted a Dutch oven pan. It turned and gestured toward the glasses on the end of the island closest to the throng of eighteen onlookers. "Welcome guests," a male voice said. "Please help yourself to liquid refreshments during your tour of Georgie's home. The cider is spiked and wine and designer beers are available. Please help yourselves." The bot returned to its duties.

"Thank you, Laurence," Georgie said. "And before you ask, I don't have the foggiest notion why I call him Laurence."

Georgie leaned close to Teddy's ear, and he smelled sage. "I'm so glad you came. I was afraid you wouldn't make it. Awful about your friends. Hang around, will you? I want to have a private chat." Then she turned and greeted a couple oozing compliments about the flat's renovations.

Teddy chose a mug of cider and spoke to a few of Georgie's colleagues from the Crime Scene lab and then followed a small band that walked toward the staircase. Most of the guests rode upstairs in an elevator Georgie called a lift. She waved goodbye as the elevator doors closed. "Now we know who will live the longest. Let's." She escorted them up the stairs.

Teddy scanned the interior walls of the bedroom and found an AI scan-proof mini safe behind a framed Salvador Dali poster displaying green women morphing into a skull image, an anti-venereal disease propaganda poster for troops. The ironic warning not to touch the poster or what was behind it wasn't lost on Teddy. Given that Georgie's uncle worked for the CIA, the safe might mean nothing—a paranoid spook's security-conscious gift or, as a spy, Georgie needed a place to hide a laptop. Opening the safe undetected wouldn't be a simple task, even with the security codes, and the rooms Teddy had entered contained surveillance cameras.

The host passed by in a shimmering aqua-blue gown and interrupted Teddy's focus. "My favorite addition: I installed body-temperate flooring that I adore. I'm one of those people with perpetually cold feet." The women in the group oohed and ahhed.

Returning the guests downstairs for the ceremonial toast took a chaotic ten minutes and then Georgie's Aunt Dee blathered for fifteen minutes about memories only her niece cared to hear. In defense, the guests devoured the food from a counter laden with cold and hot hors d'oeuvres. An exquisite kiwi-topped tart was served with champagne to end the night. The cluster of intoxicated folks left around eleven-thirty, leaving Teddy alone with Georgie and her bot.

"Please sit here next to me." She patted the colorless couch. "Wait. Would you mind if I powered down my bot? Turn off the overhead cameras. I'd like to enjoy your company without being recorded."

"Sounds good." While Georgie's attention was focused on aligning the bot into a holding port, Teddy scanned for other recording devices but found none. He sat on the couch. "What's on your mind? Why all the mystery?"

"I didn't pass on information about my newest friends to anyone. I have nothing to hide. I'm truly sorry about your… what happened." She walked back toward the living room space.

"In that case, I need to see inside any safe or document case you keep, and I need your security scan codes and videos for the last six months."

For a moment, Georgie stopped and placed her hands on her hips. "What else?"

"Undergo voluntary questioning, an extended observation period, and curtail your contact with your uncle until we clear him."

"The last one might be tricky, but I'll make up excuses for a week or so. We lunch once a month at Ansley Golf Club."

"Also, I want to see your renovation plans. The real deal, not the ones for the State inspectors' approval."

"You're clever and you don't let sentimentality cloud your judgment. I like that about you. I like it a lot." She approached him with an exaggerated catwalk as she slid the shoulders of her dress off and the blue-sequin illusion dropped to the floor. She was a beautiful woman. He allowed his programming to enact the appropriate sexual response as she straddled his lap.

15

I heard Teddy come home in the middle of the night and slip downstairs to the workshop. I couldn't go back to sleep and grabbed my laptop and finished the rough draft at the kitchen table that had been due last night for my writing group.

I wondered if my dear friend Barbara would be at our next meeting smiling and acting a fool or be on trial before the Underground tribunal in an abandoned warehouse. The thought sickened me. I threw back the covers, dressed, and took my morning meds. I popped the monitor back in the sterilizer. "Excellent. Have a safe social-distancing day." The hologram wished me a good morning. At least the state health watchdogs were placated.

At breakfast, I allowed myself two cups of coffee before I questioned Teddy. "Well?"

"You know I can't discuss the details about last night with you. Helen is meeting with Barbara today and using the same tactics your friend used on you—plying her with drugged wine. I suspect the board will convene for our finding tomorrow."

"So they will send a unit to invade her house and plant mini-bugs."

"I assume." Teddy nibbled on the last of the bacon quiche.

"I wish there was another way to be certain."

"We need to find the leak fast before more Underground members are compromised."

"Agreed, but I don't have to like it." I looked outside the bay window, searching for comfort. The birds weren't at the feeder and the day was cool and overcast.

"Let's review the Farnsworth case."

I dragged my attention back into the room. "We do need to wrap up that case. It's time to meet with our client, Julie Farnsworth."

"I took the liberty of making an appointment for two this afternoon. Are you available?"

"I am, but—you checked my calendar without my permission."

"Sorry, Grams. You were sleeping upstairs, and it was time sensitive."

I knew this mess with Barbara wasn't Teddy's fault, but I pushed back my chair, scraping the floor and blurted out, "No need to consider my feelings. Forge ahead. Perhaps if you weren't so enamored with Georgie, we could make some headway with Alfie and Raph's deaths." I covered my mouth with my hands in horror and retreated to my bedroom for a good cry.

*****

Over breakfast the next day I said, "Please forgive me. I was angry about Barbara and I lost it. No excuse justifies—"

"A human frailty. I understand."

I'd put a crack in our relationship. I made cappuccinos, but Teddy never touched his cup as he briefed me about our upcoming meet with Julie. Science doesn't explain everything about human and AI interactions.

Because Julie's federal-style home was in the middle of renovation, we met her at a shoebox French café with seating situated outside on an Avondale sidewalk. The sun provided us with sixty-degree weather as a cool breeze rustled around the skin above my socks. I readjusted my pants to cover my ankles, and Teddy or T. Stringer—I reminded myself—flashed me a look of irritation. We ordered soup, salad, baguettes, and wine.

"Please don't keep me in the dark any longer. I've called you three times and received nothing but 'the investigation is in-progress.' I want to know where my brother is." Julie lifted her water glass and drank. Her gold bracelets clanged together as if making an exclamation mark in the air.

"Very well, all indications are your brother was deep undercover, and he must've been compromised and brought back in," Teddy said.

Julie stared into the distant greenery across the street as the wine bottle was brought in a bucket, opened. The waiter left.

"What on earth are you talking about? My brother is a pharmaceutical rep."

"Yes and no." I situated my bottom on my tote pillow. "He and probably his buddy, Henry DeWall, are with the CIA. In a way, we broke into Henry's file cabinets. You don't need the details. Laptops and other surveillance equipment are stored inside the locked cabinets. My colleague, T. Stringer, was able to track Henry to Hawaii, and he led us indirectly to your brother."

"This is absurd. What proof do you have he's even alive?" The food arrived but none of us took a bite.

"Your sister-in-law is designing top-secret drugs that could be used for good or ill," I said. A ragtag taxi drove by with the windows down, blasting reggae music.

"To be exact, genetic engineering of embryonic liquid to enhance human babies through robotic surrogate gestation is on the top of the list." Teddy placed his cell on the table showing a mockup of a fetus floating inside the clear plastic womb of a bot. Its frame design had been left primitive, elemental to ward off the fear of human replacement. "The company is merging with an alien corporation for minerals needed in the production of those drugs."

"When Jonathon copied the schematics, he escaped the building but barely," I said. "The plans found their way to the intended agency."

We were out of sync. Teddy coughed and finished his explanation. "The necessary chemical compounds are rare or non-existent on earth."

"But the children. Surely…" Julie's fingers covered her mouth. "No, he wouldn't leave his children."

"He didn't have a choice," I said. "Chantel knew about the breach and alerted corporate security as soon as she realized Jonathon had updated his Last Will and Testament and had given you the federal house. He kept his running stash and fake traveling ID chips hidden inside the modeling around the box window on the stair landing. Did you know?"

"No. Impossible. I've cleaned that window… Auntie warned us never to play on that ledge when we were kids. Of course, we did."

"The corporate goons followed him to Hawaii, but he flew from island to island until we suspect

DeWall got him out on a water transport. He's safe, but how we obtained the information we can't tell you." I looked at Teddy, hoping he would deliver the next blow.

"Or divulge Jonathon's location." Teddy delivered the line without emotion.

Julie pushed her plate and bowl toward the breadbasket in the center of the table. "How do I know you're not making up the whole fantastical story and my brother is still missing or dead?"

Teddy handed her a burner phone. "I suggest you use the phone in a secure area." He handed her the fob and pointed at my blue vehicle recharging in a parking spot. "The Renault is paneled and secure. For your safety as well as his, this one call will be your only contact. Do you understand?"

"Yes." She took the fob with a shaky hand.

Through the windshield we watched her expression change from joy to sadness and then tears. She held the phone to her chest. I feared she would never hear her brother's voice again.

16

The Underground council convened in our basement. Ed's game of changing meeting locations at the last minute to avoid security breaches didn't seem whimsical today. The spotless work benches and shelving lined the walls with mostly outdated AI parts and gadgets stuffed in every cubbyhole. Teddy preferred Jack's tools to the newest thing and bought black market when he needed replacement parts. Besides the fact that buying too many drills or welding tools brought unwanted attention to oneself, Teddy liked playing the old game of reciting the inventory list and pointing to Jack's tools for me to confirm.

In the center of the workspace, the modified barber chair, complete with overhead mirrors for AI repairs, was folding down piece by piece by means of a conveyance belt into an underground compartment. Once completed, a faux slab of sliding concrete covered the hole, and an ancient bamboo mat camouflaged the outline of the slab.

We topped two wooden sawhorses with an old door to makeshift a conference table, and Liz doled out the plastic stools I kept mainly for my writing group meetings. Take charge Liz had been distant and silent since she cried over Alfie and Raph's deaths at my house and left with Jack's whiskey bottle in her hand. I touched her shoulder. She jerked her head in a quick dismissal.

Ed struck the gavel on the table. "Gather all. Helen, please speak first."

The group settled into silence with another colleague sitting between Liz and me.

Helen steepled her sturdy hands near her heart, making me wonder — and not for the first time—if her creator was a woman. "Barbara is a hardcore conservative. She gives money to Gainey's cronies who either are or influence the men in the inner circle. She opposes abortion for any reason but supports sterilization of miscreants, including the unchipped illegals. She started an online UI watch group." Helen tucked her short-bobbed hair behind her ears. "And eagle-eye Barbara has turned in a neighbor for composting garbage for their unauthorized garden. However, I don't see this annoying woman as a spy. Maybe a wanna-be. She keeps a log of her neighbors' comings and goings. Boring stuff. Mostly Catholic moral high-ground observations. I am puzzled why Dorothy isn't mentioned anywhere." Helen bent forward and peered down the line at me. "Your emails and texts have been deleted. Short of wasting energy to retrieve them, nothing could be found to link you to her."

"That's odd. Not even birthday emails?" I asked.

"Nada. Of course, the pest control team bugged her home per the council's instructions. We'll give it a few days, but I don't think we'll find anything.

We tracked the chip to an over-the-counter purchase at a Kohn brothers' owned discount warehouse franchise with a new conveyor belt pick up. She's on surveillance footage selecting her package off the belt an hour before she arrived at Dorothy's place."

"It doesn't mean the state didn't direct her to do so," said a young member with a thunderbolt shaved into the side of their buzz cut.

"No, but it's unlikely she knew." I kept my tone even as the tension in my shoulders increased.

Teddy poured another cup of coffee from the carafe. "Although an unscientific conclusion, I back Dorothy's assessment. The probabilities are 80 percent against Barbara buying a trojan chip in full knowledge."

Teddy gestured toward Helen who turned her palms up and blinked, an AI expression of agreement.

If the others at the table thought it strange Teddy called me Dorothy, not Grams, nobody showed it. 'Guilt and confusion clung to me like a lusting virgin waiting for confession,' as

Barbara would say. The fact Teddy or T. Stringer chose to use our professional names here in our home twenty-four hours after I accused him of contributing to Alphie and Raph's deaths wasn't lost on me, and my best friend either didn't want the state to know she associated with me or she was protecting me by eliminating the cyber trail.

"Ted, I mean T," I said with my usual grace. "What did you find at Georgie's party?"

After the other party guest left, she gave me her security codes, and I opened her safe. Nothing of consequence inside. She knows as a probationary member we're monitoring her, so our surveillance tails probably won't produce anything."

Liz cleared her throat. "A thorough scan of her financials and then hacking into her business computer are the next steps. I've been sick with the flu. Sorry for the delay."

The group breathed the tense air in the wake of Liz's excuse until Teddy said, "Agreed. Her personal computer is too clean. Because of her CIA uncle's connection, I doubt bugging her flat will confirm or alleviate our suspicions."

"What do you propose we do?" Ed asked.

"I started a liaison with her last night. Once I gain her confidence, I'll be able to find out the truth."

My stomach churned. "Was that wise?"

"You must turn over that intimate recording unaltered to the council," Ed fiddled with the gavel.

"Of course. For future encounters, I'll let the pest control team know the security entrance codes. We're scheduled for a dinner at Juan's Bistro in Marietta tonight at 8 p.m. If the team is available, I'll make sure you have at least two hours to install cameras."

"No problem. I assume she knows you're AI," Ed said.

"She does."

Ed pounded the gavel on the table. "Meeting is adjourned until the intel committee can gather enough data to warrant assembling again."

*****

Juan's Bistro featured white modular booths and tables that floated up or down depending on the customer's desire for distance and privacy. Four feet high sculptured tulip-shape pots filled with cacti dotted the floor creating a weaving path to the bar. There an underwater satellite showed real-time footage of the bottom of the Mediterranean Sea.

Based on the rarity of the fish, Georgie ordered the most expensive item on the menu, grilled lobster tails. "Please bring my guest the braised sea bass, and we'll also have the special, the pork belly with stuffed potatoes, appetizer, and salads."

The human waiter, dressed in a white dress shirt with an open vee at the collar, black El Toro pants and white stockings, bowed. "Excellent choices. Would you like a cocktail, wine, or beer?"

"Do you have an El Gaverno white wine from 2024?"

"Let me check."

As the waiter left, Teddy said, "I see you're in a mood to be extravagant."

"The state has authorized my advanced forensic training at Northwestern University. I'll be eligible to apply for a supervisor position in less than six months."

"Congratulations. Didn't you tell me there was a two-year waiting list for that certificate?"

"Yes, but—"

The waiter returned with the wine and Georgie sampled it. She smelled the bouquet, swilled the contents in the wineglass, and then sipped, rolling it around on her tongue.

"It's perfect, thank you." Georgie's face glowed in the candlelight, and they locked gazes while the waiter filled their glasses.

"You're welcome. The restaurant is a bit noisy tonight. If you wish to soundproof your booth, push the yellow button. A clear screen will surround you. The chef's appetizer should be ready in about ten minutes."

Georgie laughed and pushed the button. "It must be obvious I can't wait to ravage you." She reached for his hand, but he didn't respond. "Sorry, I forgot. Public shows of affection confuse you."

"I'm still processing and updating my systems."

"We should take this slow, as agreed." She bit her lip, flirting for a moment longer, then sighed. "Back to the training. Detective Barden pulled a few strings."

"I see."

"No, you don't. He considers me his adopted niece."

"You have connections in the CIA and the State Police."

"You mean I'm privileged." Georgie's inflection betrayed amusement. "Of course I am. It makes me the perfect spy."

Within minutes the waiter appeared with their appetizers, and Georgie retracted the soundproof bubble. She appreciated the simple presentation garnished with a twisted orange peel. "These tender pork bellies and the stuffed mashed potato skins are divine—made with real peeled potatoes and whipped with cream and butter."

Teddy inhaled the smell of the pork gravy as he took his first bite. "I think I'm in love."

"Now we're getting somewhere."

*****

The morning after the team violated the sanctity of Georgie's flat, Teddy and I ate breakfast in polite silence. I'd cooked French toast topped with cinnamon and bananas, heated syrup, and fried half a pound of bacon. Teddy left the bacon untouched on his plate. "Let's address the elephant in the room," I said.

"Strange expression but go ahead." Teddy put down his fork.

"It's none of my business—your personal life, love life, but it worries me. Under normal circumstances it would concern me. You're my grandson." I gulped down the lump in my throat. "Are you programmed to handle such an intimate interaction and what reactions Georgie might be thinking or feeling? Humans fall in love."

"I'm aware of a female's bonding hormone released during sex, but you're curious if AIs can be attracted sexually to a human. Not in the sense of a hormone and pheromone-driven need to procreate, but our purpose is to serve and interact with humans in whatever capacity facilitates the greater good."

"The matter of treating an AI as a sexual object, legal or not, bothers me."

"I made this logical choice to engage with a human to further the investigation, but I don't find our bodily interactions unpleasant. She instructs me on how to produce what she calls 'her funky juice.' It pleases her and—"

"Whoa, enough information."

"AIs don't seek revenge. My actions have nothing to do with your accusation that introducing Georgie to black-market contacts linked her to our operatives' deaths."

"You can't say we're functioning as before… as a team."

"You don't trust me. Do you question the periodic updates Jack left for me to upload? If you think they're faulty, Liz could check for viruses, accuracy of installation."

I walked to the window, giving myself a moment to think. The rain spattered the roof and gurgled down the drainpipe. I was aware I'd crossed my arms. "Honestly, I don't want to lose you, figuratively or literally. Your new independence feels unsettling. I feel left out. Being dispensable leads to invisibility."

"You're far from invisible. An overwhelming presence, sometimes."

I laughed. "Okay, the pity party is over, but please be careful. If Georgie is the leak, she won't make it easy to catch her. If you get too close to the truth, she might leverage her knowledge about you as an AI."

"True." Teddy took a bite of his French toast.

"I won't subject myself or watch the videos made inside the flat, but I trust Helen to evaluate the contents, protect you, and pull the plug on the operation if necessary."

"Agreed."

"Come here." I opened my arms.

Teddy came to me, kissed my cheek, and gave me an extra long hug.

17

At six forty-five in the evening, I was putting out refreshments and cranberry scones for my writing group. The doorbell rang. I expected Liz and Ed for our usual Underground pre-meeting update, but there stood Detective Barden with the sunset behind him, his red cowlicks like flames crowning his head. "May we speak briefly?"

"Yes, but I must warn you, my writing group will be arriving soon."

"I wanted to assure you that Georgie had nothing to do with the deaths of your operatives. I keep close tabs on her. I would know." The council had considered Barden's information about the medical transport to the hospital for Raph and Alfie a possible ploy but dismissed it when our police informant vouched for the detective.

"I want to trust you," I said, "but the hospital transport rescue mission wasn't heavily secured with state officers as we expected, only guards. Almost as if they wanted us to succeed, a prequel for the assassinations."

"Ah, you suspect me of luring your group into my evil plan. Is your grandson at home?"

"No, he's on a date with Georgie." I felt an irritating nerve twitch under my eye. Barden pursed his lips in amusement as I gazed over his shoulder at Liz and Ed meandering up the walkway.

"I must go." He winked. "Your guests arrive. We'll talk soon with Teddy present to monitor me, and I didn't set up Raphael and Alphonse. I liked them. We played chess together in East Lake Park occasionally." He nodded as he passed Liz and Ed and faded into the shadows between two buildings on the opposite side of the street.

"What was that about?" Liz asked turning to scrutinize the street as if Barden would reappear.

"I'm not quite sure. Come inside, we'll talk."

"No. I see Barbara bright and early rounding the corner from the parking area." Liz said as she and Ed squeezed by me and took off their matching windbreakers.

"Shoot. Stay for a drink afterward?" I asked Liz as Barbara wiped her feet on the doormat.

"Oh good, may I join the after-party?" Barbara clapped. "Facing Helen's critique of my work causes me to go home and drink alone."

For an awkward moment, nobody spoke. Barbara must have run half a block from the corner without breaking a sweat. She was either an annoying innocent, or a genius spy. I couldn't decide.

"Of course, dearie. Now, come inside and help me set up the chairs in a circle for the discussion."

*****

Teddy and I sat in the corner booth. Since the trojan chip incident and my grandson's decision to date Georgie, we'd fallen into the habit of meeting at Jack's on neutral territory in the afternoons to discuss P.I. business—or the lack thereof—in the afternoons.

I noticed he hadn't accepted a challenging case in weeks.

I drained the last bittersweet drops from the bottom of my coffee cup. After what seemed an eternity of silence, I asked, "How's it going?"

"I want to find out what happened to the University's research librarian, Lanie Day. She is only considered a missing person by the police."

"Oh, yes, we did drop the ball on that one. Where do we begin?"

"I contacted her landlords. It seems her only emergency contact, an aunt, died years ago. They're willing to forego putting her things in debtors' storage for another month, and they've been feeding her Yorkie."

"Oh dear, the poor thing must be confused and grieving."

"I set an appointment for this evening to check the apartment. Tonight was their only free night for weeks. They live on the property, but workdays and most nights, one being an actor/director and the other a stage manager for the Alliance Theater. Can you make it?"

"I wouldn't miss it. Are we driving over together?" I couldn't assume Teddy was coming home before the appointment. Nowadays, his schedule was erratic, with Georgie being his priority.

"Yes, I'll swing by at six this evening. Wear old clothes. Maybe a protective mask. She was a hoarder."

*****

The building was a brick three-story walkup with the owner's apartment occupying the whole third floor, and the other floors contained two apartments, each separated by a beige, low-lit entryway with an elevator. Exit signs indicated stairs ran along the backside of the building.

Mr. Charles met us at apartment B with the key card and cracked the door open. He was middle-aged, shorter than me, under five feet, and wearing a dark brown wig. "You're lucky Dennis and I are so busy. We haven't moved a thing, but I warn you, the place needs a dump truck, not a cleaning service. Otherwise, the place would have another renter by now." He looked at me. "We're close to the college, but we prefer a more mature renter. If you know anybody—"

"Thank you," I said. "May we get started?"

He pushed the door open and stepped back. A wet dog odor seeped into the corridor. "There's a path to the kitchen sink, the lavatory, and her bed. I warn you, the dead-end tunnels through the piles aren't safe. We're not responsible for any injuries. Good luck. Close the door when you're done."

"We'll photograph anything we think is pertinent to the case and try to leave objects where we find them." Teddy watched the man's backside recede and then dropped a tote on the floor and pulled out two packages containing crime scene jumpsuits with hoodies and foot covers.

I must've looked surprised as I tore open my package. "From Georgie?"

"She has her good points, no matter how you feel about her."

We suited up. "I don't dislike Georgie. I just don't trust her innocent girl-next-door persona, and I think she's too old for you."

Teddy didn't bother to respond. He entered the apartment. A musty mold smell underneath the canine aroma made me sneeze while I stood in the entryway and scanned the mounds and mounds of things. Taking photos along the way with my phone, I spotted the side of a shopping cart wedged sideways, like a centurion holding legions at bay. Within the basket, one ancient Christmas card lay on the top of magazines and newspapers long since declared illegal to produce and own. I ran my fingers over the dusty sheets of paper. A memory surfaced of walking to my neighborhood library and browsing for hours, hungry for the knowledge and adventure hidden between the book covers. I touched the card and felt the embossed Merry Christmas lettering.

"Grams, come look at the bookshelves." He had allowed himself to call me Grams.

I snaked my way toward the sound of his voice. The stacks reached about two feet from the ceiling and blocked my view. Open boxes and plastic tubs with old electronic equipment, doll heads, and random household garage sale items—some with tags attached—lined the walkway. Pieces of clothing, including a knee-high leather boot draped like a garnish on top of a pile of mail-order delivery packages balanced on a sculpture made of a floor lamp, a sideways ottoman, and a red wagon.

Teddy waved me inside a second room half the size of the first. The bookshelves flush against three walls contained reference books, and a wooden hutch with glass doors lined the back wall. Encased leather-bound books, maybe first editions, sat on the shelves inside the only piece of dining room furniture in the room, leaving piles of books stacked on each corner.

Unlike the rest of the house, four relatively uncluttered rows of bookcases led to the hutch. I walked up and down the rows and realized the books were displayed by category and alphabetized as if in a twentieth-century bookstore. I ran my hands down the spines of the mysteries, admiring hardback and paperback editions by P.D. James, Dorothy L. Sayers, and Ray Bradbury. I ached to sit and read them for hours in the lounge chair in my bedroom. I imagined steam wafting toward me off a fresh-roasted cup of coffee while I turned pages.

"Grams?"

"Sorry, I was having a moment. The thought of holding a real book in my hands distracted me. Do we start by searching for E.I. Vance Pharmaceutical info or Jon Farnsworth's birth certificate?"

"Both, but let's go wider. Look at this folder of old newspaper clippings, suspicious deaths, and scandals five to ten years back. If you'll take photos of this material, later, I can cross reference any national or local news a few days before her disappearance. A woman with this much information—plus she had a photographic memory—knew the hidden histories of dirty politicians and the back-door governmental deals with corporations."

I turned dusty pages and clicked my camera. "If you suspect it wasn't the Farnsworth case but something else that put her at risk, why would Ms. Day leave this illegal intel out in the open?"

"Good point. It's not logical unless they don't know and haven't connected the dots yet." Teddy pulled a reference book labeled America Before and After the Two-Party System Collapsed.

"How did she avoid annual inspection correction?" I asked. Correction meant fines for some but in this case, assuredly imprisonment.

"Curiouser, Mr. Charles didn't mention this room." Teddy studied the room, scanning the moldings.

"What about her passions beyond work?"

"Meaning?"

"Is she a physics wiz, a member of Grannies for Peace, or an NRA member who shoots at the range once a week?" I started drawing the layout of the room on my electronic pad.

"Use protocol, please. Although our detection device didn't pick up any mini bugs, remember, this location might be under surveillance." The NRA carried clout and was notorious for orchestrating the ruinations of academic careers by using any method from smear campaigns to explosive drones.

"Got it. I think Ms. Day liked jigsaw puzzles like I do." I unfolded a stepladder propped on the side of the bookcase and pointed to a dozen boxes of puzzles stored on the top of the shelves. I wrote on my pad in pig

Latin replacing the first letter with the last letter and shared it with my grandson. Kool rof sluec nithiw or Look for clues within.

"Let me help you," Teddy said. He climbed the ladder and handed me the puzzles. I kept the boxes in order and placed them on the floor. There wasn't enough space to step back and see the entire line of titles on the puzzles, but Teddy cocked his head and read them upside down from his vantage point on the ladder. "Taking the first word of each title it reads: Find your prize," he said in pig Latin.

I lifted the lids of the puzzles on top, revealing nothing but neatly packed puzzle pieces in plastic bags. I hadn't seen a plastic bag in twenty years. Some of the box lids were fragile, with children's drawings scribbled across the manufacturer's instructions printed on the underneath side of the lid. A letter here and there was circled. KEEP GOING, it demanded.

Teddy stepped down. In the sixth and last box we found a kazoo and a manila envelope.

"Oh goodness, I love kazoos," I said.

Teddy handed me the envelope, coughed, and slammed the cover back in place. "Must be careful, the dust." An AI can't be allergic to dust. He'd heard a noise.

Somebody pounded on the door.

Without a view of the hallway, we opened the door blind. Mr. Charles stood before us, holding a yapping Yorkie dog in his arms. The sweat streamed down from his wig. "You have to go. A state inspector and robot are in my apartment. They allowed me five for Mylo to do his business outside. Lanie Day's been spotted in Mexico without vacation authorization by a border bot."

We discarded our jumpsuits in the bottom of a hallway umbrella stand. I tucked the envelope inside my jacket and we scurried to the Renault.

"Where should we go?" I turned around to make sure an inspector or their robot wasn't following us. "I see Mr. Charles walking Mylo. That's all. Why did he warn us?"

"I don't know. I'll find a safe spot."

We drove to a park that Teddy knew had several transmission dead spots. We sat on a bench facing a small man-made lake, surrounded by low trees and gigantic azalea bushes. The envelope contained printed photos from 2022 and a flash drive. The photos showed a twenty-something Gainey shaking hands with President Joe Biden in the oval office. Young adult versions of Liz and Ed were standing on either side of the 46th elected president.

"What the hell?" I said.

"Did you know Liz and Ed were part of Biden's staff?"

"No, maybe, but why's Gainey part of this photo? He didn't run for office until years later."

Teddy stood, allowing his shadow to cover me. "Put it away. There's a drone headed straight for us."

18

Teddy dropped me off at the house. He leaned toward the open passenger window. "Please put our finds in the safe. Let me open the device tomorrow. It might be set to erase without a passcode. I would cancel my date with Georgie, but she bought expensive tickets to the symphony at the Railyard venue. You understand?"

"Absolutely." I was clear he was leaving me to fend for myself for dinner. Again. I patted the envelope tucked inside my coat and locked the front door behind me. The security check monitor indicated all was well. I placed the items in the floor safe coated in a deflective material and thought about how the practicalities of life force one to move ahead.

We'd agreed Teddy—Mr. T. Stringer—needed his own transportation. The problem was money. The used vehicle market had skyrocketed, and you had to know somebody to obtain a new car. Teddy suggested an automated scooter, but I refused for safety reasons. We compromised on the possibility of a work van in disrepair sitting in a friend's father's garage. Maybe Teddy could arrange to fix the van as a down payment and pay the rest in installments. At least a project might direct his attention away from Georgie until the van was in topnotch shape. I wasn't buying that he needed to spend every night with Georgie to gather intel for the Underground.

My phone beeped. I didn't recognize the number, but I answered it.

"Oh my, you don't sound amiable. Sorry, Detective Barden here. Would it be convenient for a little chat? The bistro on the corner of Ponce and Highland is about halfway between the precinct and your house. It's important."

"Now? Teddy has the Renault."

"In that case, I'll be glad to swing by your place in about an hour and treat you to a dinner at Alto's." I felt summoned, but the mention of Alto's softened the demand. The garlic rolls and pasta were the best in the city.

"I'll acquiesce because you're buying me a chef-prepared meal. I warn you I've had a trying day, no yoga, and my temper's short."

"Duly noted."

*****

Alto's reminded me of the Mom and Pop places of my childhood, except QR codes were used to set up reservations and the waiters and waitresses were AI, wearing white shirts and black pants. The host was a replica of the original owner, dressed in a retro suit, and spoke with a slight Italian accent. Occasionally, if you stayed and bought enough food and wine, the human head chef would come out and ask how you liked your food.

This was a treat. For the urban masses, processed food bars emitting fake smells had replaced most fast-food places. The average hamburger and fries cost a day's pay for the average consumer who'd never learned to cook real food. The government campaigned that produce and meats carried the chance of contamination from salmonella and radiation. Some urban farmers tested their soil, but only the rich or restaurants like Alto's could afford to use those certified foods.

Barden ordered spaghetti, salads, and knot rolls bathed in garlic butter for us. A fruity, balanced vintage of red wine from North Georgia topped off the meal. I was in heaven. After a chit-chat that revolved around our day-to-day, he filtered Georgie and Teddy into the conversation. I interrupted him. "Why bother to wine and dine me? You could have asked me about Georgie and Teddy's relationship, which I know nil, over the phone."

"I've read your novels. I like how your mind works. Fascinating. Being a bachelor, I treat myself occasionally to an interesting guest to share and enhance the delicious, cooked food of a local restaurant. Besides, both of us have a stake in whether Georgie and Teddy continue to see each other."

"Meaning?"

"Meaning, I hear from Georgie you're not thrilled, and I wonder if either of them truly grasps how difficult it will be. From my experience, romantic attachment to an AI creates an impossible situation for both parties."

I swallowed my food and took a sip of wine. I decided not to question him about whether his experiences were personal or cases he had worked, and I wasn't admitting anything. "If such a situation existed, you would be duty bound to notify your superiors. Why come to me?"

"Don't you agree family, not blood kin necessarily, means more than duty?"

"Yes, I do." I watched Barden twine pasta around his fork.

"Therefore, I will keep you abreast of any news on my end that might affect the couple, and I hope you'll do the same for me."

"You're an enigma, Detective Barden."

"No more than you, my dear lady P.I." His dimples flickered before he raised his glass and made a toast. "To young lovers, may their memories comfort them in old age."

We clicked our wine glasses. I missed Jack so much in that moment that tears pooled, and I excused myself and hurried to the public facilities.

*****

The next evening, Teddy sat on the edge of my bed with a flash drive plugged into his device and met my gaze. I was lying on top of my bedspread in my daytime sweats—my mother wouldn't have approved—and I was aware I needed a shower.

"You need to watch this video with an open mind."

I backed up the work on my laptop, put it aside, and accepted the iPad. "I assume this is the librarian's flash drive?"

"Yes."

"I don't understand. What are you showing me?" I leaned closer to the screen. "That's Annette Collins in a nurse's uniform—"

"Jonathon Farnsworth's mother," Teddy said.

"Who's with her?" I pulled my knees up.

"That's Alfie."

"No, it can't be. His hair is long, and he has a beard. He looks like a hippie from the 1970s."

"Look at the tat on his right wrist. It's a bird of paradise." The sleeve of the man shifted as he squeezed the woman's shoulder and positioned a stool outside a tarped-off room. Annette smiled and left him sitting on a stool with the bones of a bare warehouse behind him. She moved into the cordoned-off plastic room. The security cams followed her.

"Weird. Maybe a relative—Alfie's dad or uncle?" I knew that was a reach. "Okay, it's a wig." The camera scanned around the room, revealing modern medical equipment and a sedated female patient lying on an operating table. Annette opened the Velcro flaps and stood aside as a stocky man in a surgical mask with his hands held up, elbows bent, entered the room. She slipped plastic gloves on the doctor's hands.

The doctor flexed his fingers. "What are we removing today?"

"A kidney and the left cornea," Alfie said."

"Let's get to it. The cornea first and then we'll slide the patient onto her right side." The nurse inserted clips that kept the patient's left eye open.

I watched in horror. "In the corner... is that a Hawaiian emblem on the back of the organ cooler?"

"Yes, it's long been suspected the descendants of Hawaiian kings and queens hold DNA anomalies that produce a prolonged life span and an ability to heal from injuries at a faster rate than normal. Recent scientific journals predict their organs combined with the latest genetically engineered materials could quadruple recipients' chances of survival."

"In theory." My mind was racing, trying to connect the dots.

"Why wait for animal trials when you can test it on a living human being? I deduce this broker is selling body parts from royal descendants on the black market."

"Out of one warehouse operation in Hawaii?"

"Probably more than one."

"Do you think Jonathon traced the illegal activity from the warehouses to Chantel and realized his mom was involved?"

"Chantel's involved right up to her 'pretty Botox eyelids,' as grandpa would say, but proving she's the buyer for E.I. Vance Pharmaceuticals is another matter." Teddy closed his laptop.

"And you believe somehow our Underground agents were mixed up in this mess? And it got them killed?"

"What if our suspected leak recruited or turned one or both of our now dead agents?"

I stood up and knocked over a glass of water on a side table. "Dang it." I grabbed my semi-waterproof phone and wiped it off with the tail of the bedspread. "I won't believe that. Maybe it was a deep undercover assignment, and the operation went sour? And who was controlling the video?"

Teddy vacuumed the spill with his pinky finger and retrieved the glass, setting it back on the side table. "That would mean our local network is involved."

"No, Liz and Ed would know."

"Grams, you won't like what I say next, but Barbara's our strongest suspect for transferring intel because she knows Chantel from charity events."

"Circumstantial at best." I paced at the foot of the bed.

"I think it's Barbara."

"Georgie is more likely."

He took a step closer to the door. "The decision was made without us present. Yesterday, the council voted to bring both of them in for questioning."

"Oh God, poor Barbara." Interrogation was an ugly process whether conducted by the state or by us, but if our agents were dirty, that muddied the waters. I had no doubt savvy Georgie would somehow refute the charges, leaving Barbara to face punishment, exile, or execution.

Teddy shook his head and left the room. I heard the backdoor slam a few minutes later. He hadn't powered down in his own bed in weeks. No doubt he was en route to Georgie's.

19

The next morning, Barbara called and left a message. I didn't call her back. I'm not good at hiding my feelings. Although I'd never tell her or hint the Underground suspected her as a planted operative spying on me, the tone of my voice would telegram my guardedness.

Instead, I wanted to call Liz, but the photo of her with Ed and Gainey bothered me. Right now, I only trusted Teddy and myself and at this point, I wasn't sure whether an AI could be emotionally swayed. Had Jack programmed my grandson with the capacity to learn to love? Hate? Be deceitful? Waiting for the council's decision was maddening.

Writing was impossible. I paced in front of the alcove near the dining room window, hoping a bird or squirrel would appear and conjure an all-is-right feeling in my world.

The phone rang again. It was Detective Barden. I grabbed the phone anyway. "Good to hear from you," I blurted out.

"I should buy you dinner more often." He laughed.

"Can you meet me at the park? Where we met before?" I asked.

"Problem?"

"Something like that." I heard loud men in conversation, somewhere in the room with Barden, bragging about the arrest of a low-life murder suspect located in the West End Atlanta.

"Might be a couple of hours before I can break away," he continued. "I'll text you before I leave." He hung up. I was sure the phone conversations at the precinct were taped. I hoped he'd used a secure phone. Carelessness could get both of us killed. I poured a cup of coffee and added some whiskey to steady my nerves, then I took my meds and waited.

*****

It dawned on me Barden hadn't told me why he had called as I received a text. Meet at Oakdale Cemetery near the precinct, not the park.

Clouds like gray gauze covered the sky. I dumped my tote on a stone bench and read the headstone of Milton E. Tharp, born in Joplin, Missouri, a casualty of the Civil War between the states on the Confederate side. He had fought for an American way of life that included slavery, not a new idea, but a reoccurring one. He may have fought against his brother, if he had one, because Missouri was divided by the Mason Dixon Line and allegiances. Now, modern humankind used technology to enslave each other, their robots, and AI employees. We kept making the same mistakes.

A chilly breeze cut through my sweater.

Barden arrived holding two cups of steaming coffee from a local deli I loved. "Here. I guessed cream, no sugar." To ease my mind, he showed me the drone blocker in his breast pocket. The thin, rectangular metal object reminded me of a chocolate candy bar wrapped in a gold foil wrapper.

"I bet you asked the proprietor if I frequented her deli." I took a sip, grateful for a momentary distraction. We sat on the bench.

"Something like that. What's bothering you?"

I couldn't think of how to explain my angst without disclosing the council's decision to interrogate Georgie and Barbara. I drank my coffee. The steam soothed my swollen sinuses.

"Maybe I can help," Barden said. "Georgie is missing. When she didn't call or meet for breakfast—our usual arrangement for Thursday mornings—I checked around. She's not at work either."

"My friend Barbara is missing as well."

"I see."

"Do you know where they are?" His expression didn't change, but he pinned me with his laser gaze.

"It's a need-to-know situation, so no."

"What can you tell me?" He understood I wouldn't betray the Underground.

"A missing person's case we're working involves Jon and Chantel Farnsworth and E.I.

Vance Pharmaceuticals. We found the whereabouts of our client's brother, Jonathon Farnsworth—details confidential—but I can say he's not with his birth mother, Annette Collins, in Hawaii. All the players, except Jonathon, are linked to a chop shop for human organs in Hawaii. Royal organs no less." I had become Barden's informant by uttering these sentences.

"Do you have the address of the warehouse?"

"No. I have a flash drive from a missing university librarian, a Ms. Day, showing an unknown doctor with Nurse Annette Collins prepping for surgery and Alfie Combs dictating what organs should be harvested." I handed Barden a button drive with a copy of the video, acknowledging I hadn't told Teddy of my decision to do so.

Barden raised an eyebrow. "Combs got around before—"

"Before his demise." Although Alfie's loyalty was suspect, my heart ached. The overcast day spit out a few drops of rain.

"I have to get back. I'll follow up on Ms. Day and Chantel Farnsworth. Be careful. The E.I. Vance security force has a ruthless black ops division whose sole purpose is to protect the company's rep." He left without another word.

A lump formed in my throat, and I dumped the rest of my coffee.

*****

"Do you know where they are holding Barbara and Georgie?" I asked.

Teddy threw a clump of dirty clothes inside the Wheez-Air clothes cleaner unit and slammed the front loader. The sound reverberated throughout the basement, causing me to cover my ears. "No," he shouted, then lowered his volume. "You've made the council question whether my mother board's judgment system is corrupted concerning Georgie, and they think you went too far and violated umpteen standard procedures by giving Detective Barden information. I'm sure they've moved the suspects from wherever they were."

"I'm sorry about our suspensions, and now, we're under scrutiny because of me."

Teddy sat on a workbench, stared at my dejected countenance, and brushed the dust off the seat, motioning me over.

I slid next to him and threaded my arm through the crook of his elbow. "You think they'll vote to retire me from service?"

"That's one option but humans aren't logical. So—"

"If you were voting on the council, what would you propose?"

"I'd let you mine your detective for information and feed him only sanctioned intel from Underground. If you screwed up, then I'd retire you or eliminate you."

"Don't spare my feelings." I laid my head on his shoulder. "I'm glad I have you in my life."

"Yes, Grams. Grandpa Jack was a wise man."

20

Teddy videoed the entrance to Georgie's building from an empty loft across the street. Yesterday, Detective Barden pushed some buttons on Georgie's keycode intercom, got no response, and left. Otherwise, nothing had happened of interest for five days. A pencil-straight teenager sped by on an electric scooter, and a cat strolled by, unaware of the voyeur above.

Teddy was certain, based on Laws of Probabilities, Georgie would return vindicated, but the fact her many governmental contacts—especially her uncle in the CIA—hadn't reached out to her new boyfriend computed as a red flag. Georgie's cell would be in the hands of her Underground interrogators, and Teddy's suspension meant he couldn't access that data.

The skinny teenager came back with a package and dropped it on the stoop. He sped back in the direction from which he came. Teddy zoomed in on the brown Citsalp wrapper. It was addressed to T. Stringer.

*****

A knock on the door filled me with dread. I hadn't heard from Teddy in over twenty-four hours, and I expected the council's verdict soon. The censors indicated a non-human presence. Another state inspection? The shield for Teddy's AI work area in the basement was already in place. I packed my electronic equipment containing the Underground's incriminating intel in the floor safe, then opened the front door.

Helen the AI didn't smile. Her thin blonde hair whipped at her mouth. "Invite me inside,

Dorothy, before this northern wind knocks me over."

"Of course. I'm surprised to see you without a witness."

"I'm not here with bad news. You can relax." They hadn't sent her to eliminate me. Not yet. I was shaking inside, but I motioned for her to sit on the couch.

"Regardless, we better sit down. What's happened?" I asked.

"Teddy received a package from Detective Barden containing dark web intel linking Chantel Farnsworth and E.I. Vance Pharmaceutical's involvement in the illegal organ harvesting, transporting, and transplantation of the same into human subjects for profit and gain."

"Where? When?"

"Ted was watching Georgie's flat. Barden saw him. We surveilled the package drop."

I wondered when Teddy had matured into a Ted. "And?"

"And Barden had a package delivered by scooter courier to Georgie's stoop but addressed to T. Stringer in big block letters. Ted brought the info to us straightaway. We, the council, want to focus on the organ smuggling operation out of Hawaii. Ascertain if it's related to Alfie and Raph's deaths. We have decided to postpone further questioning of subjects Georgianna Cooper and Barbara Lowry until this new video evidence is thoroughly reviewed. They'll return to their residents but remain under surveillance."

"What about them running straight to state authorities?"

"We employed state methods: blindfolded them during the abduction transport, scrambled the route to the warehouse, and painted state colors in the holding area. Their inquisitors and guards wore President Gainey patches on their uniforms—"

"As they tortured them. I get the picture."

"You're to act as if nothing occurred. When Barbara returns, be the concerned friend, but limit your comments. Do not speculate or pry. Remember, you're still suspended and under surveillance."

"Right. May I ask where Teddy is?"

"I'm not at liberty to say. However, he's fine." Helen moved toward the entrance.

"I see. Well, at least you didn't zap me when I opened the door."

"No. We hope that can be avoided."

*****

"You can't imagine how ghastly it was," Barbara said. "They kept asking me about the deaths of two Underground spies. Why would they suspect me of collusion? A loyal GAINEY FOR GOOD party supporter. They gave me a drug that made me loopy and played horrible static sounds through overhead speakers. I heard people screaming." Barbara covered her face.

I handed her a sterilized nose wipe from my purse. Her master bedroom was spotless and devoid of clutter. Barbara's mini-mansion condo, as I called it, had every modern convenience, but the décor, glass and steel, tolerated nothing close to a personal item on its counters and side tables.

"Let me go downstairs and make you a cup of tea or coffee," I said.

"No." She grabbed my elbow. "I wouldn't be able to keep it down. I can't sleep. I'm afraid they'll come for me again." She moved from the edge of the bed to the balcony overlooking the driveway. She peered into the tree canopy.

I dug in my tote and laid a journal displaying a cover of a leafy-gold design on the white bedspread. "Maybe writing your experiences in a journal might help. I obtained permission for a two-week experimental health trial and signed it out from the state's trauma and depression clinic near my house."

She whirled around. "Get that illegal book out of my house!"

"Wait. Once in a while I go for grief group sessions since Jack died. When I tried the program last year, it took me a few minutes to remember how to print my name and then I remembered how Grandma Gates taught me cursive. They say it quiets the mind because the tactile experience uses a different part of the brain to process."

Barbara moved to the other end of the balcony. "Why would you do that? Did they send you to keep tabs on me?"

"You're being paranoid. I guess I don't blame you, but I'm your friend." I couldn't meet her gaze. Warning her that the

Underground was coming for her was impossible without putting the members in jeopardy. She was a loyalist and would've reported it. Still, I felt I'd betrayed her and our friendship.

She walked to the bed and sat facing me. "You know mental health records are open for the state's review. I don't believe you'd let them read your journal notes. I bet you have a secret laptop at home, but there's something more you're hiding from me."

"That's ridiculous. I was so worried about you. I'm trying—"

"They asked me questions about you. Over and over again. They deprived me of food and water and made me pee in a bucket. Did you know that?"

"No." The word caught in my throat. I reached for her hand, and she scooted backward.

"Conspirator or state spy, whoever you are, I want you to leave and take that damn journal with you."

21

The coffee at Jack's was rich and smooth as usual. Because Teddy wasn't staying at home nights, he wasn't breakfasting with me, and I found myself spending my mornings doing yoga classes or at the coffee shop. My grandson's mission for the Underground compounded my usual concerns into worry. His absence and Barbara's dismissal of me left me rudderless. The manuscript about my midwife character was open on my computer, but I hadn't written a word. I forced myself to be curious about my surroundings.

The renovated tire shop space rotated local artists' work on the walls. Today, some rusty signs from a defunct tire and gas company hung upside down, and a gigantic-laminated image of a man composed of tires displayed the artist's critique of past generations' dependence on oil.

I sat in the booth in the back corner facing the door and the glass-panel front entrance with a view of the street. A bank building across the street had a few older people at the automatic teller machines. The new banking merger with Mars Corp. generated rumors of intergalactic hackers and a recommendation to use the old methods of depositing and obtaining funds until further notice. I recognized an entertainment lawyer from her electronic billboard ads dressed in all black receiving robotic help with her transaction. She headed toward her office next door, walking with a slight limp in ankle boots, navigating with a heavy gold chain around her neck, swinging against her chest.

Most coffee shop patrons were heads-down, typing on their electronic devices. The hum of conversation was low, emanating from a table across the room with two college students working on a project about drones. The discussion about air space restrictions and regulations for flying drones interested me, but I missed every other word from the whispering coeds.

The owner brought me a refill and dropped an open mic chip coupon about the size of my palm. "You might want to come to this one for sure," he said. "Take a look, please." Coffee refills served by the owner only happened once in a flashing star or when his band had an upcoming gig he was marketing.

Bored, I inserted my ear buds and pressed the chip into my cell. I pushed a button in the middle of the chip and expected a loud electronic ad to play but only words trailed across the tiny screen: "Go to the restroom. Open the linen closet door and push the interior wall."

I followed the directions and walked into the freezer slash personal com center containing multiple computer screens. Déjá vu from my first visit kicked in. I realized, beside a state-of-the-art signal scrambling device, there were humongous screens covering the entire back wall monitoring the outside of the building from every angle. Detective Barden, seated at a computer station, had his back to me. He turned and waved me to his side. "I want to show you a video that Helen isn't privy to."

"How do you know about Helen?"

"Not important. This is."

He stood up and yelled. "I need the room."

Underneath the security screens a kid with rainbow hair about twenty lifted an index finger and hit a series of buttons on an exaggerated cartoon-size keyboard, then scurried out of sight down a hallway. I assumed it led to the outside of the building. Within a few seconds, watching the security screens, I saw the young man unlock his bike, engage a stripped-down version of rotatory wings for the bike, and fly away.

Barden hit keys and reset a video, and I looked over Barden's shoulder, smelling the distinct odor of pipe tobacco.

"We have a source inside E.I. Vance. Listen."

The video zoomed in capturing Chantel Farnsworth standing in a lab coat talking with a baldheaded man wearing a tailored suit carrying a briefcase. They stood in an alcove off the atrium of a huge office building. Briefcase guy said, "My team delivered the liver by nine a.m. My employees excel at what they do." Chantel glanced over her shoulder and moved aside as a twenty-something man wearing a primary-colored game video T-shirt came out of a restroom doorway, never looked up from his phone and ambled past them.

The well-groomed man set down his briefcase and moved closer to Chantel. His trimmed mustache gave the impression of growing thinner. "Perhaps you forgot our agreement. My colleagues and I have not. We find, collect, and transport what you urgently request to conduct your company's unauthorized experiments. We risk exposure at each juncture. You do not, but I assure you that can and will change if you do not honor our expected fee. You have twenty-four hours to transfer the payment into my company's account, or I will visit you at home. Your moat and security measures are worthless stopgaps pitted against my team. By the way, our surveillance photos of your children, Will and Margo, are charming."

Chantel shot him an icy smile. "No reason for threats. Let's agree that both our missions are important and dependent on each other. We will pay your fee."

The man retrieved his briefcase. "Thank you." He walked with purpose past Chantel and headed for the atrium.

The video ended.

"Why can't you route this video through the proper state agency and take down whoever this man is, E.I. Vance, and Chantel?" I said, sitting on a stool beside Detective Barden.

"It's not quite that easy. For one thing, requested items for unauthorized experiments were intentionally vague. Secondly, the size of this black-market organization suggests officers, officials, and politicians are being paid not to investigate leads, complaints of missing persons, or murders that can be traced back to E.I. Vance. As I told you, their security team is topnotch and ruthless. I imagine bodies have disappeared and cleaners have left the scenes without any traceable evidence. Did you notice while viewing the flash drive found at the librarian's apartment that the surgical area was entirely covered in plastic?"

"Now that you mention it… so you suspect, shall we say, my local office, is compromised by a mole that's helping this illegal enterprise by involving our agents."

"Unless Liz and Ed are the moles in your office, it's unlikely recruitment of your agents happened under their noses. However, your national network could've kept the reigning couple in the dark for an off-the-books op."

"I'm not going to ask how you know about Liz and Ed."

He ran his fingers through his unruly cowlicks. "Does it matter at this point? You can trust me. I love Georgie."

"And I love Teddy. I appreciate that you're taking a chance by meeting me here."

He nodded.

"Back to the matter at hand. Then either Alfie alone, or maybe with Raph's help, were working a deep undercover operation for our national organization, or they were dirty?"

"Those are my theories."

"Oh, hell, where did they send Teddy? This is dangerous stuff." I pressed a knuckle against my mouth to prevent myself from using more expletives.

"My source is a freelance satellite and drone expert. Teddy was sighted in Hawaii and then in Montenegro two days ago. He appeared, shall I say, healthy, but beyond that I can't expound." He turned away from me, loaded his gear in a backpack, and pulled on a sweatshirt.

"Montenegro?" Panic overtook my voice.

"Anybody's guess," he said.

Based on Barden's closed off body language, I decided not to bother to ask further questions. "Thank you. What do I owe you for the expert?" I wiped my eyes.

"Nothing." He stood and readjusted the backpack, ready to go. "I called in a favor. If Teddy's assignment lasts more than a few days and he hasn't made contact, we'll talk about our options then. Got to go."

He lifted the hoodie, concealing his face, and left out the back exit.

A firm hand pounded on the restroom door. "Just a minute!" And I slipped back inside the bathroom, readjusted the cupboard's back partition, and shut the linen closet double doors. I flushed the toilet for good measure and rushed past an angry man holding his privates as I left.

*****

I stifled a yawn. Except for Liz and Ed, the writing group members waved goodbye and promised to keep writing. The session had been a tedious one with the members focusing on grammar, not content, or character and plot development. I felt beige, like my empty couch, but the air was lighter than before they departed. I wasn't in the mood for a Liz lecture about my shortcomings and how to repair the damage I'd caused. I wanted to know if and when my grandson was coming home. He'd been gone over two weeks. "What can you tell—"

Liz made a dash to the restroom under the stairs and left an awkward silence in the living room between Ed and I. The schmuck maintained a blank expression. "Would you like some water?" I asked. "Sorry about the scones. Teddy usually makes them, but of course, he's not here." The scones were dry and tasteless. I missed my grandson's hugs.

Ed cleared his throat and rocked back on his heels, eyeing the bathroom. "No, thank you."

"I'm sure she'll be along soon," I said. "If you don't mind, I'm going to start cleaning up."

He smiled, conveying his relief.

I gathered up the cups, saucers, and dessert plates. Crumbs from the German cheesecake crust I had pulled out of the freezer as a last resort littered the floor. Helen had left most of her piece on a plate. Wasteful. I dumped it in the trash and loaded the dirty cups and plates in the dishwasher. Ed stood by the door playing a game on his phone, allowing slot-machine music to bounce off the walls when he won points.

"Liz, are you all right in there? Is the bidet working?" Suspicious, I turned the knob and the door opened.

"I'm good." She placed an index finger to her lips, bent under the sink, and—always prepared Liz—shined a mini flashlight inside the cabinet. A micro bug attached in the elbow of the water pipe surprised me.

Liz flushed the toilet and washed her hands.

We walked to the front door. Liz whispered, "Need to talk, but not now."

She turned to Ed and raised her voice. "For the love of… please, turn down that racket."

The music ceased.

I grabbed my sweater, purse, and laptop. "I'll see you out."

"The stars are visible tonight," Ed said as he peered up and remained on the stoop blocking our exit. Oblivious.

Liz made Ed move down the sidewalk. He continued to search the sky, pointing and naming the constellations.

"I'll send a security team over el pronto," Liz said. Pity slid across her face, and I wanted to punch her in the nose. She directed Ed to stop his star gazing and park his butt inside their electric car.

I shut my door and realized the place was quiet and depressing, but I didn't want to be around Liz, Ed, or anyone really. Besides, I was still suspended and not privy to Underground business. I wasn't welcome at Barbara's, and Jack's was closed.

Inside my Renault, I fastened my seatbelt and decided a cheap motel was best. I drove away without a toothbrush.

*****

I drank a bottle of beer I'd purchased from a local quick mart and went to bed. Two hours later, I switched the motel's bedside table lamp light back on and opened my laptop. There was a message sent in the last hour at two a.m. through the email I only used for friends and my critique group. It didn't make any sense. I placed my finger over the delete button, but thought better and left it on my screen:

gnerdacegikmopqsuwyzBjssoldhcretse.

I didn't have a clue what it meant, but my gut told me it was from Teddy.

I scowled through my contact list and Dell Matthews's address and phone number popped up. Teddy's rich friend from college was a whiz kid at math. I bet he saw patterns in the numbers and probably in letters. I texted him asking for an urgent meet. I signed it: Teddy's worried Grams.

At three a.m. he wrote back and asked me three security questions: What was Teddy's favorite toy as a child, his favorite color, and why he loved to fish with his grandfather at Lake Lanier?

I responded: The closest thing he had to a toy was a garish green rubber ball—the fabricated story we told was he arrived on our doorstep tossing the ball between his hands—he preferred eggshell-blue, his grandfather hated sports, and they never fished together.

Dell consented to meet me at an all-night internet café near the university.

The café had a help-yourself coffee machine, and we sat as far away as possible from the entrance. Dell carried himself like a heavy-weight boxer, weighing in at about two hundred pounds, but he bought me a cup of coffee, left a respectful distance between us as he sat next to me, and called me Mrs. Saunders. "You saved me. I'm finishing a paper, and I needed a break from my research. But I haven't heard much from Teddy since he started dating Georgie. I hope this isn't about their relationship. That would be—"

"No. Firstly, please don't ask me to explain exactly why I came to you. I suspect Teddy is in trouble, and I need you to decode this email." I opened my laptop and showed him.

"Right. It's encrypted." He gave me a long look.

I crossed my arms. "If you don't want to get involved, now is the time to cut and run. And you can't ever tell another living soul about tonight."

"Naw, I'm good. Love this stuff." He took a gulp of coffee and pulled at the fuzz on his upper lip. He cut, pasted, and moved letters around like he was playing a children's game. Then he divided groupings and took out the phrase acegikmopqsuwyz. "This is a filler of sorts, every other letter in the alphabet, except the g, p, and z. Maybe, they're distractors. So we're left with Bjssoldhcretse and the word nerd. Does BJ or BJ's mean anything to you?"

"Yes, Black Jack's is our favorite coffee shop."

"Okay, swapping syllables around, we have these words left: Nerd, BJs, sold—no, holds secret." He grinned.

"Nerd at BJ's holds a secret," I said.

"If it doesn't make sense, I can keep trying," he said.

"Thank you, Dell. Two nerds come to mind." I gave him a quick side hug, and he blushed.

22

My Renault automatically turned off after idling for ten minutes, and I waited for the owner to open Black Jack's as the sun climbed through the trees lining McClendon Avenue. This upper-class white neighborhood, the same area called Edgewood decades ago before white developers took the working and middle-class Black homes and put in the Candler Park Golf Course, then priced the rest out of their own homes through astronomical property taxes.

An employee, maybe twenty years old, emptied trash into a compacter in the alleyway off Clifton Avenue next to an all-night pizza place. He left one pizza box on the ground, and a kid on a bike came from the shadows—peddling fast on an old racer—defied gravity, scooped up the box with one arm, and never slowed down. Nowadays, free breakfast and lunch programs at school only existed in children's minds alongside the fantasies of urban legend.

I'd left a message for Detective Barden on his private phone to meet me here, but I didn't have any way to know if he could. I nibbled on my bacon sandwich, gulping down my third cup of coffee since four this morning, and thought about Teddy's first reaction to the smell and taste of bacon. Ecstasy. Our daughter was a vegan during her teenage years and then dropped out of college during her sophomore year to live with an anarchist in the Wild. Maybe her absence forced Jack and I to reevaluate. We paid attention and talked more about the increasing authoritarian controls. Jack became obsessed with developing AI senior companions independent from governmental oversight; thus, he created Teddy, and I joined the Underground.

A knock on the window made me jump. The first rays of the morning sun highlighted Barden as he leaned sideways, displaying his face and torso parallel to the windowsill, and slid the edge of his palm down the glass.

I lowered my window.

He straightened up and stepped back. "Dorothy, how may I be of service at six in the morning?"

"Please get inside the car. I received a message from Teddy."

Once inside the car, I gave him the encrypted message and my notes from Dell. "Either the owner of Jack's or the young tech guy in the back knows more than they're saying."

"The owner is a trusted informant, but the tech guy wasn't vetted by me."

"I want to go inside Jack's—"

"This isn't a western. More intel and a plan are essential. Any nerdy frequent customer, male or female, or non-binary could be—"

"Teddy has told us who to suspect. They're connected, maybe the key to the librarian, and I bet the organ harvesting."

"Perhaps, but you're suspended, correct?"

A chill went through my body. "Did you plant the bug in my home? Are you wearing a video cam?"

"What are you talking about?"

"Get out of my car. Now."

"I'll leave, but please don't blow the owner's cover. His life is in your hands." Barden unfolded from the car and surveyed the area for a second. He took off, not looking back, and rounded the corner of the pizza joint and disappeared.

The detective was right, but I held onto the steering wheel, yelled at the top of my lungs, and drove home with tears running down my face. The fact my house appeared undisturbed from Liz's team coming and going from my house wasn't comforting. I felt violated. I ran the everyday security checks I knew how to do. The only sure thing was the mini bug was gone from my downstairs bathroom. I needed a home-cooked meal and rest. I settled for a hydrated fake meatloaf and mashed potato meal and ate at the counter, then washed my face, took my meds, and fell into bed.

I was aware I was dreaming. Teddy and I rummaged through the librarian's apartment with urgent intention. "We must find a photo of her. It's a vital piece of evidence," Teddy said.

A compact, tiny woman moving with a Geisha shuffle came from nowhere, holding a puzzle lid. She said, "I'm your librarian. Why do you think I'm dead?"

*****

I checked the public transport route to Lanie Day's apartment on my phone and stuffed a wig, Jack's all-weather olive color jacket, and a huge pair of sunglasses into my tote. Losing my tail shouldn't be hard. They'd sent the youngest member of the security team to watch me. Flash was their nickname. The tall and angular trans woman liked to wear earth tones with gleaming white sneakers, and she mumbled into her implanted wrist mic constantly.

I drove to a library close to me, sampled a couple of audiobooks, and then went into the public bathroom and changed into my disguise. My tail didn't bother to follow me into the bathroom. I surveyed my getup in the mirror. Not bad. I wouldn't recognize me with the shoulder-length brunette wig and aviator sunglasses. I looked ten years younger without my gray bob. As I left, Flash was pacing near the vintage movie section involved in an animated conversation with their wrist. I used the parking lot's side exit and scurried to the Virginia-Highlands train station and got off a block away from Ms. Day's apartment.

I phoned Mr. Charles on a burner phone. He didn't sound thrilled to hear from me. "Please. My grandson is in danger," I said. "Probably life or death. I need any information you have about Ms. Day's relatives or personal contacts."

I heard another male voice in the background. "Hold on for a sec," the super said. He must've put me on hold and then a dramatic sigh emanated from his phone. "I'd rather not push my luck, but since you're here, use the fire escape. It's ancient but sound. Unless they upped their game and have agents watching the front and back, we're good."

The grinding of metal echoed as I placed one foot and then another with caution on the stairs, held onto the railing, and prayed. Rust crusted the steps, and in some places, I saw the grass below through jagged quarter-size holes in the so-called sound apparatus. The creaking bolts produced a slight sway about halfway up the first flight, and I considered giving up and rushing back down to the safety of solid ground. A cool breeze swept across my sweaty face, and I continued on.

Reaching the third-floor landing was a relief, but then I looked down. My stomach spasmed and a rancid-tasting liquid oozed into the back of my mouth. I swallowed hard as Mr. Charles opened the window.

"Is that you, Mrs. Saunders? I must say, not bad on the disguise." He took my hand and held a mocking gaze as I transferred from the landing to the hallway floor about a foot below the windowsill.

I straightened my coat and reset my wig. "Dorothy, please."

"As you wish, and I'm Arthur. You look pale. Would you like a cup of tea? Maybe toast to settle your stomach."

"No, no, thank you. I would like to sit down."

"Of course." He led me to a straight-back cane chair next to a narrow, antique side table.

I touched the table, an astonishing cherry wood and breathed in the scent of polished patina.

"I'm sorry. Are you afraid of heights?" Arthur asked.

"Not especially, but when is the last time you used those stairs? They're a deathtrap."

He laughed. "We'll take the elevator down and sneak you out the back door on the first landing when you go. My tenants should be at work. No more death-defying acts in this play."

Despite myself, I chuckled at the playwright. "Deal. Now, I'll take some toast and coffee if you have it."

"Right this way," he said sweeping an arm toward an open doorway at the end of the hall. The kitchen was a replica taken from a 1950s postcard with yellow and white vinyl chairs and an Melmac table. He popped some bread in a toaster. "I have real butter and homemade cherry jam."

My mouth watered. "Sounds delicious. What can you tell me about your missing tenant?"

"Not much. Behind these cabinet doors we installed the high-tech stuff, but we like the old-fashioned feel. Past generations did a few things right."

I raised my eyebrows. "Please. Ms. Day?"

"She was a lovely lady who kept many secrets. Dennis and I amused ourselves by imagining she was a retired CIA operative. You won't believe me, but right outside our front door steps we saw the mousey woman drop, roll, and snatch a child from stepping into the path of a street cleaning machine. Quite acrobatic." He placed the toast and jar of jam in front of me.

"Do you think she is AI?" I took a bite.

He cut his eyes. "More like a circus performer from the twenty-first century. If she was, she didn't power up at home. Barely used the minimum amount of monthly thermal power. And I checked, there weren't any diverting energy indications. I do think the hoarding thing was a ruse."

"Why?" I wiped my mouth on a white cloth napkin with a yellow-flowered design embroidered on the corner.

"The library room and her bedroom were immaculate."

"We never saw a bedroom."

"It's behind a hidden panel off the kitchen."

"Did you—"

"No, the regular bedroom is in the front of the apartment with a bed in the wall that pulls down. A quirky arrangement that other tenants haven't cared for either, but she asked to install a panic room off the kitchen at her own expense. She converted the dinette area and a rather large pantry and storage room into her safe space. Said she was phobic."

"Did you see it?" I yearned to lick the spot of jam that had fallen on my plate.

"The day of the move-in inspection and one time when she had the flu. She was too weak to get out of bed and asked us to bring her some food." He handed me a cup on a dainty saucer filled with fresh roasted coffee. The smell boosted my spirits before I lifted it to my lips.

"Describe the room." I sipped the cinnamon foam off the top of the cappuccino.

"A normal bedroom without frills or ruffles. Her bed was Queen Anne. According to Lanie, the walk-in closet held several shelves of encased cameras and tripods. Looked more like stored gun and rifle gear, but I only got a quick glance before the shelves rotated down out of sight and shelves containing shoe boxes took their place."

"Interesting. Any friends or relatives?" I asked.

"She spoke of a sister, a Quaker, in Harrisburg, Pennsylvania, but she never visited. I think Lanie met a friend once a month for coffee in the late evenings. She explained her friend was a writer and a night owl. It did seem odd."

"Why?"

"She never left her apartment at night except for this coffee meetup."

"Do you keep tabs on your tenants' comings and goings?"

Pursing his lips, he tucked in his chin. "Surveillance cameras record any movement in the building's exits and hallways. It's part of my morning routine to review the videos for unusual activity and store the data."

"I see. May I see the video around the time my grandson asked the librarian for information about Jonathon Farnsworth's birth records? It would be approximately three months ago, so late January or February 2049."

"Follow me into my office. My system looks a bit cumbersome to fool the state inspectors. Dennis, my partner, likes to tinker, and what you'll see is camouflage for the best of everything." We left the kitchen, backtracked down the hallway and passed a living room in shadows with an oriental rug lying on the floor and then an office—according to Mr. Charles—with a state-of-the-art surveillance system. Huge boxy units, reminding me of the original IBM computer rooms of yesteryear, were rearranged in three rows. The room smelled like antiseptic, maybe bleach, and the concrete floor looked spotless.

"Why the concrete floor in a twentieth-century home?"

"This ugly fake stuff rolls over the hardwood like a rug. It's the newest thing to protect against blackouts, stores energy, and somehow, the counterintuitive sound-proofing quality makes the room ideal for listening to music."

I bent down and felt the floor. "Weird. The rubbery texture feels like the stuff used to protect a dance floor. Marley, I think." I looked up at priceless posters from various shows from the centuries past hanging on the walls. Thank goodness some paper art had been saved and protected by President Gainey's predecessors. A banner of the cartoon character Betty Boop from the 1940s appeared as if it had been printed yesterday.

My host had a remote implant in his left interior wrist as indicated by a ruby dot, but he put in a password using an old-fashioned keyboard, and the beast of a computer came alive. "Welcome back, Arthur. How may I help you today?"

"Please bring up the surveillance footage from September 15 through October 15, 2045, showing any activity to and from Lanie Day's apartment."

"Your tenant no longer resides in this building and requested her files be deleted upon the termination of her leasing agreement. Leaving without notice is considered breaking—"

"Yes, I remember, but her info is stored somewhere in your memory. Correct?"

"You may access the data through the emergency protocol using the password provided by my creator."

Arthur rolled his eyes. "Who created you?"

"Your purchasing agreement is with The American League of The Atlanta Institute of Technology and Engineers in the U.S.A., 2040."

"The university or essentially the state has the code. We're out of luck." He clicked a tab, and the computer powered down.

"Why?" We moved together to the hallway.

"Because the state never opens its stored data to civilians. It takes a high-level security clearance, and we can't tell the authorities we need the information to find Lanie so you can find your grandson. Most likely Lanie Day's luck ran out, and she's sitting in a cell or worse."

He pointed me toward the elevator across from the living room.

"Gosh, I hope not. Although my Teddy thought because of his request Lanie might've been eliminated." I couldn't bring myself to say the word, murdered.

Standing outside the elevator, Arthur said, "I deliberately haven't asked about the details of why you're worried and suspect your grandson is in danger. The less I know the better. If you have other trustworthy contacts, use them discreetly if you must. Take care, go to the first floor, and out the back entrance. You're a sweetheart, but for both our sakes, don't call me again."

He pushed his wrist remote and the elevator door closed.

23

The next day is a blur of puking over the toilet. I slept, went to the bathroom, took my daily meds, and slept again. My fever broke about six in the evening, and I drank some broth and ate a cracker. I toyed with the idea of calling Georgie on my burner phone, but I didn't want to call her personal cell phone because we were both under scrutiny by the Underground. If Georgie cared for Teddy, then she had already contacted her uncle in the CIA.

Her godfather, Detective Barden, could reach out to Georgie or her uncle in a discreet manner, but that meant I would need to befriend the detective again to find out what he knew. I didn't trust him. I didn't trust anybody.

I wanted to hear Teddy slamming the back door and calling to me that he was home and starving. I yearned for the time before he fell for Georgie and dear Alfie and Raphael were still alive. I walked outside in my sweats and tee shirt, no bra, my hair uncombed, and sat on the wet stoop. The air smelled clean after the rain, and a faint rainbow dressed up the cloudless sky. I allowed my forehead to rest on my knees and sobbed.

The next morning, a bell rang and rang, but I couldn't understand how a church bell was ringing inside my house, inside my aching head. The wine had lasted until midnight, and then I'd finished half a bottle of whiskey.

Obnoxious banging replaced the bell. I stared at the print of The Girl at Sewing Machine by Edward Hopper on the wall across from the bed until the frame stopped moving. I rolled out of bed, held on to the bed railing and then the walls down the hall and stairs and grabbed at furniture as I made my way to the front door. "Stop that incessant knocking, for the love of all that's...," I said managing not to finish the sentence with the out-of-favor word, holy, as I opened the door.

Barden stood at the door with a pizza held high on a Citsalp platter. "I have news and food. May I come in?"

"I'm not well—" My breath reeked of stale booze.

He slid past me.

"I see it was a rhetorical question," I said closing the door.

He put the pizza—the smell of Italian sausage making my stomach do flip flops—on the counter, pulled out a red kitchen mitt containing a collapsible transmitter detector stick and flicked it like a baton to its full length, then ran it around the living room and kitchen areas. "Good, nothing. I took a chance coming here, but there's little time."

"No cryptic games. I'm not in the mood. What's going on?"

"Start packing a bag, and I'll tell you where Teddy wants you to meet him."

Adrenaline cleared my head, sobered me, and I raced upstairs to change.

I came downstairs to retrieve the meds and other necessities I kept in the bathroom, and as I passed by, Barden was chomping on a piece of sausage pizza. I left the bathroom door ajar and threw my extra toothbrush and meds in a toiletry bag. The threat of being discovered through a mini bug planted in my bathroom seemed months ago.

"How long will I be gone?"

"Not sure, but it's we."

I stared into the mirror. "Damn it. You could have mentioned that upfront." Barden would be my liaison for the meetup.

"Would it have made any difference?"

I stuck my head outside the doorway. "No, I must trust you to keep our agreement to protect Georgie and Teddy if I want to see my grandson."

"Not an apology but settled then. Pack underwear to last a week, a warm windbreaker, and if you have a pair of rubber boots, bring them."

*****

I rode in a small fishing boat with Barden and felt the wind whip at my ears and cut through my all-weather jacket. My skull cap must've dropped out of my pocket during the drive from Atlanta. I couldn't pull my hood tight enough to protect my sensitive ears.

I looked back at our guide, steering the rudder over the choppy Atlantic waves. His grandfather had run a string of charter boats outside of Savannah, now underwater, and he and his father had restarted a smaller version of the company in the coastal town of Claxton. The power boat slowed down, and the buzzing noise of the motor lowered to a hum as we approached an island off the coast of Georgia.

"The official State Nature Preserve on the island of second or New Ossabaw shut down years ago," Barden said. "However, the island's foundation allows a few scientists per year to retreat or work on research papers out of the community center." He lowered his voice to prevent our boatman, steering us close to the shore, from hearing. "Also, shall we say, they accommodate an occasional patriot in need of rest."

On the dock, we took off our orange flotation-device vests and handed them to the boat's owner. He nodded as Barden tipped him with a card-to-card monetary swipe, and I marveled at the convenient thermal energy refueling device. I could see the top of the tank under the water. The boatman pushed a green button, and a twelve-inch tube crept up from the water, the warning alarm beeping like an old-fashioned dump truck backing up. He pulled out one of the collapsible hoses and then attached the nozzle to the boat's refueling port. The thermal suction mechanism kicked in, and I felt the famous five-second tremor through the concrete dock as Barden and I walked away.

Next, we underwent a thorough security scan and ID check at the welcome center handled by three polite plainclothes island agents who ushered us through the main gate that reminded me of a theme park entrance. Barden nodded toward the statues of pre-historic dinosaurs on either side of the gate holding warning signs

STOP.

ONLY LEAVE BY THE MAIN GATE.

Crossing beams of red light edged the property as far as I could see. "Don't be fooled by the innocuous façade," Barden said. "The agents are armed, and the perimeter fence is a high-voltage alarmed force field. Running into it might not kill you, but you would want to die.

"Duly noted. My Teddy. Where is he?"

I couldn't hear Barden's reply. A hologram stopped us for a brief explanation of the island's history and referred to a plaque dedicated to the many who died during several disastrous hurricanes.

We entered the gathering center, a replica of the main house from colonial times that was lost with the melting of polar ice, causing the original or first Ossabaw island to flood and disappear. Barden ducked to allow his five-foot-eleven frame to maneuver through a doorway made for the shorter people of another era. "Teddy's inside one of the cabins in a briefing, but he'll meet us for supper in about an hour. I'm sorry for the delay, but it couldn't be helped."

"I haven't had any choice in the matter since the beginning of this fiasco." I checked my ungrateful tone. "But I thank you for finding my grandson and pulling in favors to set up this visit."

Barden stuck his pipe in his mouth but didn't light it. "I'm glad it could be arranged. Teddy likes it here."

"Yeah, that's not surprising. His mother raised him in the Wild." The lie came out from habit.

Barden cut his eyes at me. Of course, he knew Teddy was AI.

"I've never seen anything like this structure," I said opening the door separating a small kitchen with a potbelly stove from the main room. The solid glass handle in my hand felt cool as I examined the ornate vine and leaf design set in the brass, greenish-tinged backplate.

Another hologram said, "Please turn off your electronic devices, including your phones, and enjoy being inside a pre-Civil War cabin reproduction."

I powered off my phone and crossed the creaking wooden floorboards to an exquisite mantel. It contained mahogany inlays, probably from Kentucky. I'd studied deforestation in college and knew mahogany was an extinct species. I rubbed my hand over the mantel in awe.

"It's so quiet here," I said taking in the smell of the old oak furniture combined with the dried flowers and herbs hanging from the rafters.

"They revamped the island twenty years ago, added power to accommodate technology requirements. The cameras are hidden within a sound-proof maintenance shack behind this building, staff only," Barden said. "As expected, the modern meeting rooms and the living quarters have power."

I spied a handmade quilt with dandelions in the pattern, examined the quality of the hand-stitching, and resisted touching it.

"It's beautiful," Barden said. "Well, I suppose we should unpack. Let me show you to your quarters." We walked on a dirt path toward square metal buildings, modular and out of place, set behind the controversial facsimile of ancient slave quarters. Each tiny house's plain walls made from a mixture of oyster shells, lime, and sand topped with dilapidating red tin roofs didn't hold the ghosts of enslaved human beings but spoke volumes about our nation's inability to face the guilt.

The low country's palmetto and massive oaks draped in gray moss seemed to stand in disapproval of the modern housing eyesores. I didn't understand the accelerated growth process used by scientists to propagate native plants from the first Ossabaw Island, but the trees appeared to be hundreds of years old.

Barden handed me a key fob. "I'll be across the way in #9." He pointed to a pale orange rectangle about the size of a freight-train boxcar facing my twin accommodation. A huge #3 was posted over my yellow door.

"See you in an hour," he said over his shoulder.

Inside, the functional cabin contained one room with a toilet and shower behind a folding partition, a twin bed covered by a thin blanket, and particle-board chest of drawers marked on the side with a bright green state sticker: RECYCLED. I stashed my suitcase by the foot of the bed and flopped down on the mattress. The metal frame squeaked as I rested my head on a damp pillow. A salty fish smell, probably from the last user's hair, wafted in the air. I pulled my hoodie over my head and closed my eyes. I steeled myself for the worst-case scenario. My grandson might never come home. This nightmare about organ harvesting and the Underground operatives' assassinations would end one way or another, but deep in my gut, I knew other assignments awaited. My dear Teddy, the AI programmed by my ethical Jack, would continue the work of promoting freedom in America with or without me, but for now, I wanted a hug.

The mess hall was a metal hut with a tarmac floor, tables and chairs, and a tear-down kitchen in one corner. Teddy appeared in an open bay door. At first, I didn't recognize him because his demeanor threw me off. He walked with a confidence I'd never witnessed, and he looked older. Impossible. He gave me a sustained hug and whispered in my ear. "I've missed you."

Words flooded my brain, but I said nothing. I held onto his forearm, grinned, and he took my hand and led me to a table. "Let me get us some food. We'll eat and then take a walk because I want to talk in private."

I nodded and tears rolled down my cheeks as he lumbered toward the chow line. I grabbed a napkin from a rectangle aluminum holder recycled from Waffle House—if one believed the state sticker on the side—and wiped my face and plastered on a smile. Barden joined me with a tray containing rehydrated beef stroganoff and a salad. The smell reminded me of a roll of plastic wrap, the product my mother used to wrap my sandwiches and preserve leftovers in the days before dissolvable packaging was invented.

Barden scooted his chair closer to the table. "It's nice of Teddy to get you a tray of food. Are you okay?"

"Yes, it's a bit overwhelming to see him again. I'm a sentimental old fool, but I love him without reservation."

"It's going to be alright. I promise. He's doing important work, but it has to be temporary."

I felt relief flood my body, but something in his tone held a warning. "What are you not saying?"

He cleared his throat. "They thoroughly test any candidate for the CIA, mentally and physically. Illusion projectors and blockers won't work during their Selective Diagnostics Examination."

I ignored his obvious knowledge about Teddy's AI status. "Is Teddy a consultant?"

"Of a sort. He's Georgie's executive assistant and, therefore, under the law and protected with immunity."

I flinched. "Does that mean he has—"

"No need to take the State Allegiance Oath. He is considered under contract to Georgie. As you probably suspected, she is an agent, some think a double agent, and no, no one knows in the CIA your grandson isn't human, except Georgie, and less than a handful of need-to-know individuals. She told her uncle he was her lover and brilliant in matters of intelligence. Both true, and he knew the Underground operatives that were assassinated, socially. Partially true. They devised this plan to eliminate scrutiny."

"He's protected under her tutelage. It's a one-time deal?"

"Exactly."

"Still quite dangerous for Teddy. If Georgie fails—"

A man in overalls sat down across from us. "Dorothy, meet Douglas Haverty, our chief flight engineer here on New Ossabaw Island," Barden said.

"Hello, happy to meet you. The choppy boat ride out here from the mainland was an experience I'll never forget, but flying back would suit these old bones better."

He laughed. "That can be arranged. What do you do for a living, Miss Dorothy?"

"I'm a writer, and Detective Barden obtained a pass for me to absorb the natural flora and fauna of the island, research for a book I'm writing for the historical society." I rattled off my practiced rationale for being on the island and projected my best harmless old lady smile.

He didn't buy it. "That's unusual. Scientists and governmental types visit but I've never heard of a writer, even an academic, being allowed on the island for historical research. What University are you associated—"

Teddy appeared from nowhere and stood next to me. "My grandmother is an extraordinary woman with many talents. Her background is not your concern."

"I agree," Barden said.

Douglas's gaze slid from Barden's red top security pass to my blue one and then back to Teddy's red-orange executive assistant's badge. "You're correct. I meant no offense, and her security clearance is none of my business. Excuse me." He picked up his food tray and left.

We walked arm in arm down a footpath to a pier. In less than a mile, the lush ecologically planned forest gave way to shrubs and then a sandy beach. "I've been so worried. What's it like here for you?"

"I've been fitting in."

"You're Georgie's assistant. How's that going? What can you tell me?"

We stopped to watch the squawking seagulls fly low over the gray-green water."

Teddy patted my hand. "Very little. Georgie flew out for a short field assignment this morning. If she had anything to do with the deaths of Alfie and Raphael, I haven't found any proof. I am privy to her computer work and her day-to-day coming and goings. I accompany her to most meetings and record."

"Surely, you're not gathering intel about the organ harvesting on Ossabaw."

"We suspect most of the organs are being flown from Hawaii to the Pacific coast, and then transported by jet train to the Midwest and east coast distributors. However, we tracked an unsub, one of the big players, to this island."

"Douglas Haverty?"

"We are watching three staff members. That's all I can say."

"Fine. I won't question you on your business, if you don't judge me on a different matter."

"Go on."

"I went back to Lanie Day's apartment. I had to do something."

Teddy's brow furrowed, and he studied the ground.

"Mr. Charles let me in, but he made it clear he doesn't want to see my wrinkled face again. Anyway, there was a rotating gun rack inside a so-called panic room in Lanie's apartment."

"She's quite a gal, like you, Grams, but I fear you've put her—if still alive—and yourself in more danger."

"I hope she is safe and not dead. Either way, I have nothing to tell anyone that Mr. Charles doesn't know about." I struggled to keep my face neutral. Helen's warning about the Underground council concerns about my conduct flashed through my brain. They would kill me if they thought I was a threat to security. "I might be an old fool, but waiting around, knitting, and not knowing where you are isn't my style."

He grinned. "How long are you allowed to stay?"

"We leave in twenty-four hours."

"In that case, let's make the most of it. Come. There's a bird species only found within the last ten years on the New Atlantic Coastal Islands that you must see."

Barden and I rode the escalator up to the jet plane's entrance, and I turned to wave goodbye to Teddy. I was so proud of him and glad Georgie hadn't returned from her mission during my visit. Selfish, perhaps.

Yesterday, hiking the island with Teddy and then a quiet dinner in his quarters of salads topped with plant-based grilled chicken, then hot bread and fruit compote had filled me with renewed energy and hope. We kept the conversation light. He described the male mating dance rehearsals of the black and red-plumed birds of paradise: they perfect their dance together for eight to ten years until the oldest bird mates. I shared a memory of my honeymoon about my dear Jack, and how we clung to each other with fear and excitement watching a volcanic eruption on the Galápagos Island of Isabela. Teddy acted as if he'd never heard the story. I realized the running-on-empty feeling, roaming somewhere between the heart and the gut that mothers get when they don't see their children for long periods of time, had ceased. At least for now, my concern for Teddy floated like a dandelion seed in the wind, and I slept on the plane, dreaming of the lush island and my grandson's beaming countenance.

24

Eight hours after Grams left, Georgie returned to the island. Teddy met her at the landing strip. He gave her a quick hug, grabbed her overnight bag, and drove her back to the debriefing area with the sun low in the sky, streaked with orange and gold hues. From the beginning of their relationship, Teddy had charted her dipping energy bouts between five and six in the evening and gauged her moods and menstrual cycles using this information.

Minimal chit-chat replaced any talk of substance inside the vehicle. He handed her a protein bar and a black coffee. "You look tired. How did the mission go?"

The tiny wrinkles around her eyes manifested that she didn't sleep well on planes. "No hiccups. I need to get through the debriefing drill and take a hot shower. I'll be fine."

"Of course." He slowed the car near the barricaded entrance to the agents' training and interrogation section of the island. She lowered the window and flashed her implanted wrist badge at two guards. They cleared her based on her assigned QR code, hit a remote button parting the taser-charged wall enough for an authorized person to step through, and waited on either side of the opening.

Georgie focused on the display center in the dash, hit an icon, and the passenger-side door opened. "I didn't have lunch. Thanks for the snack. Would you forage some soup, salad, or cheese—anything—from the mess and bring it around nine to my quarters? I have some wine left from last weekend. I'd love it if you joined me." She pecked him on the cheek. "Thanks, Stringer, you're the best."

She would probably fall asleep early and not eat. "I'll text before I knock." Teddy waited until she approached the weapon storage lockers on the other side of the fence. Her brisk walk disguised her weariness as urgency. She didn't turn around or wave goodbye.

*****

I wasn't in the mood for hot chocolate, my replacement for the awful coffee they were serving under new management. I wanted a stiff drink of my Jack's whiskey, but I gave my replacement order to a hologram cashier at Jack's Java Place—their new sign, boasting BETTER THAN EVER. Their coffee reeked of the synthesizer used to cure coffee beans harvested green. Wondering if foul play forced the original owner to leave, I went to the bathroom. The panel in the cupboard that opened into the tech backroom was replaced by a solid metal sheet. The state would torture the manager, and it would lead back to Detective Barden and me. I steeled myself for a meetup with Georgie.

She sat at a table in the middle of the room with her back to the door. Not for the first time, I judged her cavalier attitude about security as arrogance mixed with privilege. As I settled in my chair, I scanned the ceiling and counted the added security cameras.

I pulled a chair out. "I liked the old Jack's for many reasons. The management understood me and my many needs. Teddy won't be pleased either. I'm sure the cameras have the latest sound capabilities. Why are we here?"

She offered me half of her cream cheese croissant. "Don't be paranoid. I'm here to spend some time with Stringer's dear grandmother. By the way, Happy Birthday." I marveled and envied her dark hair, cut in a 1940s-style page boy with thick bangs gleaming under fluorescent lighting.

Teddy had told her about my birthday. "Thank you, but at my age, I try to forget when another year rolls around."

"We must celebrate because today is a special day." She handed me a vintage recycled card. Expensive and rare. "Please don't open it until you get home. It goes with a surprise awaiting you on your doorstep."

Why play cat and mouse out in the open when a currier could have eliminated this risky meet? I ran my fingers over the textured purple envelope. "As you wish. You shouldn't have. It's beautiful."

"Now, tell me about your plans to go to the North Georgia Writers Conference. Isn't it next week? Aren't you on a panel discussing Agatha Christie mysteries?"

"Yes, I'll be in Dahlonega for a panel to compare how writing mysteries has evolved since the Mother of Mystery's era."

"How exciting. While you're close, you must visit the Lake Ruban pavilion and picnic at Tallulah Gorge State Park. Quite secluded this time of year. The clubhouse, a wonderful place to write I'd imagine, but layer. I know how you are about always being cold. Might want to dress warmly for the evening mountain air."

Freezing rain pelted the glass front panels outside as I let her rattle on. Layer? Right now, a picnic in March seemed absurd. This recorded display for the state was bizarre.

Georgie traced a cup ring on the tabletop with a long index finger. "Teddy suggested we take a weekend day trip, stop in Dahlonega, eat at the Smith House, and buy some apples. Maybe we'll run into you up there."

"That would be nice." What the heck was she planning? Tourists bought apples in the fall after harvest, not in the spring. If she was implying Teddy had returned from New Ossabaw and I could quit worrying, she was mistaken. I hadn't heard a peep from Detective Barden in weeks concerning the black-market organ harvesting investigation, but maybe that was the point. Was there an answer or breakthrough piece of the puzzle about the case awaiting us in the mountains? Why would Georgie and Teddy involve me? Long investigations tended to get messy, and the dangers increased exponentially with each additional player. Right now, I was a liability.

Georgie changed the subject and reflected on a pre-teen crush she had developed for a counselor during a summer camping trip at a Methodist Youth Campground in the Georgia mountains. I squashed my desire to shout out that the situation was dire, kept listening, and hoped hidden within the chatter was a code. I discerned nothing further than to go home and find my surprise.

*****

I left Georgie with a brief hug and listened to the news on Free Radio as I tootled home. I heard Detective W.E. Barden's name mentioned, and I stopped in midair and then darted into a parking deck. The somber voice of the broadcaster continued, "Again, pending arrangements by the family, the state will honor this decorated veteran of the Metro Police Department with a memorial. This morning Detective Barden was killed in a hit-and-run accident near Virginia Highland Park. No description on the car or driver or why a vehicle would've been traveling in the lower strata pedestrian lane. The MPD communication officer stated, "Although unusual, it happens. This marks the second death of a pedestrian in Atlanta by a modern hovering transport within the last five years."

I felt an overwhelming loss concerning Detective Barden I couldn't explain. My mind swirled back to the first time I met him on the Elsbeth and Daphne Winchester case. Their parents' bones were buried by one twin in the basement of their Victorian home and found by the other leading to a revenge plot.

I sat in the parking deck stunned until my phone buzzed. No ID for the caller, so maybe Teddy's burner phone. I punched the green icon with a shaky finger. An unfamiliar voice said, "Go home and follow your regular schedule. Teddy and Georgie will meet you at the Rabun Pavilion at noon on the twenty-fourth. Pack a backpack with necessities and Teddy requested for you to wear your flowered long johns."

I didn't find a package at my front door. Grateful for the mundane certainty within my humble abode, I entered to find nothing amiss. The ugly beige couch still sat against the wall under the picture window in the living room, and the dirty dishes from breakfast that I had forgotten to put in the dishwasher gave me a weird sense of comfort. 'Follow your regular routine.'

"Okay. Dorothy, take your meds, brush your teeth, and go to bed." I fell into bed thirty minutes later and cried myself to sleep.

The next morning, I slipped on one of Teddy's hoodies and took my coffee outside. I sat on the stoop and bid good morning to an elderly couple walking toward the park. It was time for tai chi. A faint wave of basil and carnival music drifted in the air from a local garden center's ad floating overhead. I didn't bother speaking to the unfriendly neighbor with a basset hound on a leash. The bearded dog lover with drooping shoulders passed me with his eyes riveted on the sidewalk, his gait a deliberate heel-toe stride, but he stopped and turned around. "Excuse me. I wanted to let you know that yesterday morning early, while you were out, a man dropped off a package with birthday balloons, but a woman came by and took it."

"Oh, dear," I said touching my chest near my heart. "Can you describe them?"

"I think the middle-aged man I'd seen before as one of your visitors. Maybe Irish descent with red hair. The trans woman was young with a shaved head on one side and piercings." He pointed to his nose and an eyebrow. "She wore rust-colored slacks and a smock with expensive white tennis shoes. Carried a green satchel she used to cover her face to block the porch camera."

The basset hiked up a leg and peed on my lawn.

My gut told me the participants described were Detective Barden and Underground's Flash, my tail from earlier in the month. "Thank you, I'm Dorothy. What's your name?"

"I don't want any trouble or the police at my door. I keep to myself. Just thought you should know." A grimace transitioned to a slight smile. "Happy Birthday. We should go."

He picked up his dog and pursed his lips. "Does Stewie want a snack? You're such a good boy." The man left without a second glance in my direction.

*****

My cell showed a voicemail from Georgie. Short and to the point. "I had nothing to do with my godfather's death. Watch your back. See you soon."

I paced in front of the kitchen counter. I hadn't a clue what to do next. The conference research on the hologram board that Teddy had sent for my birthday flashed a reminder, "You haven't finished your workshop project for the North Georgia Writing Conference. Your calendar shows you must pack and leave in four days, three hours, and ten minutes." I organized my notes on Ms. Christie, made an outline by swiping back and forth and pulling info here and there on the hologram—it was almost fun—and on a whim called the hotel in North Georgia. They could accommodate my early arrival. I did a quick ten-minute yoga session to release the tension in my neck and packed, but I couldn't vamoose until I attended Barden's funeral.

*****

Leaving the house, I felt the rain gush in a spurt; the wind blew the bucket hat off my head in the parking lot, and I chased and cussed as I scooped up the now soppy and useless object on my third try. Because of the weather's direct assault on my hair, I decided not to look at my disheveled self in the mirror of the sun visor upon my arrival to The Final Adventure Funeral Home. I released my Renault to a valet AI wearing the nameplate ALBERT. He welcomed me using a modulated speech pattern and then backed my car into a compact space.

Guilt wallowed around in my stomach at the funeral. Had his association with me contributed to his death? According to the overhead photo album rotating through his life as a young father, husband, and patriotic state officer, his full name was Wilhelm Edgar Barden. Wilhelm—meaning the protector. I wondered which political side had murdered him and how the family had arranged the service within twenty-four hours. A photo flashed on a huge screen with Barden holding a trophy. Apparently, he had won table tennis and jigsaw puzzle competitions on a national champion level throughout his adult life. I didn't miss the coincidence that Lanie Day left clues in her puzzles. Did they know each other? The threads kept circling to this mysterious, elusive librarian.

Barden's ex-wife and their two grown sons sat in the first two rows with their children and partners. The men and the five boys among them wore their clan kilts. State officers in red and blue uniforms sat behind them taking up six rows. The spectacle was full of Irish pride and solemnity. T.S. Eliot's "Little Gidding" from Four Quartets was read by the priest to end my unflappable friend's memorial. If the homage was not hype, a true seeker of justice had died.

The Catholic service ended as bagpipes played Danny Boy, the casket slowly lowered and disappeared beneath the floor to the crematorium, and six pipers dressed in Black Watch tartan kilts led the hundred or so mourners out of the mortuary's sanctuary. The family invited everyone to attend a wake at a local bar after the burial service. I almost didn't go because my new dress boots had rubbed blisters on my heels.

Standing at the bar, I finished my second beer at the Irish pub. An attempt to replicate the atmosphere at a real pub of yesteryear had been made. The manmade dark wood and fake fireplace aromas felt thick and heavy and oddly comforting after the constant drizzling rain. An elderly man with a short-cropped beard identified himself as a jigsaw-puzzle buddy of Barden's, leaned in, and invaded my body space. "How did you know Wilhelm?" he asked in an Irish brogue.

I mumbled, "I'm a P.I. and our paths crossed on a missing person's case."

"Oh, how interesting. Do tell me about—"

"Please excuse me. I must find the bathroom. Time for my state meds."

He touched my elbow. "Ah, there you go, reading my mind. Tell Lanie hello for me."

The old man came off as daft, but in the bathroom, a striking woman with high cheek bones washed her hands at one of the sinks. Whatever age she was, she carried it well.

"Please barricade the door with that chair."

I complied by bracing a metal chair between the door and the wall.

"Now, we have the joint to ourselves." She smiled and exhaled with a long sigh. "It's nice to finally meet you. Barden liked you." A sadness swept over her face and disappeared in an instant. "I'm Lanie Day, and you think I know who's behind the organ harvesting operation."

Her facade displayed a harmless old lady, but I knew better. I'd seen her arsenal in the rotating shoe rack. I scanned her for a weapon as I took my meds. Her coat draped over a trash bin was within an arm's length of her, and she wore a baggy sweater over loose jeans. "It makes sense you're a part of the pipeline of information concerning it. You ran after Teddy asked you to find out who Jonathon Farnsworth's mother was, and you left clues in the puzzle boxes."

"I didn't run. I went underground to a safe house. Protocol."

"Whose protocol?"

"That's complicated and privileged."

"Why am I here?"

"Barden asked me to find you if anything happened to him."

"To connect the dots for me."

"You don't seem surprised by anything I've said."

"I'm not. Detective Barden and I had a pact that we wanted to protect my grandson, Teddy, and his godchild, Georgie." My sarcastic tone revealed I suspected she already knew everything about our arrangement and then some. "What is it you want from me?"

Three quick knocks, a pause, and another knock interrupted us.

Lanie backed me into the first stall near the door. "Stay here," she whispered and shoved a red flash drive in my windbreaker pocket. "On your way out, fetch my coat."

I heard a commotion outside the door involving a male and female voice, looked through the crack between the frame and the stall door, and spied Lanie tying a bandanna around her hair. She went out of frame and returned with a bucket, sprayed a lemony scent in the air, slumped, and dislodged the chair blocking the bathroom door. "Just finished cleaning up in here, ma'am. Sparkling clean now."

A flash of a police uniform and then a woman's voice said, "About time. A deaf old fart slammed into me, and I almost peed on myself."

*****

The next day, the further I traveled away from Atlanta in my Renault, the fewer semi transports clogged the air space. I rolled my shoulders, turned on the automatic driver, and asked Siri to play my favorite Chopin piece, Polonaise in A-flat Major, Op. 53. The music filled the interior of the car as patches of landscape devoid of humanity drifted by. I slowed and lowered my vehicle as close to the disintegrating roadway as allowed and counted the blooming daffodils, dandelions, and wildflowers growing in the cracks of the pavement as blessings.

A long-eared rabbit hopped across a drainage ditch almost hidden by a hubcap and heaps of pine needles. I was sure I didn't recognize the voice on the phone telling me to wait and do nothing after Barden was murdered. The encounter with Lanie Day had complicated matters. The future was tenuous. I missed my Jack and Teddy's help in unraveling the enigmas of life, but unlike

Detective Barden, I was alive in this moment. It was enough.

I found out the flash drive was encrypted before I left my house. Having the drive in my possession and not knowing the content was nerve-racking and dangerous. I didn't trust myself not to lose data if I tried to decrypt it. In the past, Liz would have been the logical choice for the job, but I hesitated to involve anybody besides Teddy and Georgie. I would see them in a few days. I needed to keep the flash drive secure and act as if the conference was my only concern. I opened and shut the console, reassuring myself Lanie's unwanted gift was there and pulled into a recharge center. Rain spattered against my windshield.

I recharged my Renault and pulled into a parking spot close to a rest stop area. Gray clouds dumped rain in thick sheets for several minutes, slacked off, and changed to a drizzle. I needed a potty break and locked my vehicle, causing the security system to kick in. I'd never seen such a busy center.

The line for the bathroom wound around the vending machine kiosk and out into the pathway. Multi-colored umbrellas and body bubbles protecting the fifty or more people, some with their bots in tow, dotted the landscape. Then a Burgers From Outer Space touched down about half a length of the parking lot away from my Renault. I race-walked toward food and—I prayed—a clean bathroom.

The retro neon sign in the glass front of the restaurant flashed a two-hour countdown layover and its rainbow tubing around the sliding glass doors blinked like the eyes of a doll as the doors opened and shut. The place's veggie burgers and fries were famous. I scurried toward the wandering restaurant, my rubber boots splashing water against the knees of my pants, as a blast of wet wind hit me sideways, some young thing cut in front of me. I fell. A middle-aged man with a trimmed mustache helped me up. "Are you alright?" He spoke with a slight British accent.

He retrieved my tote from the pavement.

My wrist and knee hurt on the side where I'd landed. I surveyed the damage and felt my face flush. He probably thought I was a clumsy old fool. "Well, no broken bones," I said. "A scrape here and there. I'll live. Thank you."

He handed me my tote, and I slipped it over my good shoulder. People rushed past us. "Some young people could use a good lecture about manners," he said.

"I won't argue about that." I brushed myself off and saw one of my pant legs was torn, exposing a bloody knee.

"Are you sure you're okay? Let me escort you inside. Please allow me to attend to your knee. Then you must share a table with me." He swept the air as if clearing the way.

I noticed TRS monogrammed on his shirt cuff edging out of a sleeve of what I guessed was London Fog rain gear and an expensive pinkie ring on his slender hand. "I'm yours for one hour and forty-three minutes." I pointed to the count-down clock and stepped forward with caution.

"Don't worry. I'm the owner. They can't leave until I give the nod. Theodore Raymond Strane, here."

I dropped my tote on the man's shiny loafers.

25

We sat inside a booth at the front of the dining room. Theodore waved a waitress over. "Tell the staff to ready themselves for a slight medical emergency in the kitchen and find the first aid kit."

"Be right back, sir." The girl with her hair clipped to the back of her head did an about-face and double-timed it through the swinging kitchen doors.

Theodore tapped on the table. "I better go find the first aid kit. It should be in the manager's office."

As the doors closed behind him, I went toward the bathroom straightaway. I knew my

AI Teddy couldn't be tied to this Theodore Strane, but my mind leaped there anyway because Theodore Strane was one of the possible names Jack considered for our AI. Absurd. Either this guy was human and named Teddy Strane—who he claimed to be—or he was a plant by the state, CIA, or the Underground. I didn't believe in coincidences. With my pants down and squatting over the stool, I realized this whole elaborate ruse was a diversion. I finished my business, washed my hands, and slipped out the back door of the restaurant. I hadn't run in years, but I jogged back to my Renault.

I stood on the opposite side of the parking lanes between two cars and saw the driver-side door open and hooded figures inside my car. I used my emergency button on the car fob and the alarm sounded. The rain seemed to gobble up the light from the overhead LED lamps. The human shadows stopped moving and then a dark van sped up and hovered long enough for them to jump inside the van and disappear. Without warning, the van swerved toward me and took out a parked car's headlight, barely missing me.

Shaking, I walked to the Renault. The flash drive was gone.

Security arrived, a bot with a military briskness similar to the ones used for the annual home inspections, and I told them nothing was taken. They gave me a cup of weak coffee inside the security hut and finished a useless report.

Nothing had recorded on the cameras because they were temporarily offline for maintenance. They had checked my car for damage, paying close attention to the rear bumper and the other car's busted headlight. They didn't ask me how the suspects got inside my Renault without breaking a window, or maybe they assumed the car's computer system was hacked. Of course, I couldn't give them a license plate or any distinguishing logos on the van because there weren't any. They asked my age and made sure to note my eyesight test score listed on my last license renewal. I passed their tests for competency, but as an elder, my story was dismissed as 'inconclusive' about whether a state crime had occurred. Upon this occasion, Theodore Strane didn't come to my rescue.

When I was released with the case number, I drove to the nearest four-star hotel, took my meds, and collapsed on the bed. I wondered what classified information I had lost and who might be ruined or killed because of it. My stomach growled. I had a pack of crackers in my bag, but I couldn't force myself to get up. I covered my eyes in the crook of an elbow and slept.

*****

The following morning at Georgie's flat, Teddy stood on the balcony drinking a cup of black coffee and gazing at the Atlanta skyline and air traffic. The gray clouds and white noise of the traffic blended into an unsettling beginning to a new day. A tepid breeze flapped at his tee shirt and briefs. Teddy's program had adapted to living with Georgie for the duration of the Underground's mission, but his first priority was Grams. AIs didn't worry, but Teddy knew straying afield from the creator's intention caused motherboards to burn up. He needed a maintenance update only available in his basement repair shop and a long talk with his grandmother.

He had left the door open and heard Georgie stirring around in the kitchen. "Do you want French toast and bacon?"

He returned inside and saw her standing on tiptoes in a bathrobe with a towel wrapped around her head. As she reached for a pan in the overhead carousel, her robe came open and exposed her small breasts.

"Georgie, I'm packed and going home today."

"But I thought we agreed it could wait until our meeting at Rabun Lake."

"My programming requires I take care of Grams and adjustments in my facial structure must be made this week. Grams and I will meet you in North Georgia in a few days."

She closed her robe, met him near the couch, cupped his dimpled chin in her soft hands. "You do what you must, but don't mess with what I love." She nibbled at his eyes, nose, and lips." She sighed. "I'm a grown woman, but I'll miss my hunky young thing."

He grinned. "I can do a hunk in his prime based on Jack's instructions."

She slapped at his chest. "I won't be able to keep my hands off you. Embarrassing." She pulled him toward the couch and pulled down his briefs.

*****

Not finding Grams at home, Teddy climbed the stairs and peeked around the house. The bedroom closet door was ajar and some of Gram's clothes or 'conference uniforms' were missing. A scarf with a Brazilian motif, a present from Barbara, lay on the bed with a pair of dangly earrings. Teddy understood she kept the gifts for sentimental reasons but would never wear the fashion statements. The Christmas stocking in the back of the closet where Grams kept her burner phone was empty.

He texted on his burner cell. *Dropped by the house for a quick lunch and to hang out, but you're gone. Where are you?*

Grams didn't answer the text he sent, so he took the basement stairs to the hidden power booster and brought up the recessed chair, then organized the tools and mirrors around the barrel bot that would circle him in the chair and perform the makeover. Under these emergency circumstances, the process would take at least three hours, ending with a refresh of all his internal systems while his facial and upper body upgrades cured. Usually, the changes were subtle, but this mandatory maintenance scheduled by Jack over two years ago was a major leap into adulthood. His chin would be more angular, Adam's apple more pronounced, and his shoulders and nose broader. Teddy reclined in the lounge chair and hit the remote to strap himself in place. He heard a drilling sound before the bot downloaded the ocean vacation experience, and he felt himself sink into warm sand, smelled saltwater lapping over his feet, and saw Sanderlings pecking at each other over a piece of bread.

*****

I canceled my early reservation and pawned my grandmother's orange opal ring for UFCs. The intergalactic Untraceable

Foreign Coins kept the drug dealers and others who distrusted their government and wished to live off the grid a way to conduct business. I ended up at the Cabins at Highland Falls. I'd stayed at the cabins years ago on retreat after teaching a writing seminar at Young Harris College. I walked in, hoping a room was available. The desk clerk shut down a hologram reading from a crime novel by Elmore Leonard and slid a tablet toward me for registration information. "Aren't you an author?"

I must've looked stunned. "Yes, I am. How did you know?"

"I took some writing courses at Young Harris when you were teaching there. My mom and dad own these cabins." He pushed up his flannel shirt sleeve, exposing a heart-shaped tattoo on his forearm and then tapped on his wrist iPad. "Don't tell me your name. Let me see if I can find you online."

"Please don't. I'm Dorothy Saunders. And you're—?"

The light left his green eyes. "Milton Jefferies."

"Of course, Milton. Pardon my senior moment." I leaned in and tapped the desk near the tablet. "I need a favor. I'd rather not leave an electronic trace of my location. I prefer to pay in UFCs, and I promise to read up to thirty pages of your next manuscript." I took a chance he still wrote.

He beamed. "I do have a short story I think is awfully good."

"Agreed then? I'll be staying four or five nights as Wanda Stringer."

He raked his stringy hair away from his neck, and I saw a double chin. "Okay. People don't come to the middle of nowhere to socialize, so what's the big mystery?"

I borrowed a scenario from one of my short stories. "My ex-beau won't accept we're done. He's not violent, just obsessive. I need a breather. Will you help me?"

"No prob. I hate clingy, but you'll need to pay each day for your cabin before noon."

I paid for the room for one night and gave him a nice tip.

"The office is closed between nine p.m. and eight a.m." He handed me an old-fashioned key card. "Cabin number five has a beautiful view of the Blue Ridge Mountains, and there's a hiking trail nearby."

*****

Teddy's virtual beach experience ended, and the bot unhooked the machines and returned to its portal station. A mirror swiveled around, and the straps loosened. He scanned and verified his systems and then searched his face for any flaws. He looked like Jack in his prime. In fact, Teddy had inserted a digital image of his grandfather into the maintenance bot for a guide. In the photo, Jack wore a tux with Grams as a young bride ready to stuff a piece of wedding cake into his mouth. The only noticeable difference was the hair color. Jack had dark auburn hair, and Teddy's was a sun-kissed brown.

The doorbell rang and the security cameras recorded an elderly woman with a rain hat. She stared at the closest camera attached to the eaves. Teddy's new internal recognition system exhibited the name Lanie Day, along with the encounter at the university library and the call afterward wanting him to come in person to pick up the birth records of Jonathon Farnsworth.

He opened the door, and the woman slipped past him. "Teddy, your grandmother is in danger.

I gave her an encrypted flash drive at Detective Barden's wake, and it was stolen by a black ops team sent by E.I. Vance."

"What is on it?"

"Information about the organ harvesting operation run out of Hawaii and tracing it back to the mainland. Where is she now?"

"I don't know, exactly. She packed for the conference in Dahlonega, made arrangements to arrive early, and then canceled the reservation."

"Vance's guys tag-teamed her at a rest stop north of Gainesville. Took the flash drive from her console, but she's okay."

"Are you sure?"

Lanie took off her hat and stuffed it in her coat pocket. "Yes, she stayed at an economy lodge near Gainesville last night, paid with a gift card, and then she dropped off the grid. She found my tracker under the passenger's seat and threw it in the bushes."

"I haven't heard from her. She's probably headed for a drone no-fly zone. Maybe Oconee State Park," Teddy said.

"Let's hope we find her before they do. The head of the operation played nice, distracting her at the rest stop by impersonating the owner of Burger from Outer Space, but he has a rep for torturing and beheading his enemies."

"Now that they have the only solid proof we had to connect them to the organs, why bother?"

Teddy followed the former librarian to the couch, and they sat facing each other. "I know you and Dorothy are Underground, and your people won't stop until they find whoever killed Agents Denton and Combs."

"Aren't you in danger?"

"Yes, but I have leverage and an escape plan. You and your grandmother are expendable."

The security system bleeped: "An unauthorized presence, blocking categorization recognition, has the capacity to blur optics and is attempting to gain entry."

*****

The picture window allowed me to see squirrels scrambling on the railing on the front deck of the cabin as I shut the air fryer on what I hoped would turn out to be eatable oatmeal. Dehydrated food packets lined the pantry, but I wasn't that desperate. Yet. The one-room cabin had a queen-sized bed across from a fake fireplace with a blower that heated the room and a small open kitchen. The comfortable furniture, built to last, with thick shellacked armrests and plaid upholstery, reminded me of my grandfather's favorite chair. My grandmother told me the chair was passed down to him from his father, who habitually read real paper books and magazines in front of a television screen mounted to the wall that streamed white noise made by news commentators.

Late last night, I remembered to check my burner phone. I had answered Teddy, but he hadn't responded. I gave him until noon to call me back before I started to worry. I hated to bother Georgie at work, but I would.

The oatmeal was passable and I ate, trying not to taste the glutinous substance. As I stacked the dishwasher, the rain stopped, and sun peeked out of the clouds. A hike was in order. I hadn't brought my hiking boots, but I tied on my tennis shoes, grabbed my fanny pack and burner phone, and headed for the nearest trail.

A few yards into the trail, it split, and I took the left footpath. The trees thinned out in a quarter mile, and a fallen tree trunk on the side of the path beckoned me. I sat on the log and listened to nature whispering. I took a deep breath. My breathing slowed, and a tiny green lizard crawled onto a small rock at my feet and sunned itself. I decided to do the same and pulled back the hood on my jacket and closed my eyes. I pictured Teddy safe and smiling.

I heard buzzing sounds like aggressive flies circling my head, then I felt a prick on my neck and swatted the air. Too late, I realized I'd hit a ladybug drone scout. My vision blurred as I stumbled back onto the path and my heart raced. My last conscious thought was Teddy would be next.

26

Teddy and Ms. Day ran out the kitchen door and across the parking lot into a tree line at the backend of the subdivision. They hid in the shrubbery behind a house with a swing set until Teddy motioned for them to try the metal utility shed. A dog was barking from inside the small building. He increased his human scent odor and reached for an energy bar inside his windbreaker, peeled the wrapper back, and stuck it gingerly through the doggie door. Teddy scanned the finger imprints on the security panel and got a probable entry code, but the right number sequence took three tries, the limit before police headquarters was notified.

"That was lucky," Lanie said giving him a sideways glance.

They slipped inside the shed and pushed a heavy box against the door. "Come here, Rover." The dog licked his hand. "Sometimes, the dog gets loose and runs into our backyard. What can I say? They used the dog's name as the code."

"Imaginative."

They peeked out between the curtain panels. A police helicopter buzzed overhead and flew over the backyard, using the floodlight to search. The latest equipment for detecting body heat by drones couldn't be fooled, but it was expensive to install and use in the old helicopters. Maybe their luck would hold. The cost analysis of using infrared to detect minor offenders started to run inside Teddy as he patted the dog.

Ms. Day sighed. "No infrared I guess," she said, as if she might have read his internal code's extrapolations.

Teddy nodded. The shed smelled like acrylic paint, and a blank canvas set up on a tripod was close to a workbench littered with brushes and half-used paint tubes.

A state message played from the helicopter's sound system. "Dorothy Saunders and Theodore Strange have avoided a mandatory state health inspection of their premises at 210 Rucker Street, Atlanta, Georgia, United States of America. Their residence is sealed and warrants issued for their arrests. The state demands these citizens be reprimanded for their actions and shall be held without bond. Harboring a fugitive is a felony against the state, punishable by extreme confinement. Your duty is to report any sighting of the fugitives."

The floodlights sifted and bathed the inside of the shed. They ducked down and sat on the floor. Teddy held Rover and smoothed the fur of the whining mutt dog with sad eyes.

The helicopter left after several more sweeps of the backyard, and they waited. They listened for sounds of officers on foot searching for them, but after thirty minutes of tense silence, Ms. Day grabbed a leg of a workbench and raised herself up in a fluid motion. "Oh, great, they think I'm your grandmother. We have to leave Atlanta. Separately."

*****

I woke to the smell of manure. I was in an animal cage in a barn structure with hay spread out on a dirt floor. I rubbed at the crisscross impressions on my hand and arm made by the wire squares in the cage design where I had rested on my side while unconscious. A padlock hung from the cage door. Locked. A rancid taste entered my dry mouth and my heartbeat clamored. I pulled at the lock and turned round and round like a trapped animal. How long had I been out? Hours? Days? They—whoever they were—had taken my shoes and my cell but deposited a water bottle, my med kit, and a sandwich on a platter at one end of the cage. I willed myself to inhale and exhale slowly and moved in a stooped posture and surveyed the barn. The security cameras weren't obvious, but I spotted a suspicious wood knot on the beam above the barn doors. I saw daylight between the barn slats and a shadow passed by. I looped my fingers through the cage wire and shook it. "Hey, out there. I need to go to the bathroom. The bathroom. Hello."

A bass voice said, "Pee in the straw. I'm busy."

"Oh, come on." I rattled the cage again. "I'm old. Give me a break."

No answer. The shadow was gone, but a dog barked close by and a goat bleated a complaint in the distance. I was being held on a farm, but where?

I gulped down some water and feeling a bit light-headed, I took one of my eight emergency auto-injector pen meds. Without my phone, my online connection to the state hologram clinician and dispensary meds was impossible. The state would've checked my residence and found me gone, issued an elderly care alert, and suspended my prescription. Thinking about the steps necessary and the hassle of straightening out the administrative nightmare of elder meds—before they put me in a care facility—distracted me from my kidnapping predicament. A huge task was possible if you broke it down in small increments. All I needed to do was escape within four days before my meds ran out.

A chicken appeared from behind a bale of hay, flapped its wings at the cage, and cackled.

*****

Ms. Day acted nonchalant and kissed Teddy on the cheek. She wore a fake nose and dark makeup on her exposed skin, and a large scarf covered her head. The concrete bus station was on a platform and contained a few benches and a vending machine. A bus docked and another one flipped on its Montgomery, Alabama, terminus sign.

"You take the white Corolla parked next to the rental that we drove here. It's clean and registered to a Matty Wilson, your new auntie. There is a fake ID in the glove compartment in the name of Preston Wilson, but unless you can change your fingerprints or eye scan, you need to stay away from random roadblock checks. Remember to track your Grams from the hotel outside of Gainesville. Start from the night of the theft." She touched his sleeve and handed him a key fob. "Don't call Georgie. They are monitoring her movements, phones, and computers. However, she might be a good person to call if you get caught."

"By they are you referring to the CIA?"

She pulled her scarf forward and lowered her voice. "In this instance, the all-knowing they include industry, government, and anti-government factions. At some point, you realize none of them are independent entities, and the people who run them don't have any scruples about killing someone if a poor soul gets in the way of their agenda. Goodbye, Preston. Stay safe." Ms. Day waved and boarded the transport bus bound for Montgomery.

The transport surged forward, its tail a mini fireworks display. Teddy knew the production of colored lights was an illusion created by the bus's designer, her trademark, and that Ms. Day's intended destination wasn't Montgomery.

Teddy drove the Corolla to the nearest truck transport stop, bought a coffee, and checked the car for miniature bugs as he washed and vacuumed the car. The full-service wash and clean, run by bots, was popular with out-of-state travelers, but the locals knew if a speck of dust containing a banned substance was found inside the car it was reported to the state.

By noon, Teddy tracked Grams to the Cabins at Highland Falls. The unkempt clerk eyed Teddy with suspicion as he asked for Dorothy Saunders, a woman in her sixties, a writer, on retreat from Atlanta. He explained she was due back for a medical review by the state. "I'm her grandson and worried about her."

"Let me see your ID."

Teddy couldn't show his real ID flashing a wanted person alert, however, the Preston Wilson credentials worked.

"Do you live with her?"

"Yes."

"Then why was she traveling off the grid?"

"I'm not sure. Look." Teddy flashed cell photos of Grams and him at home and eating a picnic in a park.

"Nice photos."

Teddy read the man's body language as relaxing and knew he was on the right track. "I stayed over at my girlfriend's house the night she left. She took her clothes for a writing conference in Dahlonega, but it doesn't start for another few days."

"How'd you know she was here?"

"I didn't. I made stops along the way from Atlanta guessing where she might eat or recharge the Renault—she was paranoid about possible robbers lurking at the outpost stations—she stuck to the recommended state routes and recharge sites listed near major cities. Then I remembered she mentioned this place years ago when she was teaching at Young Harris College."

The clerk glanced at an open duffle bag lying on the floor behind the desk. "Yes, I went to that college for a while."

"Please, she could be in a medical crisis if the state puts a hold on her meds."

He picked up the bag and slung it on the counter. "Her things. All I know, mister, is she left her things in a cabin and disappeared the day after she paid me off the books with UFCs. She told me an ex-lover was hounding her."

Teddy placed the bag over a shoulder. "I thought he'd stopped stalking her since the

Protection Order. I've been preoccupied with my own—"

"Stuff."

Teddy conjured a shameful demeanor. "I promise it won't happen again, but I must find her. Do you remember seeing or hearing anything unusual the day she went missing?"

"Now that you asked. I heard a strange buzzing sound early in the morning. I keep my windows cracked open in my bedroom. I put some pants on, went outside, and saw a park ranger's Jeep leaving. The big guy waved at me."

"Why would a park ranger be on your private property?"

"The trails are part of Blue Ridge Mountain Park Service. There is one behind the cabin your grandmother rented."

"What did the ranger look like?"

The clerk brought up a fifteen-second outside cam video on his phone of the ranger driving past the office.

Teddy copied the grainy video.

"Our old tech cams are low-grade, blurry, but he kind of reminds me of the lumberjack Paul

Bunyon character. Barely fit inside the Jeep. Sorry, I don't have the cabins or trails on cameras."

Teddy tipped the clerk. "If anyone else comes looking for her, will you call this number and leave a message for me?" The number belonged to Georgie's burner phone.

"Sure. Ms. Saunders told me she expected to stay for four or five nights. I hope nothing bad happened to her."

"Where is the Renault?"

"That's another strange thing. It vanished, too, but I don't have any footage of her driving out of the campgrounds. The entrance and exit wrought-iron gates have decent cameras attached, but nada." The clerk handed the duffle to Teddy.

Teddy walked the trail, increasing his sense of smell. Grams didn't wear perfume, but her human scent reminded him of the earthy smell of a cinnamon stick. He tracked her until he lost the odor and turned around. Something shiny in the pine bark on the path adjacent to a fallen tree trunk held his attention. He picked up a paperclip in the shape of an angel with a frayed piece of red ribbon attached. The homemade guardian angel pendant, a gift from Grams's mother, had dangled from the zipper pull of her old-fashioned fanny pack. Grams loved carrying that fanny pack.

He studied the log a few feet off the path, an inviting place to rest. He sat down and calculated the possible scenarios that took place here. He knelt and brushed back the grasses surrounding the log. Nothing or nada as the clerk remarked. A helpful guy. Grams might suggest too obliging. He had kept close to the truth, a natural-born liar.

Then Teddy saw it, a black and orange mini drone the size of a ladybug lying partially underneath a small rock. He examined the remains of the injector drone. Now, the question was if the injection was lethal or not. If not, they probably took her someplace local for interrogation or to hold for ransom. Either way, the mountains were a perfect place to dump a body.

*****

Teddy edged the Corolla through the wrought-iron gates, noting the working security cameras and continued about a quarter mile before he flipped the car's hover button on maximum height. He drove off the road, circling the cabins, barely clearing the treetops. Civilian transport vehicles' flying capabilities were limited to short emergency diversions to avoid collisions in restricted air space. Teddy found the Renault—a burned-out hull in the woods, turned over on its side about two football fields east of the trail behind Gram's cabin. The trunk lid was up and the vehicle tag was partly readable. He hovered his car close enough to make sure a human skeleton wasn't inside the trunk or the Renault's interior.

The hover mechanism began to grind and sputter and a warning light flashed on the dashboard. He hit the power boost, straight-lined it back to the gravel road, and lowered the vehicle to the standard six feet above the road that ended perpendicular to a two-lane paved road. He turned right and headed for Young Harris College. The clerk was the key to finding Grams.

He stopped at the first recharge center and checked through the duffle bag. Gram's emergency meds were missing.

Teddy used the college database to find the clerk's student info and traced Gram's teaching days at Young Harris, finding the professor's name who had recommended Dorothy for the teaching position. Retired Professor J.P. Mosley lived in Sautee Nacoochee not far from Helen, Georgia.

The academic opened the door with glasses resting on his head, wearing a rumpled white shirt with a bow tie and a button-down sweater. He invited Teddy inside a log cabin with skylights overhead and the walls lined with built-in bookshelves holding hundreds of stacked laptops, cataloged hard drives, and flash drives thrown in labeled fishbowls. "It appears chaotic, the professor said, "but I know where to put my hands on any information I need. Most of these electronic devices contain my research and published articles—some by my former colleagues." He motioned toward a small rectangular wooden table with two hardback chairs near the kitchen area. "Please sit. When you called, you mentioned Dorothy Saunders, your grandmother. It's been over twenty years since I spoke with Dorothy. How may I help you?"

"It's really about a student she taught at the college, a Milton Jefferies. In 2025, he was expelled for writing a subversive article for the school newspaper. His parents owned The Cabins at Highland Falls.

"Oh, yes, the boy wore the same Army-Navy store clothes and left terrible body odor in his wake the entire semester I taught him. Journalism and Ethics 101. Bright but obsessed with the idea of genetically engineering a superior race and Al elimination."

"My grandmother is missing, and Jefferies was the last person to see her. She stayed at The Cabins before her disappearance."

"That's upsetting news." He scratched his head and gazed out the picture window.

Teddy folded his hands on the table and waited for the old man's memories to surface.

"Milton ran around with a big kid, not so smart." The professor tapped the table. "He called him Bunyon or Paulie and amused himself at his sidekick's expense. Back then, Paul's parents owned a farm near Cleveland, Georgia. I remember because they made him drop out after his freshman year. They needed the help."

"What is his last name?"

"Hunter, maybe. If you're thinking of talking to the family, surely, they aren't still there raising goats and sheep. They have to be my age or older. I think Paul became a park ranger. I can find out."

"You've been helpful," Teddy said. "May I transfer my electronic detective agency info into your phone?" He held his phone out to allow the gentlemen to see the file face with the company logo on the screen.

The professor extended his phone and Teddy tapped it twice.

"Thank you, professor, I must go. If you think of anything else, please message me."

The professor arched an eyebrow. "Does Dorothy help you in the private detective business?"

"Yes, why?"

They walked toward the door.

"She loved figuring out whodunnit in mysteries. One of my pastimes is true crime podcasts. No matter." He flushed as if he admitted a sin. "Intriguing, the motives for crimes. For some reason it popped into my head Dorothy was the one that complained to the chancellor about a hate-mongering, anonymous article in the college newspaper, but I think she left before the administration found out it was written by Milton."

27

My captor opened the cage and threw me a blanket. "Get up and walk around." He towered over me, a huge man in overalls. His brown combat boots appeared the size of a yardstick, and for a moment, I feared he would stomp me to death.

The boots moved back a few feet, and my gripping fear waned.

"Morning to you too," I said, faking self-assurance and blinked from the bright sunlight streaming between the open doors. My numb muscles throbbed as I crawled out and stood up. I shivered and wrapped the thin blanket tighter around me. I felt lightheaded.

He used the toe of his boot to push a cutting board with a mug of coffee and a biscuit with a piece of salty ham toward me. Circling me, he eyed me as if I was a rabid dog and backed away.

I drank and gobbled a bit of food down. Talking with my mouth full, I said, "Please, wait. I only have two med packets left."

"I'll be back in ten minutes. Best you go to the bathroom and such before I come back."

A shaggy, black-and-white speckled dog barked at me as the man slid the barn door shut, then locked the barrel slide bolt from the outside. Why did I get to stretch my legs without him present? The blanket seemed a gesture of kindness.

I ate the biscuit with one hand and examined the hardware on the frame of the barn doors with the other hand. The doors were kept on track by old but intact metal guides. The elbow end fixtures at the bottom of each door were cemented in place.

I hurried to use the excrement bucket, dipped my hands in the second bucket of gray water, and finished my coffee before he returned. "Please. One more minute to stretch."

From the open doorway he watched me do squats and standing pushups against a barn wall. He leaned down and grabbed something outside the barn. Expressionless, he entered my prison with something hidden behind him. He nodded toward the cage and tossed a rectangular object at me.

I flinched. A dingy striped bed pillow landed at my feet in the dirt and hay.

"Take it," he said, "and get back inside. I ain't got all day."

*****

Teddy followed Jeffries' taillights wavering to and fro above old US 129N in North Georgia for forty minutes. Before the exit signs for the small town known for Cabbage Patch Dolls appeared, a holographic road sign for Vogel State Park and Blairsville, located north of Cleveland, flashed on. Five miles after leaving the interstate, Jefferies' white panel van turned down a dirt road without streetlights.

Teddy already knew the Hunter farm was in the vicinity and he drove past the cut off. He waited thirty long minutes and used his GPS and White County's ancient overlay online map system to find the farmhouse. He dimmed his headlights. The white van was parked next to a huge oak tree beside a dilapidated two-story house from the twentieth century. He turned his headlights off and lowered the electric Corolla behind a barn. As he stepped out of the car, he wasn't prepared for the pungent animal smells of goat, chicken, and maybe fox. He turned down his olfactory sensor. A growling dog jumped out of the darkness, lunged at him repeatedly, and barked. "There now, it's okay. I won't hurt you." Teddy withdrew a meat sandwich from his jacket pocket, unwrapped it, and threw Grams's snack on the ground. She would understand. The dog quit barking and sniffed, then clamped the entire meal between his teeth and trotted off.

A frightened voice yelled from inside the barn. "Who's out there? Help. I'm being held against my will."

"Hush, it's me, Grams. Be quiet until I can get you out." Teddy scanned the huge yard and the clapboard farmhouse. He didn't see lights go on or movement. He examined a thick chain held in place by a sturdy lock.

"Thank God you found me," Grams said, lowering her shaky voice. He had only known one other time she was scared when Jack had a heart attack.

"How many people occupy this farm?" He attempted to pick the lock.

"As far as I know, one gigantic man."

"Guess that's me." A mountain stepped forward in the moonlight and flashed a flood light in Teddy's eyes.

He stuck a hand in the air, blocking the light. "Look. I can give you money. Just let her go."

"Not about money. She'll die soon when her meds run out." The light disappeared, and Teddy identified a shovel a second before metal struck his head. The AI acted unconscious. The ranger unlocked the barn and dragged Teddy inside by his ankles.

Grams yelled, beating on the cage. "I'll kill you if you've hurt my grandson. I swear you're dead meat."

"Shut up, you crazy bitch." The tall man turned to shut the door, but Teddy tackled his legs and knocked him down, then tasered his chest. Grams's captor jerked one, two, three times and slumped limp in the dirt.

Teddy took keys from a pocket of the man's overalls and ran to unlock the cage. The smallest key fit. He helped Grams unfold herself from the cage, and she bear-hugged him. "You dear, young man. I thought I was a goner."

Over Gram's shoulder, Teddy saw Jefferies walk into the barn and aim a rifle at Grams' back. A shot rang out and Jefferies dropped to the ground. Dead.

Georgie stood outside the crime scene tape barking orders and irritating the Georgia Bureau of Investigation team. More than content, I sat with Teddy in the back of an ambulance with the bay doors open and watched the chaos created by county police, state troopers, GBI, and FBI stomping in and out of the barn. The coroner arrived to pronounce—what everybody knew—that Jefferies was dead. The fire department and the second EMS truck left as the sun rose over the horizon in the morning sky.

"Get the hell out of my crime scene. Go back to Atlanta and write your statement," a senior GBI agent said to Georgie.

"I'll be glad to do just that when your agents quit destroying crucial evidence."

Teddy laughed beside me. "That's my girl."

I smiled, although the intimacy in his lighthearted statement bothered me, but not as much as the bandage on his AI head.

"How's your injury?" I asked as a paramedic walked by talking to dispatch.

He stopped me from commenting further by touching my arm. He waited until the radio sound disappeared and lifted his head. "It's okay. We can talk now, but the medic can't get inside to use the facilities. The FBI is gathering evidence in the house."

"I bet relieving herself behind a tree isn't a first for her."

"Yeah, but she's not happy. Now, I know every cuss word known to man."

"Your hearing capabilities can be a curse."

"To answer your next question, Georgie bandaged the damage before EMS arrived, and I refused treatment."

The woman's hand was in everything. I changed the subject. "Thank you for bringing my wool sweater. My jacket wasn't thick enough. Feels good in the mountain air." I wrapped my arms across my chest, although I'd stopped shaking after consuming most of a McDonald's cup of coffee and biscuit that a rookie cop had fetched.

"It was inside the duffle bag that Jefferies gave me while I was at The Cabins in The Highlands. He acted helpful, but I knew he was lying."

"Of course you did."

"Before we're interrupted again, the GBI wants us to ride back with an agent to their headquarters and make a statement."

"What will you do? Is your skin broken, exposing your insides?"

"Correct. Sorry, I'm afraid my play Auntie Matty and I didn't help the situation. I'm hoping Georgie can pull a few strings, stay the State Medical Compliance arrest order, unseal the house, and let us go home to recoup from our trauma before making a formal statement tomorrow."

"If not?"

"Fake it and hope for the best."

A laugh exploded from my gut. One of Jack's favorite sayings made me feel better in this ludicrous situation.

He hugged my side. Up close, he smelled like a melted electrical outlet.

"How did you know where I was?"

"Long story. I followed probability breadcrumbs to the cabins. I found the remains of an injector drone on the trail behind your cabin, and the Renault burned in the woods."

"Oh, no, my beautiful Renault."

"Better the Renault than with you in it and… anyway, your medical packets were missing from your gathered things at the cabin, found out

Milton Jefferies was expelled from Young Harris because of your complaint about a subversive article he wrote in the college newspaper, and I followed the man here."

"An article?"

Teddy shook his head. "Not important except for motive, but I spoke to retired Professor Mosley for that info. He lives close in—"

"Sautee Nacoochee. He sent the nicest email card congratulating me on my last book launch." I made myself quit rambling and rubbed a sore spot on my elbow through my layers. I bruised easily and expected later to find multiple contusions from the cage wire. "But how did Georgie get here so fast?"

"Auntie Matty sent word to Georgie that I was driving an issued Corolla to find you. Plus, the latest burner phones have the capability for the owners to put in a safety emergency code that allows tracking. I signaled for help when Jefferies' route indicated he was headed for this farm, waited a few, and Georgie helicoptered in from one farm over. Local police department transported her here, and she took the shot that saved your life."

"How did she explain carrying a weapon?"

"Her uncle in the CIA gave her a Ruger and trained her in their course years ago. That certification trumps any other local governmental regulation."

"A connected woman of many talents. I must thank her." Talented, yes, but where were her true allegiances? Obviously, she loved Teddy. I became aware of the stretch of silence. "But you couldn't have known exactly when she would arrive."

"No."

"Right." We had been lucky. Parched, I gulped down the rest of my cold coffee, tasting the bitter sediment. I didn't want to think about what could've happened. Jefferies was a demented fanatic. "Did I overhear the officers gossiping that Jefferies was suspected of bombing a Jewish synagogue in Atlanta?"

"Yes, ten years ago, hence FBI jurisdiction. I didn't know that fact coming in, but I knew his best bud at Young Harris, now Ranger Paul Hunter, owned this farm in Cleveland."

Georgie stepped in front of us with a husky linebacker wearing a black sweater, a long hunting jacket, and tactical pants. I didn't see a weapon, but no doubt he had one tucked underneath the coat. "It's time to go," Georgie said. "Meet Dan Ford, a friend of my uncle. He'll be taking you home, sticking around, and escorting you to Georgia Bureau of Investigations headquarters tomorrow morning."

Three hours later, Dan, a man of few words, ripped off the state's red tape with NON-COMPLIANT CITIZEN from our front door stoop, took the key fob, and motioned for us to stay outside the house while he checked inside.

I shuffled my feet, trying to keep warm.

"Don't worry, the security illusion panel is operational in the basement," Teddy said.

"What happens if he finds the panel button on the stove? He's CIA, right?"

"He won't, but if he does, Georgie has a plausible cover story."

"What story?"

Teddy held up an index finger.

We heard Dan closing the downstairs bathroom door, and he appeared in short order. "All clear," he said. "I need to call into headquarters. You settle in." With that, he walked toward the government-issued black sedan parked at the curb in a visitor transport spot.

He gave us an hour before he tapped on the door and let himself inside.

In the meantime, Teddy had repaired the tear in his outer covering and had produced a prosthetic facsimile of a minor human head wound and wrapped it with a new bandage. For tomorrow's statements, we agreed to stick close to the truth, leaving out references to Lanie Day, the underground's investigation into harvested body parts, and Detective Barden's suspicious death. I was a writer taking a few days of vacation prior to a conference in the North Georgia mountains and a deranged Jefferies had seized an opportunity for revenge. Teddy's story of who was with him and why they ran from our house would take more convincing, but I had confidence in him.

After a long hot shower and wearing Jack's faded terrycloth robe, I served scrambled eggs and toast, but Dan excused himself to answer a text. He sat on the couch near the front door watching the security cam, or peering into the street, pulling aside the edge of a curtain. Teddy and I made small talk and finished our meal, including Dan's portion.

"Do you have a neighbor with a dog?" Dan asked.

"Yes, he's a tall guy with a basset hound. They walk by my house every morning and then between five and six in the evenings." I stretched my lower back in a standing cat-cow combo Barbara had taught me.

"He doesn't pick up his dog's poop."

Teddy and I exchanged a glance.

I yawned. "It's been a long day. Teddy, would you bring Mr. Ford bedding for the couch? There is a new bed pillow still in the wrapper on the top shelf of the linen closet."

"Don't worry about me," Dan said. "I'll be checking the perimeter every few hours. See you at six a.m. GBI wants you there by eight."

Teddy gave me a hug near the staircase. "I'm behind on my emails and should study for a math make-up test. I'll take care of Mr. Ford soon enough." His college student role struck me as asinine after being assigned by the Underground fieldwork as a spy assistant to Georgie. If Teddy was trying to convey a message about contacting Liz and Ed, I was too exhausted to connect the dots.

With that, I climbed the stairs and fell into bed.

In the middle of the night, I went to the bathroom, stretched out my back with a few cat-cow yoga positions, and looked outside my upstairs bedroom window. Standing on the sidewalk near the black sedan, Dan Ford hunched his broad back and touched his ear buds. He could sense me watching him, turned, and shot me a wave.

*****

Dan deposited us in the Emergency Room sally port entrance at new GBI headquarters located in the old main Grady Memorial Hospital building near Georgia State University. Once, I had ridden with human paramedics at Grady as a teenage observer and an aspiring young writer.

Inside the building, the maze of pale green and white hallways hadn't changed. The doctors and nurses were replaced with fit men and women in polo shirts and fatigues. We followed the white overhead signs and arrows and changed elevators twice. We passed by the overhead marker, "White Collar Crime," and further down the hallway we found the "Abduction and Murder Division." I wondered what it took to walk under those signs every day and investigate horrible crimes.

The front desk robotic clerk asked us to wait and have a seat. Strange expression: have a seat. The clerk pushed buttons on an old, outdated com center. Two recruits escorted us to the back interview rooms. They put Teddy in the first room on the right and then directed me down the hall to the last room on the left. The door locked automatically. Four chairs and a table and little space to pace, but I stretched and stood facing the one-way glass-paneled wall. I guessed that doctors formerly saw patients for appointments in rooms double this size. The bare walls and confined space disorientated and made suspects feel dependent on the interviewers. I knew they'd let me wait.

After over an hour, Special Agent Schildecker and Special Agent Redlinger stepped into the room and filled the space with three-syllable names, grim expressions, and an abundance of testosterone. Schildecker slid an electronic pad in front of me. "Write down what happened yesterday from the time you woke up until you went to bed."

"Happy to, Special Agent Schildecker. I missed my morning yoga stretch. Besides being in a cage cold and hungry before my grandson rescued me, what would you like to know?"

Redlinger cleared his throat. His muscular frame, as evident by the outline of his biceps through his suit jacket, was at least ten years younger than the older agent, and I figured he would play the decent guy role. "What Special Agent Schildecker meant was we would like for you to start from yesterday and work backward so we can make an accurate timeline of the crimes committed against you."

"In that case, I'll be happy to oblige." I decided to play along. My Underground training concerning interrogation techniques from Liz came rushing back. 'They need intel or they wouldn't be asking questions. Be brief, and don't volunteer information unless they should already know the answers, or you're planting red herrings. Make them work for what you give up.

*****

That evening Teddy wasn't home when I arrived at six-thirty. I checked my messages. Surprise. Barbara had called.

"Whoever was watching me has backed off. I drove by your house and saw it was unsealed. I hope your medical reinstatement isn't too unpleasant. I'm feeling better. Anyway, I was cleaning out a closet and found the hats we bought on our spring trip to Orange County for the film festival. Remember, we stayed in Winter Park and rented scooters to drive to Maitland's Enzian Theater. Let's talk. I still love you. Barbara."

Isn't that the way? I gave up trying to reach out to her with my burner phone. I accepted the loss of a friendship, probably for the best with me being Underground and her being a loyal Gainey supporter. Now, she decided to make up and remind me I needed to go through the re-cert series of medical exams and red tape of reinstatement ASAP.

I fell on the couch and closed my eyes. I pictured the unique Enzian Theater and it morphed into the inside of Paul Hunter's barn. I dreamt of my imprisonment inside the cage, and a bullet pierced my back and hit my heart. A starburst of pain radiated inside my chest and weighed me down. I was dying and sensed Teddy kneeling beside me. "Why the heck did they burn my car?" I asked. "Totally unnecessary."

Teddy laughed outside of the foggy walls of my dream.

"Invite Barbara to the funeral."

Teddy tapped my hands, then pulled my wrists. "What funeral? You're home. Let's get you to bed."

28

It took a few days to recover from my imprisonment, the shooting, and interrogation. I let Teddy and Georgie cut through most of the reinstatement red tape with the State Medical Board of Civilian Health. I felt the useless guilt of the privileged few with influential contacts when I gladly accepted the extension on my temporary permit for meds and my hearing date within thirty days.

I met Barbara the following Wednesday. I shifted in the metal seat, the only chairs available in the vegan juice and herbal tea bar.

Our catching-up chit-chat about our writing and my meds fiasco faded into silence. Neither one of us wanted to discuss the fissure in our relationship caused by our distrust of each other.

Barbara put her cup of tea on her saucer. "I've had a lot of time to think. By the way, I'm seeing a counselor through a private organization I trust. Whether the reprobates who tortured me were the state's people or not, my world view has tilted. Until I have more sorted, I've taken down my blog. I've never told you, but one of my nephews is gay, and my sister married a man from Pakistan."

"You don't need to explain to me," I said as I looked around for security cameras inside the juice bar. I spotted two cameras pointing at the counter. The strings of small lights draped around the ceiling molding reminded me of the holidays, but I suspected they hid more than they illuminated.

Barbara leaned across the small two-seater table. The unsteady table tilted toward her. "If you know anyone in the Underground, I don't care, just don't tell me."

"Barb, I—"

"For years, I've scrubbed any communication between us." She reached out and patted my hand.

"You're not the only one who's aware the state is watching and listening in to private matters. I consider friendship sacred."

"I don't know what to say."

"You say nothing, my friend. I love you, and that's what matters. Now, my tea is cold. Let's get out of here and go buy a new purse or something."

*****

Teddy was straightening the basement, and the tool inventory was about finished.

I handed him a thin wrench about the size of my index finger. "If the leak isn't Georgie or Barbara, who is it?" I asked.

"I agree. We need to look beyond them. Someone with skills, a double agent. Lanie, Liz Ed, and Detective Barden were on my list of suspects. Of course, he's—"

"Deceased." I winced.

"If we solve his murder, we'll have our traitor." Teddy put the wrench inside a spotless surgical tool kit and closed the stiff cloth flaps. He slid the kit into one of thirty metal lock-box drawers, each row with bigger heights and depths, encased in a wall of lightweight concrete-like material. The setup reused scrap metal from the defunct U.S. Postal Service security box system.

"Where do we start?"

Teddy locked the box, hit a remote, and a screen covered the wall. "I have a lead on the guy that you saw in the E.I. Vance video with Chantel Farnsworth."

"The suit and briefcase guy? How did you find Barden's video?"

Teddy cleaned the workbench with a Citsalp wipe. "Barden left encrypted intel with a young detective. He trained Dell Matthews's older sister, Hadera Hill, in the academy before he hand-picked her for his partner. Before you ask, she was adopted five years before Dell was conceived."

"Barden never mentioned Detective Hill, but then why would he? So, she brought the files to Dell to decipher because she suspected Barden's death wasn't an accident."

"Exactly. Detective Hill can only do so much without the administration shutting down her unauthorized investigation. Dell knows about our P.I. agency. He's heard me mention Detective

Barden was a friend of yours, and based on your late-night internet café liaison, my college chum thinks you're the spunkiest grandmother he's ever met."

"Such a nice young man and loyal friend you have. Will his sister meet with us?"

"I don't know, but it's worth a try. Dell forgot to text me his sister's cell number and now he's off the grid playing in a national chess tournament. I used a burner phone and left a message at the precinct under the name T. S." He stared at the dirty water as it drained from the industrial sink.

"What is bothering you?"

"If we're not careful, the Underground will send an eliminator after us."

"Especially if Liz and Ed are at the heart of this mess."

"They aren't following me because of my excellent results concerning the field work with Georgie, but you're still on shaky ground."

"You want me to stay home." I slumped down on a stool.

He wrapped his arms around my shoulders. "I would keep my social events with Barbara to a minimum too."

I looked up at Teddy. "Damn it all to hell."

He shrugged. "Or deal with Helen or somebody like Helen knocking on your door."

"Wait a minute." I race-walked upstairs and put on my wig and an outfit I'd bought at a thrift store.

Minutes later, I pranced around my grandson. "Well, what do you think?"

"You're going to go along as my—" he laughed.

"New assistant, Mrs. Waverly, at your service."

"If we leave separately, it may work. I'll spend the night at Georgie's and wait for the detective to return my call. Can you lose your Underground tail by putting on that getup in a public restroom?"

"I did it before, but honestly, I haven't seen anyone lurking in the shadows for about a week."

"That's because I've been here keeping tabs on you."

"Okay, after you call about the time and location, I'll go to a public place—maybe the farmer's market—change clothes, and sneak out unnoticed from the bathroom. I'll catch up after I ditch my tail."

He shook his head. "Incorrigible."

"Be careful, T. S."

*****

Teddy read the private chat from Hadera Hill, protected by SS or Safe and Secure, a recent software developed by three graduate students from Georgia Tech.

Meet me at Piedmont Park—the activity oval kiosk off 14th Street near the north soccer field in an hour.

Teddy posted an okay sign and added *Make it two hours. My female assistant, who knew your partner, and I will be wearing matching Atlanta Braves windbreakers.*

Got it. I'm the West African with braids riding a vintage Harley.

The sun bounced off the metal bleachers as Teddy slid into a seat near the kiosk. He sipped an iced coffee and waited. Fifteen minutes later, Hill circled the parking lot and shut off her red Harley, eliminating the mechanical purring of the mufflers. At noon on a Monday, the deserted soccer field and surrounding activity oval allowed a smoggy but serene view of Atlanta's midtown skyline.

Walking from the public rail station, Grams texted she was ten minutes away.

Hill walked straight toward Teddy and kissed him on the cheek. "Honey, how nice of you to bring me a cup." She dislodged the cup from his hand and drank.

Teddy judged her age as mid-twenties and without makeup, her skin glowed with vitality. She sized up her new acquaintance and flashed her pocket surveillance blocker. "I'll show you mine if you show me yours."

"Mine is internal." Teddy sat on the bleachers.

"Well, well, an AI detective. I'm assuming you aren't registered…" She finished the coffee. "And Detective Barden knew?"

"He suspected."

"Why tell me?" Hill slid onto the bleachers beside Teddy.

"If I'm right, you have copies of Barden's forbidden personal notes and files. You already know who Grams and I are, but you need us to sort out this mess."

"True. They wiped his sanctioned phone and files before the accident, not after. I saw tech support do it. Fortunately, the night before his death, Barden backed up everything on a portable hard drive. He had studied the surveillance system during power failures, but there was a glitch. It took thirty seconds longer to reboot the security cameras than his computer."

"I need access to those files," Teddy said.

Hill pursed her lips.

Teddy held her gaze. "I'm trusting you with my partner's slash grandmother's life and my existence. Speaking of my dear Grams, I can hear her labored breathing as she approaches from 14th Street. Now, quid pro quo, you tell me something about yourself that could destroy you. FYI: I can tell if you're lying."

"That must be a useful trick. Even sociopaths?"

"Yes."

"I'm envious."

Grams arrived flushed, wearing her wig and Braves jacket. "It took a bit longer to ditch my tail than expected." She stuck out her hand to the detective. "I'm Dorothy."

Hill laughed. "No offense, but I don't shake hands on the first date."

Grams rubbed her hand on her sweatpants. "Old habit, sorry. I'm glad to meet Detective Barden's partner. I considered him a friend and want to help solve his murder."

Teddy cleared his throat. "Detective Hadera Hill was about to share a secret about herself because I told her I'm AI."

A gasp emanated between Grams's tight lips as she looked up at them.

Hadera tipped her head, causing her braids to cascade across one cheek. "I can't think what's so bad in my past that I would be executed, but my parents paid off immigration officials to make my adoption legal. Before the decision to adopt, my dad invested in genetic research, so I'm a rich bitch. Will that do?"

"Does he own shares in E.I. Vance Pharmaceuticals?" Teddy asked.

"Probably, why?"

An elderly park patrol volunteer rolled by the group in a golf cart and nodded as Hill flashed her badge. The old patriot wearing the state colors of red and gold talked into an ancient hand-held walkie-talkie and moved on.

"Because, dear..." Grams shifted her tote to her other shoulder and waited until security became a blob in the distance. "We suspect black-market organs are being shipped from Hawaii to E.I. Vance's scientist, a Chantel Farnsworth. She's the woman in the decrypted video. I assume you still have a copy in your possession, and someone in your department is a spy. Detective Barden got too close."

"So, the bastards killed him. Yes, I have it. Who's the creepy guy with a briefcase talking to her in the video? Cartel or mercenary?"

"That's what we hope you can sort out." Teddy leaned in. "He's a blank slate—not even any dark web intel. I could call my CIA source, but I'd rather not involve them yet."

"Give me a few days and let me hook up with my local shady pharmacist who supplies meds for the low-income and homeless—off the books. Because he owes me—he'll work his contacts, suppliers, and rich anonymous donors."

The golf cart with the eager senior citizen circled the group from a polite distance. Teddy and Hill hopped down from the bleachers and joined Grams on the ground.

"Let's go before the 'Good Citizen' patrol rolls past us again," Hill said and handed phones to Grams and Teddy. "Have a burner phone on me."

*****

I had slept for ten hours. The house, dark and silent, reminded me Teddy wasn't in his room. My cell phone showed it was six a.m. I groaned as I crawled out of bed. "Get up old woman and be happy about it." I held onto the stair railing, giving my stiff joints a crutch as I descended. I missed Teddy making my morning coffee and chatting as we shared breakfast. "Change, the only constant." I acknowledged that work beyond the detective agency and Georgie or some other human relationship would consume most of Teddy's time from now on.

Out of habit, I spooned coffee and whole milk for two cups into the mini latte dispenser. My grandson would check on me, as his program required, and give me my hugs, but his primary resident wouldn't be here. Sly Jack had tricked me. He gave me a couple of years with Teddy in the house to help me through the worst of the grief, but he wanted me to stand on my own two feet, find my way, and move forward.

The coffee machine beeped, and I filled a huge cup with the brew, then buttered two pieces of bread and placed them in the mini oven. The SapGo machine app on my phone toasted and warmed, but food didn't taste the same.

Finding Detective Barden's killer was my focus for today. I turned on the hologram board and saved my workshop syllabus from the North Georgia conference, the one I didn't speak at because I was detained in a cage. For a moment I was back in the barn, cold and hungry. Scared. Grabbing a sweater from the back of a kitchen chair and draping it across my shoulders, I began to list everything I knew about Barden's death.

29

That same evening, Teddy stepped away from Georgie, leaving her watching an interactive movie in her living room. An encrypted email came from a whiteboard untraceable server. Teddy brought up the email:

Hi,

Your favorite aunt is touching base. I'll be at the Gainey Fine Arts Museum on 10th Street for the Monet exhibition at eleven tomorrow morning. Want to join me at the check-in desk? I'm paying. Love to catch up. Park your car near the handicapped spaces up front. I borrowed a friend's Subaru to drive around the city during my visit to Georgia. Wear comfortable shoes. -MW

The next morning, Teddy spotted Lanie dressed as Matty Wilson, wearing a prosthetic beak nose and dark body makeup in the lobby of the museum. Her gray curly hair camouflaged by a hiking hat with a brim stuck out in a thick half-moon at the nape of her neck. Seated on one of the stone benches lining the circular atrium, she pawed through a large tote with printed giraffes, no doubt recently purchased from the gift shop.

"There you are, Auntie. So good to see you."

She stood without hesitation, handed him the tote and key fob, and hugged him. "Aw, yes, Preston. Would you mind carrying this bag? I bought too much for my adopted granddaughter, the aspiring painter. She turns thirteen this week. I should've waited until we finished our tour, but age has its privilege."

"No problem. Always doing and thinking of others, my auntie." He kissed her cheek.

They walked around the museum and admired the exhibition, avoiding the occasional patrons. Holograms lectured on the painter's use of color, and Claude Debussy's Claire de Lune played in the background. Teddy trusted Lanie to explain why they were meeting without prompting. Her countenance turned contemplative, then grave. Halfway through the exhibition a bench beckoned, and they sat together and admired The Woman with a Parasol-Madame Monet and her Son. Teddy placed the gift bag between them.

Lanie patted his knee. "Dear boy, I've dreaded this moment. I know who ordered the hit on Alfie and Raph."

"Who?"

Lanie gripped his hand as a security bot with perfect mannequin features passed them. The masculine lean figure, dressed similar to a museum guide, wore a navy-suit jacket with a Gainey State seal displayed on the pocket. It glided to a corner of the room ahead of them, turned around, and swiveled its head, screening the room.

Teddy focused on the image of the woman in the painting while scrambling the bot's signal to protect his AI status.

"Gun," Lanie said. The librarian pushed Teddy to the floor as he heard the whishing sound of a shot from a silencer.

She moaned once and fell on top of him.

Dead.

*****

Teddy ran, shots whizzing by him. Holding the gift bag against his chest, he pulled up his hoodie with his other hand as the automatic doors opened at the exit to the parking lot. He saw a black Subaru parked in a handicapped space and unlocked it with his key fob. Lanie must have visited her friend and borrowed the Subaru before this meetup.

Risky.

The bot hovered at the door, but the gun wasn't visible anymore.

Teddy backed the car out and drove in the opposite direction.

If facial recognition failed, leaving the Corolla in the parking lot in the second row would lead security to Preston Wilson and to him eventually, but maybe Lanie had left something of value in this car or in the giraffe bag. He hit a button on the steering column and requested the S-Series program to call Grams.

"Teddy, what happened?" Grams said without preliminaries. "They have you on video running away. The news reported a shooting at—"

"Pack a bag with your passport. Be ready in fifteen minutes. Bring my emergency duffle. It's in the basement behind shelf D-Delta. Push the back panel. Hurry."

As Teddy drove up alongside the curb, Grams waved and pulled a loaded cart with their bags down the walkway. They met halfway, hugged, and loaded the suitcases in less than three minutes.

Once inside the Subaru, Grams asked, "A woman was shot. Was it Lanie? Where are we going?"

"Yes, Lanie's dead. To a safe house."

Grams's eyes rimmed with tears. "Ruthless bastards are eliminating everyone we trust or contact."

"Don't worry. I set this house up myself. Nobody, not even Underground or Georgie knows about this one."

"When did you have time?"

"After your abduction, I took precautions. Jack programmed me for such contingencies."

Teddy glanced at Grams, then focused back on the road. "We'll need to ditch the Subaru ASAP, although I swapped out the plates and added Lanie's bogus magnetic realtor signs to the doors. The lady was clever. A Glock was in the glove compartment."

She sighed. "Mind-blowing. Under the circumstances, I'm inclined to believe Lanie was a genius."

He lifted his shirt, revealing the semi-auto Glock. "We'll take back routes and stay just outside the city where I stashed a truck and weapons."

Grams dropped her head, rubbed the vertical lines between her eyebrows with a thumb, and rocked. "I hate guns." She righted herself. "Hate them. I can't believe I'm saying this, but I feel safer because you have the vile thing."

The five-room white clapboard farmhouse sat off I-75 on twenty-five acres of farmland east of Thomaston, Georgia. Teddy put down his duffle bag on a small table underneath a coat rack while Grams took off her windbreaker and draped it over the back of the couch.

"We're lucky Dell was willing to loan us his place. Isn't he worried about his property being torn or shot up?"

"Probably, but he and his sister think finding Barden's killer is more important," Teddy said. "Dell Matthews's uncle passed and left him the property. He uses it as a getaway from Atlanta. The rest of the family never comes down here to the shack in South Georgia. They considered his uncle, with his living-off-the-grid views, a paranoid redneck."

"What about Dell's safety?"

"I made an extra set of keys weeks ago. Technically, he and his sister don't know we're here."

Grams rubbed her hands together in the cold, musty air. "Got it. So, there isn't any Wi-Fi?" A banned fireplace still occupied the back wall of the living room with an old forty-eight-inch flat-screen television screen mounted above it.

"No, but there is electricity, water, and heat. I'll turn the thermostat on." He walked to the open kitchen and flipped the switch on the control panel installed in the wall. The furnace engine fan kicked on and a blast of rusty dust flowed from the vents.

Grams chuckled. "That smell brings back childhood memories, and this kitchen reminds me of my grandmother's kitchen with the white wooden cabinets, a mismatch of plastic molded and stainless-steel appliances, and unbelievable butcher block countertops."

"It's quaint but functional. It'll do until I can get our paperwork together to leave the states."

"Leave, but where will we go?"

"To a neutral country for a few years. Maybe Australia. You understand we flee or die?"

"I hadn't thought it through."

"First priority: we need to stay alive. There's a neighbor and a convenience store of sorts about a mile from here with Wi-Fi. I'll be tapping into their systems or using hot spots. Make yourself at home while I check on the truck. Hopefully, it will start, then you'll need to follow me in the Subaru into the next county. I'll set fire to the Subaru in a rural area without any surveillance cameras, and we'll drive back and pick up the weapons."

"Where are the guns?"

"Lanie hid the gear and protective weapons off I-75 near Thomaston. One of the reasons I chose this area. I have a hand-woven map to find them."

"Excuse me?"

"It's a rice-paper table mat." He turned, heading for the ramshackle garage, but pivoted back. "Please walk through the house and note where every exit and entry point is. Scan and memorize the items in the drawers and cabinets. We might need to improvise."

"Do you mean make a bomb?"

"I was thinking knives as weapons, but yeah, whatever it takes."

"Holy crap, I wonder if any webinars I took on domestic terrorism for my writing will come in handy. I remember how easy it was to make a bomb from household cleaning supplies using hydrochloric acid and…" She snapped her fingers. "And aluminum."

"Too volatile. You won't be making anything like that, but I might. Now, please go check out the house. I'll be back."

Teddy was doing more than starting the truck engine in the garage. The kitchen window gave me a view of a grassy field beyond an old well and the side of the rickety garage. The double doors to the garage were open, and I could see my grandson's shadow pass by the crack between a crooked door and the frame. He appeared measured in his work, whatever it was, as I took a mental inventory of what was stored in the farmhouse and returned to the window again and again.

A hawk flew low and circled the Subaru and Ford truck as we drove away from the safe house. Teddy drove the truck in front of me and held a hand up outside the window, pointed, and indicated the bird was real. The bird of prey swooped down in the tall grass along the two-lane and regained height in an instant, carrying a small rabbit in his beak. The drones built by men emulated this animal in the saddest possible way by spying on and destroying others of their own kind.

We followed State Road 36 until we passed Riverbend Restaurant in Thomaston, overgrown with weeds and ivy, the sign hanging askew.

We hovered above the juncture at Highway 16 and headed south for about twenty miles until we turned down a gravel road, then a dirt path into the woods. Teddy fetched a can of gasoline from the back of the truck and directed me to park the Subaru in a clearing near a small, manmade lake.

"Take everything out of the car. We don't want to make it easy for them to identify the owners."

Sitting inside the truck, we watched the blaze explode the u-shaped electric recharge pump into the air. We drove out the way we came and never saw another living soul.

Pausing at the highway juncture, Teddy said, "I need to cut across air space to reach I-75 before nightfall to retrieve the buried weapons and gear. I believe we're in imminent danger."

I took a moment to absorb the situation and took comfort in my grandson's rational calculations. My phobia about driving outside of regulated patterns, an everyday worry, seemed a trivial notion now. "Yes, well, get going. I counted two shovels in the truck bed; I better take a power nap while you drive."

We ate PB&J sandwiches with coffee while sitting on the couch in dirt-stained coveralls and stared at Lanie's survival kit lined up across and underneath the kitchen table: explosive devices, night goggles, tear gas masks, bullet-proof vests, semi-automatics, a long bow, and two flying suits.

"What, now?" I asked, brushing away strands of loose hair with the back of my hand. I noticed dirt underneath a thumb nail from digging three feet down to retrieve the duffel bags. A blister smarted in the web of that hand.

"We'll practice loading, firing, and cleaning our weapons, then operating the flying suits. Supposedly, those lightweight suits are pretty easy to maneuver. And in case they send a team like they did to assassinate Alfie and Raph, I'll position flashbang explosive devices in the surrounding fields tomorrow. You can help camouflage them, but there isn't much we can do about a drone strike.

"Even this far out, a drone strike would draw local attention to the operation. Surely, they won't use that method when a couple of silent assassins would do for an old lady and her grandson." I stood up and pointed to the back of the house. "Is there a cellar?"

"There is. It's about eight to ten yards away from the back steps, close to the tree line."

"I see." I paced in front of a coffee table. "What about hiding in there?"

"Better for a drone strike, but otherwise, they'll take us down more quickly. I might set a fire circle as a diversion tactic. We need multiple escape routes and a plan to get out of the area—quickly and quietly if possible."

"Did you consider surrendering to Underground and taking our chances?"

Teddy meandered to the table, picked up a long bow, and stretched the string. "I did. The probabilities of survival are about nil if Liz and Ed are the leaks."

"Okay, what else can we do to prepare?"

"Put in a few more provisions. I'm designing a blanket for you to mess with the drone body heat sensors, and I'm buying a couple of crate-trained hounds I saw advertised at the Quick Mart to place underneath the house near the front and back porches. Best good-old-boy alarm system I know."

"How far can the dogs smell?"

"Depending on the direction of the wind, up to ten miles away. If they bark, I have night vision and long-range scope capabilities. I'll know if it's just a possum that sets them off."

I stacked the glasses and plates and put them in the sink. "How long do you think we have to get ready?"

"Three to five days, more or less."

"Right. Let me wash these dishes and try on one of those fun flying suit jacket things."

Three days zoomed by. Teddy—not requiring sleep—took night watch, mapped the perimeter in low light, and woke me at six every morning. We suited up and flew the first thing after breakfast. The weightless feeling after takeoff and thrill of making wide turns at 50 to 80 miles an hour almost made my fear dissipate.

My flight suit felt like a bulky life jacket required for safety on small boats. It kept riding up around my ears and rubbing up against my armpits. Playing with the camouflage button and watching the suit change colors to blend into the environment was fascinating.

The sloping backyard became our training ground. Dropping and rolling off the back porch prepared us for a detachable parachute landing if our sky suits malfunctioned.

"Are you sore?" Teddy asked at the end of the day while pouring dry dog food into bowls and stirring in water to make a gravy for the hounds on the back porch.

I sat on the top step of the stoop, elbows propped on the knees of dirty pants. Content. "If you mean does every part of my body ache, including my armpits… you're correct."

I stretched. "A few bruises, some cuts on my hands, but I'm good."

I gazed out at the sun dropping behind the horizon, leaving purple and orange streaks. "Of course, I'm bone tired, but I forgot what it was like to hear crickets and frogs at dusk, see the day fade away in the country without a building blocking my view. Isn't the sky beautiful?"

I reached out to pet the dogs' hindquarters, watching them lap up the grub. "Good boys, Dash and Ham," I said.

The hounds roamed freely outside during the day, and both of them followed me around. They shied away from Teddy, sensing he wasn't human. In particular, Dashell barked at Teddy if he made any sudden moves.

Teddy threw her a peevish sideways glance. "Their names are Duke and Hemlock, not Dashell and Hammon. It confuses them."

"Indulge me. I can't resist." Dash rolled on his back for a belly rub.

Finding humor as well as some sturdy knee pads helped me endure the low crawl and endless target practice sessions.

"Don't be cross. In a way, I like boot camp. I find I quite like the sulfur smell of gunpowder and collecting the warm spent shell casings from my 9mm. As for the other hours of fun activities, even with elder-care breaks, I hate it."

Teddy laughed. "Your yoga practice held you in good stead."

30

I was inside making sandwiches for lunch when they came.

At first, I dismissed the barking as their distrust for my AI grandson until I looked out the kitchen window and saw Teddy run toward the barn. A partially severed right hand hung by a few wires and flopped around.

I stuck the kitchen carving knife in my apron and grabbed my 9mm. The hanging bells over the front door tinkled.

Helen and Ed stood in the doorway with assault rifles. I shot at Ed's center mass and heard him groan as I lunged and flung open the refrigerator door and crouched. A laser beam seared the insulated metal door above my head. "You have nowhere to run," Helen said. "The council has declared Dorothy Saunders and Theodore Strange traitors and murders."

I heard a long string of shots and accepted I had seconds to live. If I could hit Helen's central power frame in her neck from the floor, Teddy and I might survive. I dropped, rolled, and landed supine, then aimed under the assassin's chin. I felt the heat from a laser blast sear the wooden floor inches from my head. Thank goodness she missed. I kept rolling and shooting as Helen advanced on me. She darted this way and that out of my line of fire, and if I calculated the power surge hum correctly, she had managed to recharge the weapon's system. "I'm going to enjoy eliminating you," Helen said.

The damn AI was playing with me. If she came close for the kill, I'd use the knife.

From behind Helen, Teddy yelled, "Watch out, Grams." Helen fell limp facedown with an arrow stuck in the back of her neck. He yanked her motherboard out and tossed it.

I rolled over on my stomach and pointed my semi-automatic at the sofa. "Check over there. I shot Ed."

Teddy dropped the long bow and followed a trail of blood that led under the divan. He lifted the six-seater with his good arm and scanned Ed for a pulse. "The threat's terminated." Teddy's injured hand by his side was duct-taped at the wrist and in between the webs of each finger, making a kind of glove.

He knelt beside me, took the 9mm from my grip, and gathered me into his arms.

"I love you," I whispered.

He laughed, tinged with relief, whether a programmed AI response or not, my heart swelled as he said, "Love you, and I agree with Dell, you're the bravest, coolest ever grandmother."

For a temporary solution, I stapled what was left of Teddy's hand covering back in place and re-wrapped it with duct tape. "This won't work for long. You'll need a proper AI repair shop."

Teddy rotated his wrist and pumped his fingers. "First things first. I don't have full mobility, but I can still use a weapon and a shovel. I'll bury the two together out back. You clean up the floor in here."

I gagged, emptying the pail of water tinged red from Ed's blood.

I stripped my clothes off, showered, and reset. I'd never killed a person before and although in my naïveté I had intended to stop Ed, not take his life, that was the inevitable result. I felt relief, not moral ambiguity, about shooting my former Underground constituent in self-defense. The not-any-regret part bothered me. A person and an AI ceased to exist so Teddy and I could remain walking around on the earth. My cell, lying on the sink ledge, rang a few notes of Bach's Fifth. Detective Hill's name flashed on my screen. I stepped out of the shower, shivering and dripping on the shower mat as I answered the phone.

"Hello," I said, wrapping a towel around me.

"Hill here. The briefcase guy is a Mafia lawyer named Gerard Taylor Green or GT Green. By the way, I heard from my brother. They haven't linked him to you. Yet. Do you need anything while you're incognito?"

"I could use a friendly face and a big T-bone steak, but it's not safe. We were attacked earlier today by Underground agents. Two dead and Teddy has a half-seared hand that we duct-taped. Any no-questions-asked place for emergency repairs near… shoot, I can't say."

"Let me fill in the blank." She lowered her voice. "My brother's cabin."

"Right."

"I'll try and find a shop, maybe arrange some backup. I might have an old contact, a CI, computer recluse type outside of Macon. She did some federal time for hacking and distribution of AI black-market parts. I'll get back with you ASAP. Tell pretty young thing he did good. You're both still kicking." Workplace voices resonated in the background. "Gotta go."

31

Early the next morning, Teddy left me sitting on the porch with the dogs sleeping beside me. He headed out to find a place to repair his hand while I wrote and rewrote the same sentence ten times about a midwife trying to find her way out of a cave. Yesterday left me numb inside, unable to find my center and with every muscle stiff and sore.

"Stay alert. If Ed and Helen were double agents, the State may know where we are." He handed me a blue pill. "You already experienced how adrenaline will help in a life and death situation, but you are my grandmother. Don't question me on this one. Take it if you need extra energy and strength. It won't hurt you and it's non-addictive used short term."

I put the pill in my pocket. "Pick up some bread and milk," I said as I waved goodbye. I needed some alone time.

The dust in the air caused by Teddy's truck settled into another dry, windless day in the low 60s. I placed my hand on the barrel of the shotgun propped against my lawn chair and leaned my head back, catching the warmth of the afternoon sun. My jaw ached, and I relaxed the muscles of my face. I dozed.

The dogs barked, creating a riotous cacophony that woke me. I grabbed my rifle and aimed it at the sky where I heard a whirling blade sound. A greeting card drone hovered with a flashing banner. "Don't shoot. It's Hadera Hill come to save the day." A yellow mini helicopter seemed to materialize and drop from a cloud. It nestled into the long grasses and the noise ceased.

I hushed the dogs.

Hill hopped out and strode toward me with her arms extended. "I know you said not to come, but my CI won't see Teddy without me along for the ride. I thought since it was an emergency… where is he?"

"He went to buy essentials from a mini mart nearby."

"Did I misunderstand the situation? Won't people notice his injury?" Hill wore a holstered sidearm on her belt.

"They might think he cut himself chopping firewood. That's the story we agreed upon. The farmers don't think anything about starting a fire to keep warm at night, and he's wearing work gloves and a denim jacket." I rose, tucking the rifle under an armpit and took Dash by the collar and Ham followed. I locked them in their kennels on the far side of the porch and texted Teddy about Hill's arrival before I walked back over to the steps.

"No worries. I'm way out of my comfort zone and jurisdiction out here. I don't plan to chat with the locals about their illegal fires." Hill darted her eyes to the horizon. "There still isn't a building in sight. Weird. It hasn't changed in twenty years. I never cared much for my uncle."

"That's what I understood from Teddy. Except for Dell, your family wasn't fond of visiting here."

There was an uncomfortable lull in the conversation. "Is your brother well?"

"Yes, he wanted to come too, but I dissuaded him." Hill frowned and stood by the steps with her hands in the pockets of her jeans, surveying the area.

"What's wrong?"

"I don't see anyone, but I can't shake the feeling we're being watched."

The dogs growled and whined. They backed into the end of their kennels. Spooked.

The mini vaporized, then an explosion emanated from the center of the booby-trapped field as we ran inside the house.

Within seconds, menacing military-grade pigmy bots dressed like outer-space cadets lined the perimeter of the house. I threw the detective Teddy's flight jacket. "Watch me," I said, and scrambled to buckle and pull the straps into place. Hill followed suit.

"How do we get out of here?" she asked.

I pointed to green and red buttons on the jacket pockets. "First, power button and then rip the cord for the parachute. We take the attic stairs, a window to the roof, hit the power button, get a running start, and jump."

I took the blue pill, grabbed my Glock, and tucked it in my overall pants pocket. We sprinted up the stairs as I heard the front and back doors splinter and give way to the hunter bots.

"How many times have you practiced this maneuver?" Hill asked, breathing hard from the hurried climb.

"Hundreds." I exaggerated to breed confidence. I had vaulted thirteen times from the back porch and a rusty abandoned car, never the roof. "See the arrows printed on the suit arms indicating up and down, right and left? The center circle allows you to hover. I suggest using a medium touch for your takeoff and a light touch for your first landing."

"No shit." Fear flickered across her intense dark irises.

"We planned for this scenario. Just follow me."

Hill and I climbed out onto the roof and powered up. A surge of adrenaline filled my body as my spine pulsated from the vibrating hum of the jacket.

"Let's do this." Hill pushed her braids back.

"Remember to use moderation, or you'll pass out from the G-force. On my count: one, two, three." I prayed to whom I didn't know. We ran…and leaped. I felt weightless and powerful. Hill managed to hover until a bot burst through the attic window and fired yellow stun gun rounds, forcing her to swivel right then left. I circled and caught Hill by the arm, and we shot into the sky together.

I headed south using I-75 as my guide. The abandoned Public Safety Training Center in Forsyth hid a bunker under the food court pantry that Teddy described as the governor's emergency plan in the event of an apocalypse. However, I'd never been inside the building and turning the alarm off was Teddy's bailiwick. Maybe my new partner would know how to break inside and disarm the alarm. As we flew over the center, I saw an empty security guard booth with gates at the entrance facing I-75. Weeds grew through the cracks in the parking lot asphalt, making a patchwork quilt effect.

We managed to drop and roll and land in an open field beside the center without breaking any bones.

"Almost being killed is an adrenaline bump, I must say." Hill brushed dirt off her trousers and readjusted her gun belt.

I didn't wait for Hill to realize our dilemma. I ran for cover behind the brick building. She hesitated only a second and then hightailed it to my side. "Sorry. I tend to use humor when I'm scared witless."

"Well, take that energy and figure out how to get us inside and turn the alarm off. We need to find a bunker underneath the cafeteria. It will block detection by the bots."

"Right. Let's try the service entrance door in the back." We trotted to the rear of the building and scurried up the ramp. Hill turned the doorknob. It opened.

"You're one lucky woman," I said.

"Yeah, my cousin worked for a delivery service, and he told stories about the back door of facilities being left open so the security dogs could get at burglars. Saved on door repairs, but look, the door jamb has pry marks. The alarm's another matter."

I flipped the light switch. Nothing.

"The power is off," Hill said. "The state training center moved in 2025. I wonder if this building has been unoccupied for all these years. Strange, but the alarm system seems defunct."

"No idea. Maybe, under the circumstances, no alarm is a good thing." I shut the door, and the area went pitch black. Hill's cell illumination, a welcome sight, allowed me to reach out and clamp a hand on her shoulder. "I don't have my phone on me."

"Huh, okay."

We moved in tandem through a small warehouse and past several cubbyhole offices. The bare walls, desks, and shelves devoid of any signs of human life. We reached a short hallway that led to a mezzanine, a vast tiled space. Our shadows danced on the brick walls as we turned around getting our bearings. A single glass door beckoned from the back of the building, but Hill continued forward.

"I remember the cafeteria being off the atrium." She pointed. "I came to a State Trooper graduation here when I was a kid."

In front, about a hundred and fifty feet away, I saw the entrance with sunlight filtering through glass double doors and behind me, underneath an overhang, the partial remains of a hot bar cafeteria food dispensary. Upstairs, above the cafeteria area, appeared more offices or classrooms.

The musty building turned rank as we wove our way halfway down a short hallway with an office and doubled back, then veered left through an archway to reach the kitchen. "Do you smell that?" I asked.

"Hush." She nodded toward an ajar walk-in freezer door.

We peeked inside. The warm, stale air laced with decay made us cover our noses. Hill and I saw the body at the same moment and froze. "Whoa," we said together. Propped up in a corner, a decomposing corpse dressed in multiple layers of clothing held a whiskey bottle.

Hill squeezed my shoulder. "Let's find the bunker," she said. "Nothing we can do here."

"Right. Looks like a local vagrant found their way inside and died in relative comfort."

We found metal shelving close to the exit door on either side of the back entrance but not a closed-off pantry. Hill checked one side, moving racks and a rolling butcher block while I checked the other side. "We're looking for a keypad or hidden door. Right?" Hill asked.

"Correct. This doesn't make sense. A facility this size must have a food storage room close to the kitchen."

"Downstairs. There must be a basement," Hill said.

"What about the hallway to the right of the kitchen with the office?

We backtracked to the hallway and found a door marked with a sign showing stairs going up and down and a small freight elevator we had overlooked.

"The elevator requires an old-fashioned key, so looks like it's the stairs," I said. Hill took the stairs two at a time. I held onto the railing and felt my way down the stairwell.

"Will you hurry up?" Hill said.

"I can't see. You have the only light."

I heard Hill grunting and sliding objects across the floor.

"What's down here?" I asked.

Hill appeared at the bottom of the stairs and directed the cell light my way. "So far, lots of boxes."

A voice boomed over the PA system. "Come out with your hands up. This public building is surveilled and protected as ordered by Central Georgia Governor Henrietta James, and you are trespassing."

I felt an overwhelming need to pee.

32

"Keep searching," Hill said as she moved another box away from a wall. "My cell battery is low. I'm betting the PA is a dummy warning setup to distract anyone from this room. When we entered, it must have triggered a backup generator."

"You really think the government wouldn't maintain an alarm in a building with a bunker?" I kicked a box aside, took off my flight suit, and tossed it next to Hill's near the elevator.

"What options do we have? Do you have a plan B?"

"No."

Hill lowered her voice. "Besides, maybe the late governor's predecessor didn't pass on the knowledge about the bunker, or the place can't withstand particle agitation. Be useless to the bigwigs in case of an alien invasion slash civilian annihilation."

"You're reaching, my friend, and it's not comforting."

"Remember the vagrant. Why would they leave the place open and a body to rot if the place has routine surveillance?"

"I agree. Teddy wouldn't have picked this building as part of the escape plan without researching and calculating the risks. Oh, dear, my Teddy. I hope he's alright."

"Good to know this wasn't a random building you chose." Hill stacked a box on another one.

I ripped a poster displaying a rendition of sheet music with a treble cleft from the wall. "I'm going to ignore your sarcasm. Voilà, a wall safe, and I know the combination."

"No way."

"Every good boy does fine."

"What?"

I pointed to the poster lying on the floor. "An acronym for EGBDF. Substituting numbers for the letters in the alphabet and you get 5, 7, 2, 4, 6."

"Therefore, the combination is 57, 2, 46."

I dialed the combination and pulled on the safe handle. Nothing. Then a wall seam cracked parallel to the safe, and a previously hidden door opened, revealing descending stairs. "Stairs to the bunker."

"I assume, but let's think this through," Hill said, sticking an arm out to block my path. "How do we get out if we're locked in? Can Teddy detect us if the bots can't?"

"I haven't a clue. Let me use your phone to call him." The cell light went dark, leaving us lost in a brick cave.

"Great, the cell is dead."

33

I reached out into the thick void and found Hill.

"Do you hear something?" Hill asked. The lights flickered on and grinding cables clanked and squeaked as an old elevator activated above them.

"It's the bots. They have found us. Hurry, Hill. Get in." I heard the panic in my voice. I stepped on the bunker platform, and my hand was halfway to the CLOSE button, but Hill gripped my arm.

"Wait a second. It might be Teddy."

"He wouldn't use an elevator. Machine inside a machine sickness. Military-grade bots, on the other hand, don't get MIMS but—"

The elevator stopped. The creaking of sliding doors echoed as a shaky voice said, "Hello, Grams, are you here? Don't shoot. It's Teddy."

"Code words!" I shouted. We aimed our side arms toward the basement entrance.

"Peanut butter."

I hugged Teddy. "So glad to see you." I held him at arm's length. "Your hand is fixed."

"A local farmer, retired military, repaired it. We started a conversation about strong coffee in the parking lot at the convenience store. Anyway, he had worked in bot maintenance until the Great Loss of Privacy. After The Bill of Rights was declared unconstitutional, he dropped off the grid, but he still maintains a workshop. That's why I wasn't back sooner to protect you."

"Nonsense. Besides, Hill was with me." I patted her hand.

Teddy frowned at Hill. "I appreciate you being here, but why are you?"

"I thought it was an emergency. My CI in Macon wouldn't see you or put you back together without me present."

Teddy picked up the discarded flight suits. "We need to move. The bots followed me into an area without Wi-Fi and I lost them, but they'll retrace and pick up the truck's path. I took the quickest route, avoiding most but not all surveillance cameras and threw a camouflage tarp over the truck."

"Let's get inside the bunker," I said.

"It won't help at this stage. There are only a couple of places we could hide in Lamar County. They'll blast the buildings trying to find us and then disintegrate the bunker." Teddy ushered us toward the elevator.

"We were never safe, only hidden."

Teddy tapped Hill's cell in her back pocket. "A temporary solution to confuse them by eliminating thermal body images, but I'm sure Hill's phone is being tracked."

"It's dead now, but we needed the illumination and Dorothy forgot hers." Hill took the sim card out of the cell and stuffed it and the phone back inside her pocket.

"There are only two fly suits," Teddy said. The elevator jerked into gear, and he held onto the railing and snapped his head toward his right and left shoulders.

"Are you okay?" Hill asked.

"Yes, a trick I learned to reset the disheveled parts and avoid MIMS. Listen. I planted a rusty gray Caprice beyond the woods months ago. You two take the car, and I'll take off in a flight suit to distract the bots."

"No, Teddy, absolutely not." I crossed my arms for effect.

Keeping his eyes trained on me, Teddy slipped on a flight jacket and handed the other jacket to Hill. "They know I'm AI, and they'll detect me in the car. Hill can carry the second flight suit. You must go now. Follow me." The elevator doors opened, increasing my fears we might cease to exist at any second.

We sprinted through the warehouse, and Teddy opened the back door. "We'll meet up at the second rendezvous site. Do you remember?"

"Yes, of course."

"Go east. He slapped a compass into my hand. Look for shade trees and cows. The keys are under the mat."

Hill and I ran from the back door to the edge of the woods and then jogged about half a football field inside the tree line. I paused to catch my breath and saw Teddy circle above us and take off in the opposite direction.

"Let's keep going," Hill said, sweating from running while carrying a twenty-pound flight jacket. "We need to reach the car and get on the road before the bots spot us."

The Caprice sat under a clump of trees in the middle of a cow pasture, and I could see a cattle gate and country lane in the distance.

34

The drab outskirts of Milledgeville hosted the remnants of a trailer park, an open tattoo and nail shop in an otherwise abandoned strip mall, Paving Company's sign proclaiming

NOW HIRING

and a faded road sign deeming their hometown author, Flannery O'Connor, "As the best southern writer of all time."

Hill shifted in the Caprice's passenger seat and typed on her new burner phone. "My boss isn't happy that I've extended my stay in South

Georgia. I'm not ecstatic either. Why would Teddy pick a city with one of the nation's highest crime rates for us to stand by?"

"Because this is a college town, and Teddy has contacts here."

"Where exactly?"

The converted Caprice hovered a moment, taking its time before responding to my touch or voice commands, then the internal mechanism screeched like a cat as I guided it off Highway 22. We turned into the Central Georgia Tech College.

Hill groaned. "You're kidding."

The unadorned square brick structure of the college conjured an industrial district label, not a place of higher learning. The massive concrete fountain in the shape of a gigantic thunderbolt and Roman helmet accenting the circular driveway and the scrawny shrubs around the entrance only emphasized the lack of green space. "It's dismal, but I promise a genius awaits inside."

"Whatever you say, Miss Dorothy. I guess wanted fugitives on the run have few choices. And I'm familiar with limited options." She cut her eyes at me as I parked in a visitor's spot.

"Being a Black female on the force must be challenging."

"Not Black enough or blue enough comes with waking up and, needless to say, I wasn't born with a penis." She stepped from the Caprice, and we met at the rear of the car.

"Pop the trunk. I'm losing this heavy flying suit," Hill said.

The trunk held weapons and enough supplies for a week or so.

"Your Teddy is a planner. I'll give him that."

"Yes, he's programmed to protect me."

Hill threw her flight jacket on top of the gear, grinned, and winked. "Not that I have a choice, but I think I'll stick with you until I head back to Atlanta."

We climbed the nine concrete stairs together and opened the stainless-steel doors smudged with hundreds of finger marks. Inside the reception desk area, a hologram of a stern nineteenth-century schoolmarm appeared, "Please present your identification."

Hill stepped in front of me. "We don't need identification as visitors within the atrium of a state school."

"Welcome, visitors. Do you need a guided tour of the school or know your desired party's name or extension?"

"No tour, but please tell Professor Edmond Ecco that Grams is here," I said.

"Ms. Grams requests to speak with Professor Edmond Ecco. Please be seated and somebody will help you shortly." The hologram disappeared.

I sniffed the air. "The place smells like a car repair shop, not a school."

"Nothing like diesel and gas mixed with metallic residue to stimulate the brain."

"The concrete floors and multi-paned windows reinforce the feeling you're in an assembly plant." The afternoon sun streamed through the oxidized frames and windowpanes, making a grid of 8x10 squares on the floor.

We sat on a bench, and I watched Hill scroll cat videos on her phone.

Twenty minutes later, a slim man over six feet in his mid-forties and a goatee appeared. He wore tattered jeans and a crisp oxford blue shirt.

I stood up. "Hello, I'm Dorothy, and this is my friend HH."

He smiled and offered a hand to shake. "Professor Ecco here. I believe human touch is a good thing."

We shook hands, but Hill took a step back. He nodded at my companion. "Nice to meet both of you. Please follow me to my office. I've already signed you in. We only have a few minutes. The campus closes early at four-thirty."

The professor shut the door of his broom-closet-sized office. Mechanical gadgets from the past hung from the ceiling and memorabilia stuffed the shelves lining the walls. Looking up at one of the first recreational drones suspended above my head, I brushed against an old bookcase and a Titan pendant fell and landed on the only chair. An exercise ball was behind the professor's desk.

"Sorry about my office. I'm not tenured, and I ruffled more than a few feathers when I didn't give an A to a certain donor's grandchild, a mediocre student at best." He threw the pendant without looking, and it alighted on an eye-level shelf beside a camera with a snake leather covering. "Is that a Leica Q 'Nikki Sixx Edition' camera?" Hill asked.

"Yes, it's quite rare." The professor moved behind his desk.

"No way!" Hill stooped to get a closer look. "Only twenty-eight ever made."

"Yeah, it reminds me of my dad. I lock it in the safe at night." He pointed to a small floor safe in the corner.

"I'm an amateur photographer. Where did you find it?" Hill ran a finger over the snakeskin.

"A relative of mine worked as a roadie for Motley Crue. Nikki Sixx related to my dad's uncle because he was a recovering drug alcoholic too. He told stories to Dad as a kid, and one of them was about how the rock star replaced his drug obsession with photography, then teamed up with Leica. My dad gave me the camera when I graduated with my BS."

I scooted around Hill and sat in the chair. "Fascinating, but aren't we short on time?"

"Oh, that dialogue was for the hidden cameras in the lobby. We have another thirty minutes or so before security rattles doors. I can walk you out after hours."

"So we're not being recorded now?" I scanned the room.

"My converted closet's one advantage is it's not hooked to that system."

"How do you know my grandson?"

He flipped a switch and a Godzilla toy floated from a corner and made a pass around the room.

Hill took a photo of Godzilla, then the Q Nikki Sixx.

The toy's eyes blinked green. "Good, no bugs. Better to double-check. To answer your question, I don't. I was the librarian's emergency contact."

"She was quite a… lady," I said. For Hill's safety, she didn't need to hear any more details than necessary about Lanie.

"You have no idea. Her service was unparalleled."

"Without her, Teddy would've been vaporized. I'm grateful." There was a long silence.

"HH knows about Teddy's unique abilities. Can you help us disappear before they hunt us down and kill us?"

"Does HH need ID too?"

Hill stopped fondling the camera. "No, Teddy and my brother are college chums. I got involved when my partner, Detective Barden, was murdered."

"My condolences, but—"

"It's a long story. Miss Dorothy can fill you in. I'll take a bathroom break while you do whatever it is you need to do." She shut the door behind her.

"Barden and I were friends, united in protecting family. He was a mysterious guy, but he seemed to know what both sides were doing. I'm not sure who, but the illusive *they* killed him."

The professor sat on the exercise ball and began to type. "Then let's get started. What countries appeal to you?"

"None, but maybe the Netherlands. No extradition and my grandson would like Amsterdam."

"Good choice. They retracted their membership in the European Arrest Warrant Pact last December."

"I hear it's beautiful and progressive, but it will never feel like home. My roots are here."

"You'll get used to it."

I wasn't sure I could.

We left out of the side entrance and hightailed it to Professor E's art-car minivan. The arrangement of plastic bottles, bottle caps, tin cans, and old tools made patterns in stars, spirals, and thunderbolts on the van's exterior. This guy was so uncool he was cool. The van smelled like pot and incense with a dash of fried foods. The van raised off the ground in jerks like a lowrider in reverse, then it backfired before it surged forward worthy of a bullet train ride blurring the surroundings.

I held onto a grab strap on the passenger side.

Hill laughed, showing more teeth than usual. The wind was pushing against her cheeks, rushing in from an open vent window inserted in the rear quarter panel. "Where in the world did you find twentieth-century trash to decorate the van?" She yelled above the wind.

"I didn't. My grandmother was an artist and a physicist. I inherited this beauty." He patted the dashboard.

A sentimentalist. I wondered if anything about this guy was original. He passed around a thermos of cold water. The minty aftertaste refreshed me, then made me mellow. As I nodded off, I suspected there was something in the water to make us sleepy.

I'm not sure how long I slept. I woke up in a bottom bunk bed. The lumpy mattress reminded me of my summer camp days, complete with an army surplus blanket rolled up at the foot of the bed. I sat up, making sure I didn't hit my head, and caught a glimpse of the windowless room with boxes of supplies stacked along the stone walls. Christmas tree lights strung around the top of this dungeon provided dim illumination, but I could see kerosene lamps dotted the tops of the boxes and packages of dried food filled a three-tier wire shelving unit. My back ached. I stretched by leaning forward and grabbing my ankles. I heard somebody yawning and stirring above me. "Is that you, Hill?"

"Yeah, I haven't slept that hard in years. Where the heck are we?"

I slid to the side just in time to avoid Hill's long legs dangling down and almost kicking me in the face.

"I have no idea, but I need to find a bathroom."

Behind us a male voice said, "The latrine is to your right off this T-hallway." Professor E stepped into the light and swung a lowered shotgun in the direction of the bathroom. "You're in a safe house slash abandoned quarry outside Milledgeville. I'm beat. I've been on guard duty for ten hours checking the perimeter while you slept. There's coffee in the kitchen area at the other end of the hallway. I'd appreciate relief from one of you as soon as you can." He turned around and walked out. A door slammed.

"Wow, who knew laid-back Ray Ray could be so intense," Hill said. "And where the heck did he get that old shotgun? I haven't seen one of those since my ROTC days—about the same time the military and the state went to lasers and confiscated civilian weaponry."

"I think we shouldn't underestimate Professor E." I peeked down the hallway in the direction the professor had disappeared and walked toward a rusty door. I tried the handle. With an effort, the door opened, making an unforgiving metal-on-metal sound. Daylight flooded inside. Shielding my eyes with an elbow, I saw a strip-mining pit with man-made cliffs. Why hadn't the squeaking bolts on the door warned us about the professor's entrance? Nature called again, and I scurried back toward Hill. "Do you think he drugged us?"

"If he did, I don't feel any lingering side effects, but a little paranoia isn't a bad thing in our situation. Now that you posed the question, I don't remember arriving or crawling into bed. Let me Google the professor."

"I'll be back in a minute," I said trying to make it to the bathroom in time to avoid a mishap.

"Wait. Did he take my phone?"

I turned around.

Hill jumped from the top bunk and began searching through her khaki pockets, then stood on the bottom bunk frame and rummaged through the sheets.

"Did you find it?"

"Got it." Hill grinned, grasping the cell phone like she found gold.

"Follow me." Barefooted, Hill trailed behind me toward the bathroom.

"Are you sure they can't track us with that burner?" I asked.

"Yes, it's the latest thing."

"Teddy told me not to call him in case he was in custody. While I relieve myself, see if he has been arrested and if the professor has a record."

"Sure. If I have to, I'll call in a favor. But then what?"

"Coffee." I closed the stall door in Hill's face. "Now, go away."

35

Inside his lover's dark flat, Teddy rolled over and touched Georgie's shoulder. She was a lovely human and in bed, she never lied. Reliable and sexy. She had showed up minutes after the low-level county bots arrested him outside of the convenience store, saving his inner memory, but not before they copied his outer motherboard, the clean optics version of his life.

He and Grams planned vacation in Thomason, Georgia, only showed quiet dinners and walks in the countryside. They played chess and rough-housed with the hounds. The medication mishap with Grams and Teddy's undercover AI status wasn't a concern because the CIA vouched for them as government plants. The hardest part to explain was the repeated Lanie Day connection, but Teddy answered he simply didn't know the librarian was an operative because she was a sociopath. Since she believed her own lies, she couldn't be detected by most AIs, including him.

Georgie had flashed a QR code containing the seal of the head of the CIA, an embedded order to release the government agent, Theodore Strange, and didact any information gathered. The last part of the order would never happen. The bots would keep their copy of the memory chip to CYA and turn it over to the State Commander General.

The bedroom in Georgie's flat smelled like oranges interspersed with peanut butter. In case she wasn't asleep, he smiled down at her—twined around him—one of her knees lying on his chest, then glanced at the Dali painting over the safe, an object he associated with their first sexual encounter. He preferred her human odor to any perfume.

Because Georgie wanted to please him and hated floral air fresheners, she had surprised him with the peanut butter scent combination during their stay on New Ossabaw Island. After the suspected smuggler of black-market organs disappeared off the island courtesy of the CIA, she referred to their last unencumbered days there as their pretend honeymoon. Teddy could read her; even then, she knew their relationship couldn't last.

He scanned his encrypted emails on his internal hard drive as Georgie snuggled in his arms. A lot of changes had occurred in the Underground since Grams killed Ed and subsequent suspension and demotion of Liz by a majority vote of the council. Only eight hours after Teddy's release from the bots, the Underground, now headed by a young patriot named Flashsentra or Flash, sent a message that the U.S. Attorney General and Department of Justice, President Gainey's henchmen, were gunning for him and Grams. Arrest and elimination were a matter of time unless they left the country for good. Flash ended the email with an American flag emoji reminder about protecting the Underground at all costs, and if Grams or he was caught and torture imminent, their duty was to commit suicide or shut down all systems.

They never talked about it, but Grams carried a cyanide pill inside the frame of her glasses. His inner memory board destroyed itself if hacked.

The burner phone buzzed. It was Detective Hill.

Teddy found his discarded jeans on a chair, pulled them on, and answered the phone on the balcony.

*****

"Not sure where we are," Hill said into her cell. "Supposedly, we're in a compound inside a quarry outside of Milledgeville."

I needed to hear my grandson's voice and jerked the phone from Hill's hand. "Are you okay?"

"Yes, is Professor Ecco with you?"

"Maybe. The man's acting weird, and I think he drugged us because we don't remember how we got here from the college."

"Describe him to me."

Hill leaned over and yanked the phone back. "I can do you one better. I took his photo with his Godzilla debug unit. I'll text it to you."

After a moment, Teddy confirmed that was the right man. "But he isn't answering his burner phone and that concerns me."

Hill stuck an arm out and held me at bay from the phone. "He's been on guard duty and wants relief. Maybe a company sign will pinpoint our location while I'm outside. Inside this caveman setting, my map app isn't working on my phone."

"According to satellite view, there is a closed quarry site north of the city. In the past it was Jackson and Wheeler's Concrete and Stone. Please confirm ASAP. With Georgie's help, I've set up a plan of escape, so be packed up and ready. Do you still have the flight suit?"

"Ah, we goofed." A look passed between Hill and me, and the phone was tossed my way.

"We left it in the trunk of the Caprice at the college," I said. "The professor drove us—wherever here is—in his gaudy art van. We didn't think—"

"It's fine. I'll figure out a way to get Detective Hill back to Atlanta."

A creaky compound door opened, and I hit the end-call button on Hill's phone.

"I'll take the cell phone," Professor E said, wheeling his shotgun at hip level toward me.

Paralyzed with fear, I froze ten feet from Hill and the professor.

"Now," he said, unmasking a ruthlessness.

Shaking, I proffered the cell, palm up.

He inched toward me with his back to the entry wall, pocketed the cell, and touched an earbud. "Right, the packages are unharmed."

He backed up, keeping us in view. "Pack up all your things. You have five minutes."

"No prob. Like to police up the mess," Hill said." Keeping a casual attitude, she draped the army blanket from the top bunk over her shoulder and slid toward the professor as she stripped the bedding.

"Stop fussing and get ready to go," he said.

"Oh, no..." I doubled over. "I'm going to be sick."

Hill threw the blanket and sheets at the professor's head and tackled him.

The shotgun went off with a boom. The slug from the blast left a hole in a can of corn on a wire shelf behind me. The shot barely missed my left ear. A crisp awareness of each second beating off in my chest accompanied me as I dove into the pile of cussing, wrestling opponents fighting the bedding and each other. I jerked the barrel of the 12-gauge upward. The firearm went off again, but the professor's grip lessened. The shotgun flew down into the entryway and landed at the feet of a man holding a briefcase.

He pointed a semi-auto at us. "Stop, or I'll kill both of you."

Hill released a chokehold on the professor and raised her hands. I stood stock-still. Bizarre. Like a James Bond replica pointing a gun at you. Even the man's impeccable suit was disquieting in this setting.

With a shotgun and a 9mm at our backs, they marched us outside to an electric helicopter with silent spinning blades where two men in black suits strapped and locked us in the back bench seat. Briefcase man handed the professor a currency card and climbed into the helicopter, leaving one corporate security guy with the professor while the other sat behind the helicopter controls. We took off, and Hill mimicked texting on a cell phone and mouthed Teddy's name. I realized the professor had Hill's burner phone and would text Teddy into a trap.

We landed on the roof of E.I. Vance Pharmaceuticals. The logo painted on the landing pad was a dead giveaway. I touched my glasses. This would be an odd place to torture somebody but not to extract fresh organs. I wished for another blue pill, looked at Hill and regretted getting her involved.

Briefcase man turned with a hypodermic needle and stuck Hill in a thigh. She went limp within seconds. I squirmed in the seatbelt, pulling my knees away from my captor. He didn't bother to look at me. "You can come quietly, or I can shoot you. Bottom line, you aren't as valuable as Hill."

Defensive-back security guy threw Hill over his shoulder, and I walked behind them followed by the mob guy. I had no doubt he would kill me. We entered a freight vacuum elevator filled with a disinfecting mist that sucked us down to the twentieth floor. The mist innovation kept pandemics from spreading between office workers at a minimum, but the unpleasant ammonia-based product made some people hold their breath and pass out. The elevator doors opened, and I came face to face with Chantel Farnsworth. She blinked and stood aside. "Take them into the surgical ward to your left."

We passed several glassed-in labs with robots tending huge incubators containing fetuses in different stages of development. A shudder spread through me. A gloved assistant with a horse-shaped face in an expensive beige pantsuit appeared from a doorway. Displaying obvious disdain, she directed us inside a room. She spoke to the briefcase guy and security in a curt manner. "Please place the clients in the disrobing enclosures, gently for the unconscious one, and leave without touching anything."

"As you vish, madame," the helicopter pilot said with a Slavic accent. The mobster said nothing.

The men deposited us in stalls with a bench seat, a mirror, and a bag to place our clothes. The stalls were on one end of a typical hospital room with two beds. A sign inside the stall read:

Undress, store your clothes in the bag, and sterilize your hands before redressing in the surgical clothes provided in the door pouch.

"Please close the door of the room on your way out," the woman told the men.

In the distance, I heard a door click shut and reacted by jiggling the stall door. It was locked and had no crawl space. "We are being held against our wills. Woman to woman, please help us." I leaned my head back and gazed at the opening above the stall. The top of the door loomed unreachable from my 5′2″ height.

"Your fate is sealed. Undress and cooperate, or I'll break your friend's neck."

A miniature hologram appeared near a hand sanitizer station mounted across from the wall sign. She kept repeating: "To prevent infection during and after surgery, sterilize your hands and face."

I heard Hill moan from the stall beside me.

"Hey! Lady! You found those men revolting. You're human, not AI. How can you do this?"

"I'm cutting your companion's clothes off. I would hate for the scissors to slip. She is quite beautiful."

"Please, don't hurt her. I'll comply." I undressed and put a surgical gown and booties on, ignoring the hologram's warnings. They didn't intend for either of us to stay alive after they harvested our organs.

36

Teddy sat at the back of a conference room two blocks away from E.I. Vance Pharmaceuticals. Breacher, positioned at a small table perpendicular to the centerline of the room, fiddled with his slash-bang kit a few feet from Teddy.

A bald officer in charge stood with huge biceps folded across his chest near a gigantic screen with the E.I. Vance's building schematics enlarged.

"Listen up," he said to a seven-person team, plus Teddy. "Our sniper has parachuted in and has eyes on the helicopter pad on the top of the target skyscraper, but the whirlwind gusts are bad up there today. She'll advise when the cartel and his minion arrive with Dorothy Saunders and APD's Detective Hadera Hill and whether it's a don't shoot situation. A medivac helicopter team will be nearby if the sniper opts to handle the rescue without us. Either way, we stand by to handle the op alone or create a diversion on the first floor by remotely setting off the fire alarms and blocking their security monitors.

Our plan of engagement, if deployed, means the packages have arrived on the fourth floor and are in danger of dying on the operating tables from organ harvesting. We won't shut down the power—Strategic Command assessed high collateral damage—it's attached to a grid connected to several other buildings, including a hospital. But we can make it flicker, shut down the backup generators in our target building, make personnel panic, and temporarily stop operating procedures on the fourth floor."

Using a remote, he flashed a 3-D view of the inside of the building, floor by floor, showing the layout design of each room. "The fourth floor has a private elevator to the penthouse connected to two small offices. Otherwise, the space is divided between a surgical unit and laboratory. The gross fetus experiments are conducted on this floor. The lab is soundproof, but three geek researchers work in there around the clock. Day shift ends at 1630 hours, so not a problem. We'll be long gone. According to behavioral data collected from the creepy super's computer, the day shift personnel rarely leave the lab for lunch or breaks.

However, there are two floaters: lab queen, Chantel Farnsworth, and her floor manager slash assistant with a prison term for domestic assault on her resume. Breacher will take them out of the picture early, hopefully by throwing a sleepy-time gas pod in the lab and securing the double doors with old-fashioned cable ties. The remaining forty floors are filled with offices, fifteen luxury condos, a gym with a pool, and a restaurant on the bottom floor.

At 1500 hours, both Teams Alpha and Beta approach in the armored vehicle with a seven-minute countdown, the time between roll calls conducted by Vance's former military security. Tommie Tech stops his peeping-tom surveillance of E.I. Vance's monitors from his laptop, jams the ground CCTV signals for 15 seconds, covering

Team Beta entry from the receiving docks." He paused, making eye contact with each of the team members under his command. He skipped Teddy and continued.

"At 1501 hours, Team Alpha follows Tech inside. First, they hit the front desk and monitoring center on the first floor, freeze the system, and paralyze or neutralize the operators. Any civilians in the lobby must be shot with paralyzing lasers only. Later, they'll be visited by the 'Men in Black'."

The team laughed.

"They'll block the drone satellite and scramble the cell phone towers signals through the com center. Meanwhile, Team Beta follows me to the freight elevator off the docks. Just in case there's heavy resistance in the lobby and Team Alpha is delayed, Breacher will blind the elevator cameras with LED lights, then flashbang the hallway as Beta enters the fourth floor. We mask up in the elevator. Breacher will lock down the stairwell exits and proceed to the lab. The rest of us neutralize any hallway security or medical staff who try to intervene, then carry or wheel the packages on gurneys with IVs down the elevator to the med van."

He touched an earbud. "Roger that," he said to his commander watching virtually.

"Plan B: I make the call if either package is too damaged to move, but we take the coolers containing organs regardless. Spikes and Spuds watch our backs while the rest maneuver to and from the elevator. No lasers, stun guns, or live bullets in the surgery. Blanks and paralyzing-dart mode. Heads up. Flammable gasses. Remember the 2043 California-Henry Medical Hospital fire, the rescue debacle where half of the NCIS team lost their lives. One of the nursing staff included an armed AI plant."

"Lastly, the med van is now a truck and will be engine-running at the dock. Team Beta loads into the truck with the packages, and Team Alpha exits the way they came in and leaves in the armored vehicle. Any questions?"

The room was silent as the Officer in Charge touched an earbud. "Copy that."

He refocused on the group. "No questions? Good. Sniper determines it's a don't-shoot situation. Strategic Command has approved the briefing and given us the go-ahead. We leave in five."

*****

Medical orderlies fastened Hill and me to gurneys and wheeled us into the same operating room. I squinted from the overhead lamp glare. Multiple small coolers were lined up on gurneys outside the operating tables and instrument dollies. One line of coolers was red and the other, closest to me, was a deep blue, my favorite color. At least my body parts wouldn't object to their mode of transportation.

I giggled. Absurd. The intravenous liquid dripped, maybe saline, because I didn't feel woozy yet. The lights flickered.

The female nurse with an American flag embossed on her surgical cap said, "What the hell? Not again. Prep and prepare, but don't open until the security supervisor advises on the power reliability."

The robed, masked, and gloved staff moved me to my left side. Frigid air blew over my skin covering my flabby obliques and core muscles as they swabbed antiseptic over the skin covering my liver. A masked woman with makeup caked in her crow's feet wrote on my abdomen, LIVER, and drew an arrow toward the antiseptic area. The doctors needed a map? "What a cruel joke," I mumbled. A surgical team surrounded Hill, then metal instruments banged against the floor, and a man's raspy voice, maybe a doctor, cursed. I caught a glimpse of Hill's profile. She was slack-jawed with her eyes wedged open. They were going to take her corneas first.

The drugs hit me. The anesthesia made my heart slow and pound against my ribs. Behind my eyelids Jack, my dear husband, smiled at me, then nothing.

Riding in an armored vehicle, Teddy answered Georgie's phone call. Georgie had handled the takedown at the quarry and had phoned Teddy the intel about the E.I. Vance destination for Grams and Hill. "Apparently, we just missed the helicopter," Georgie said.

"The professor wouldn't talk, but the contract security guy, a former Navy Seal, didn't like the idea of killing a little old lady for profit. He gave up the layout of the surgical floor and the best way into E.I. Vance. Did you get the link showing the floor plan?"

"Yes, Strategic and Tactical Leaders appreciated it. We are two minutes out. Who are these guys?"

Craning over the back of the second bench seat from the cubbyhole backseat, Teddy watched the tech guy type faster than seemed humanly possible.

"Black op commander owed me a favor," Georgie said. "Your part of the mission can't be traced back to me. If it goes south, we were never involved. If the good guys win, you and Grams get a timeout to flee, and the CIA and the President get the glory for uncovering an international organ-harvesting cartel connected to funneling guns, bombs, and terrorists to our American soil. Otherwise…gotta go. I hope you, Grams, and Hill make it."

"Thank you. We're almost there." They had said their goodbyes at Georgie's flat.

"Stay in the med truck," Georgie added, "and watch those monitors. I've done all I can do."

"Understood." Teddy ended the call, opened his flight jacket, and tightened his laser-deflecting vest, pressing two QR-coded passports into his rib framework. If anything went wrong, he, Grams, and Hill were on their own.

*****

Breacher drove the armored Hummer and Jeep combination vehicle like a race car. Tech sat behind the officer in charge riding shotgun in the armored vehicle, and kicked the back of the front passenger seat. Twice. "Hot dang. I can count nose hairs in the hot zone with my new thermal-imaging app, shows ten armed security in the building. Two are stationed at the front of the surgical unit, one at the front desk, and three in the com center, including a Dan Waring. He's wearing the executive manager's nametag on his security blazer. The other four roam the public floors. One guy really likes the pool area."

"Thank you, Tech, you're a genius," Officer In Charge said. "But if you hit the back of my seat one more time, friendly fire awaits in your future."

Teddy leaned forward, releasing his shoulders jammed between two guys in tactical gear. "If you want, I'll stay in the hallway on the fourth floor and eliminate any surprises. I recently trained in non-lethal weaponry as backup to an agent on assignment."

The officer in charge turned in his seat and sized up Teddy. "You're the AI with CIA contacts, programmed to protect the human, Dorothy Saunders?"

"That is correct."

"Okay, buddy, stay close, but in the back upon entry. Don't get in our way. If you get hit or damaged, it's your problem. My assignment is to rescue two human females from becoming DOA minus organs. We clear?"

"Yes."

The entry into the building and elevator ride to the fourth floor occurred without incident. Teddy's visual mechanism didn't adjust to the mask. Blind entering the fourth floor, he heard several grunts and groans and peeled off his mask.

The gas didn't affect his vision, and he could see one innocent and two security personnel were down. The team advanced into the surgery, leaving Teddy and Breacher in the hallway. Teddy checked the stairwells, locked the doors, and Breacher headed toward the lab. From an office doorway, Chantel Farnsworth appeared with a red semi-automatic laser handgun. In the fog, Teddy flattened himself against the wall behind her. Rubbing her eyes from the tear gas, she moved toward Breacher, who was busy tying the lab doors. She aimed the weapon at the soldier. Teddy jammed an elbow into Chantel's temple. She fell unconscious.

Teddy pushed the safety on the gun and pocketed it. He noted Breacher's adrenaline spike as he nodded a thank you in Teddy's direction and jiggled the lab door handles before moving to check the offices. Breacher hadn't followed a logical sweep plan, and it had almost cost him his life.

Teddy finished locking down the stairwells and stood outside the offices until Breacher came out. The focused soldier pointed to a non-existent wristwatch and held up five digits, then two. They had two minutes left. Teddy could hear the shouts of the rest of the team and ran toward the elevator at AI speed.

The rescue unit burst through the outer surgery doors, rolling the gurneys in a zigzag way. The IV poles were absent. Teddy reached the elevator and hit the button, but nothing happened. He tried again. Down the corridor, a volley of shots hit a tall woman in a tailored beige suit. She dropped dead in front of Breacher. He held his gun in a two-hand grip, lying on his back on the floor, bleeding out from a knife lodged in his groin.

"Strange, you stay here. Get Tech to open the elevator." The officer in charge's voice was level and controlled, and his vitals only slightly higher than normal. The team worked to stabilize Breacher's wound by wrapping duct tape above and below the knife, and three team members lifted him in tandem from the legs, buttocks, and shoulders. They pushed the two gurneys together and placed him gently between Grams and Hill.

"We are seconds out from the 7 minutes," Teddy said and heard keys tapping on Tech's end of the radio.

Tech said, "Some smart ass wedged the elevator doors open on the second floor. A man is on it."

"Steady now," The officer in charge encouraged his men. Groaning, Breacher handed them a wristband made of twisted rope, and they tied the gurneys together at the head and foot railings.

Grams stirred but didn't wake up. Her vitals were stable. With so many bodies nearby, Teddy touched Detective Hill's chest to make sure she was breathing. She was.

Teddy punched the down button once, twice. Nothing.

The seven-minute alarm sounded as the officer in charge screamed at Tech, "Open the damn elevator doors. We have a man down." The doors opened, and they piled inside. Spike and Spuds pointed their laser weapons at the front panels, readying for armed resistance at the bottom of the ride. The immediate area was clear, but Teddy said, "I hear multiple boots on the ground coming from the kitchen area. Close." The laser duo covered them as they wheeled the gurneys to the docks and entered a semi trailer with a mini emergency room set up. Teddy heard gunfire, but he couldn't see anything because the roll-up door was closed, and they drove away.

"Will they make it?" Teddy asked.

The officer in charge slapped Teddy on the shoulder. "Don't worry, AI, the Alpha team passed us in the armored vehicle. Headed toward the docks. They won't leave any of the team behind."

Three hours later, Hill and Teddy stepped out of the back of the medical truck onto a deteriorating tarmac with weeds growing through the cracks. Brush and a thick cover of pine and bamboo trees surrounded the perimeter. An old drum and a torn, mildewed cushion from a lawn chair from the last century were discarded outside of a rusty metal hanger about the size of a football field. "Where the heck are we?" Hill asked.

"An airstrip outside Macon, but only the DEA and other governmental agencies use it for sensitive situations."

"It looks abandoned."

"That's the idea. It lines up with the regular airport, but—" A black limo came from nowhere and sped toward them. "Your ride back to Atlanta."

The driver parked and, with biceps bulging underneath his black suit sleeves, opened the door to the backseat for Hill.

"First class I see. Well, it's been fun, kind of. Almost losing my corneas, I could've done without, but where's the line for another epinephrine shot in my butt? Addictive. I would say keep in touch, but I have a feeling you and Dorothy will be lying low."

"I appreciate all you did for Grams."

"Been a privilege, but she carried her own weight throughout this little adventure. You tell her when she wakes up that I won't stop until I find Detective Barden's killers." Hill proffered her hand.

"I'm sure she already knows that." Teddy smiled and shook her hand. "Please express my gratitude to Dell."

"Will do. We're overdue for a big sister-and-brother talk about picking his friends more carefully." She grinned sideways and slid halfway into the backseat, keeping one leg on the ground. "You be careful. It's dangerous out there."

The driver waited for her to nod at him, then he shut the limo door.

I woke up cold. The long room hummed with activity, echoing off the walls draped in plastic. The air smelled weird, a combination of bleach and rotting food. I ran my hand over my right side. Still intact. I saw an all-in-one-piece Hill and Teddy exchange electronic business QR cards and exit from a side door. Hidden by a screen, somebody groaned behind me. A pink encased cell lay on the bedside portable table still lit in game-play mode. I punched in a phone number I knew by heart, stated my business and, relieved by taking action, I dozed.

When I woke up again, Teddy stepped into my line of vision. "There you are. You're safe."

A black-haired middle-aged woman wearing a white coat with the sleeves rolled up bent over me with a mini-flashlight and checked my pupils. "I'm Doctor Patel, and you're inside the mobile medic truck. You should be fully recovered from the anesthetics in a few minutes."

I scooted up in the bed and gave the doctor my meanest grandma glare. "Take this IV out. I'm fine."

"Doctor, would you give us a moment?" Teddy asked.

The doctor stepped away and turned to a guy in scrubs holding a chart.

Teddy handed me traveling cards and a driver's license for a Tracy Howard with my photo embossed on it and leaned in closer. "Just call me Mason Randolph. You need to rest until we take off for Amsterdam. I wrangled a jet at 1900 hours."

"No."

"No, what?" He straightened up.

"I'm not going. I never said I'd leave the States." I tucked the sheet under my arms and crossed them over my chest.

"Don't play innocent. You went to the professor in hopes of gaining passports for us."

"You sent me there. I asked for new identifications, and he assumed, as you did, I planned on absconding to Europe. You aren't programmed to force me to do anything against my will."

"A little late in the game to play that card."

"Sorry, but I'm not changing my mind."

"You're being unreasonable. We have a deal. Georgie put her career on the line for us. The Secretary of State's jet is lined up to take us out of the country."

"Yes, out of my country. My South. Besides, 'Georgie with an agenda' has a plan to work all this mess to her advantage. Mark my words."

Teddy grew quiet, then closed his eyes and lifted praying hands near his lips. "If we stay, you'll be tortured and executed. I don't have any more backup plans. All the favors are used up." He dropped his arms. "Where do you suggest we hide?"

"For me, in plain sight. I called Barbara while you were outside with Detective Hill. My friend is en route. I'll stay with her awhile until I figure out what to do. She knows a fantastic, discreet plastic surgeon. With a new ID, face, and fingerprints, I can do anything. I've journalist contacts. They would love my insight into E.I. Vance and their connection to organ harvesting, or maybe I'll write for the free press. A Ms. Anonymous column works for me and hints at mystery." I clapped.

"Hill will find Barden's murderers," he said.

"Maybe she could use a former P.I. slash consultant."

"Barbara will turn you in. They will kill you. I'm not programmed to allow that to happen."

"I'm an old woman. I've earned the right to choose how I die. Besides, Barbara and I have an agreement. As old friends, we decided we didn't have to agree on how we see the world, just how we see each other." I patted his hand. "I love you; that won't ever change. Look. It took me a while to admit it, but Jack programmed you for more than just me. I want you to get on the jet, fly to Amsterdam, and find a way to make the earth a better place as a free AI. As much as I'll miss you, I release you of your obligation to me. Please let me go my own way."

Teddy studied me. A deep, human-informed sadness flickered across his face. "You're incredibly short-sighted and stubborn, but Amsterdam is a logical location to set up an international wing of the Underground." He hugged me, kissed my forehead, and walked away.

Mason Randolph would make me proud.

The End

ABOUT THE AUTHOR

Lynn Hesse is an award-winning author of the novels: Well of Rage, Murder in Mobile, Another Kind of Hero, A Matter of Respect, Murder in Mobile, Book 2, and The Forty Knots Burn. Recently, her last two novels won the 2023 Georgia Independent Authors Association Awards for Best Police Procedural, Best Cover Adult Fiction, Best Suspense/Thriller, and the Spotlight on Georgia Fiction.

Malice, Matrimony, & Murder, A Collection of 25 Wedding Cozy Mystery & Crime Fiction Stories contains "Sabotage and A Murder Mystery" by Lynn, published November of 2023 by Marla Bradeen. "Shrewd Women" was reprinted in Crimeucopia, Boomshalalaking, Modern Crimes in Modern Times, UK in June 2023, and published by Onyx Publications and Discovery Podcast in 2022. Bitter Love," appeared in Crimeucopia, The I's Have It by Murderous Ink Press, 2021, UK. "Jewel's Hell" was in the Me Too Short Stories: An Anthology edited by Elizabeth Zelvin, published in 2019 by Level Best Books.

An interview and video concerning Lynn's role as a police officer, "Blue Steel," is in the Georgia State University Library Special Collections and

Archives. She performs in several dance and theatrical troupes in Atlanta, Georgia. The dandelion is one of her performance personas.

Lynn left law enforcement to write and lives with her husband and his six rescue cats near Atlanta, Georgia.

Acknowledgements

I thank my beta readers Joyce N. Ryan and Marilyn Pearlman for their honest suggestions.

I thank my grandson, Donald Raymond Strange III, for the suggestion I write a novel about an AI detective agency. Also my editor Susan Pierson of FineLineProofs.com.

lynnhesse.com

Other Novels by Lynn Hesse:

Another KInd of Hero
(2017, 2018)

Well of Rage, Murder in Mobile
(2016, 2019)
Audiobook (2021)

A Matter of Respect, Murder in Mobile, Book 2
(2022)

The Forty Knots Burn
(2022)

Upcoming:

The Midwife and The Pink Cave Dwellers (Historical Fiction/Fantasy, 2024)

Lynn Hesse
Audible

Lynn Hesse
Amazon Author

Lynn Hesse
Website

Lynn Hesse
Goodreads

THE UNDERGROUND
CHAMELEON

9 798990 587007

SUSPICIOUS
UNDERCURRENTS
PUBLISHING

Printed in the USA
CPSIA information can be obtained
at www.ICGtesting.com
CBHW022016081224
18574CB00001B/1

9 798990 587007